IMMORTAL SOULS

IMMORTAL SOULS

PHOENIX VIEIRA

KOA TALES

Published by Koa Tales

Cover & Map Illustration by Koa Tales
Developmental Editing by Erin Young
Line Editing by Karin Cox
Proofreading by Michele Perry

ISBN 979-8-985162-50-9 (e-book)
ISBN 979-8-9851625-1-6 (paperback)
ISBN 979-8-9851625-2-3 (hardcover)

Printed in the United States of America

First Edition

To Christ.
Et regni ejus non erit finis.

In loving memory of Isabel. And to JP with love.

To Isvenfen

To Oldterra

SEPTENTRIO VEL BOREAS

APELIOTES

AUSTER

Sinenibus

Stella Islands

Parhon

PART I

CHAPTER 1
THE CRYSTAL PALACE

The Sun Empire will be ours.

Out of the carriage window, the palace's sky-high crystal walls loomed closer. Its starlit reflection, crowned by a crescent moon, shimmered in the calm waters of the lake. I ran a hand through my raven hair, wondering if I would succeed.

Tonight, I had two crucial matters to attend to: the fate of my childhood friend—now a beautiful princess for sale—and the fate of the entire Empire.

I looked away from the mesmerizing moon. A pair of swans left a glittering trail through the lake's surface, guiding my gaze to a lone figure standing close to the forest. Gilded by moonlight, the cloaked person's attention was fixed on the hundred courtiers celebrating the princess's birthday behind the crystal walls.

Who's spying on the palace?

Gravel crunched beneath the carriage, and the figure turned toward me. The cloak fluttered to the ground, and a raven flew out, soaring up and disappearing into the night.

As I searched for the fleeting spy in the stillness of the forest, tales of foul, otherworldly creatures came to mind. Humanlike immortal fairies who feasted on lost children. Pure nonsense. Fairytales. Nothing but lies to keep the children at bay.

I dismissed the oddity as a trick of the light. Fairies could not exist in my world; the wickedness of men was enough to ruin an Empire. I focused on the palace.

My carriage halted, and the coachman opened the door. Stepping out, I filled my lungs with the crisp evening air and faced the Crystal Palace.

I ascended the steps and stopped before the shining doors, smoothing the lapels of my black overcoat lined with gold. I raised my chin at my reflection in the crystal doors, steeling my silver eyes, ready to flaunt myself before the scrutiny of a Court that rarely saw me. Bleeding, crying, or smiling would throw me to the royal pack of hyenas. Preserving my stoic image was key to dethroning the Emperor.

Pages swung the doors open, and the orchestra inside halted. The herald struck the floor with his staff, and two *thumps* echoed against the floor, making my skin crawl.

"Corvus, son of Colthus, sole heir to the House of Alba." The herald announced my presence. Although I was not royal, they still announced me—the absent heir to the most affluent house. The acidic scent of clean crystal hit my nostrils. I stood masking my anxiety, holding my wrist behind my back, and staring icily beyond the crowd.

When I stepped forward, whispers rippled through the hall. My steps reverberated as I descended into the rotten Court, ignoring their spiteful stares. Their wealthiest heir gone rogue, a walking threat to the rich underlings of an incompetent Emperor who exchanged their honor for riches or bloodstained trade deals.

The moon shone through the vaulted crystal ceiling. I examined the hall, searching for Saphyr, but she was elsewhere. The polished floor reflected the silhouettes of the courtiers, gathered in groups by the windows. They resumed their drinking and chatting as the lively music filled the hall again.

"I thought I would have to go and get you dressed myself," Kanis greeted me, his emerald eyes glinting with mischief. The fifth son to the House of Phoebus, and my dearest friend, squared his battle-hewn frame. Like me, he defied the lingering gazes of the courtiers.

A slow smile crept up at the corner of my lips.

Suddenly, the courtiers found the starry lake far more interesting than us.

"I would not miss it for the world." I patted his shoulder affectionately.

"I've missed you."

I scowled at him, scanning the crowd around us, hoping the music had drowned out his words. Members of the clandestine Alliance nodded almost inconspicuously from afar, glad to see me alive. They were among the few

3

who still cared for the wellbeing of their Houses and their subjects. I knew them by name, having grown up with many of them, although never as inseparably as with Kanis and Saphyr.

"Where is she?" My foot jittered against the floor. I could not remember the last time I had seen her. The Emperor had kept her away from me after she came of age because he saw me and the influence of my House as a threat to his rule. He only cared about upholding his power, even if it was at the expense of his own daughter. I had been working to free the Empire from its corrupt Court and Saphyr from her gilded cage ever since.

"She hasn't come down yet. Perhaps she has been waiting for you?" Kanis threw me an impish smile.

I chuckled, doubting it was true. "She doesn't know I'm here." It reminded me of the second reason I had dragged myself to the palace. "Let's go."

Kanis nodded and followed me toward the back of the crowd. While the courtiers chattered mindlessly or focused on their drinks, an undercover guard by the wall removed the curtain and opened a hidden door. The Alliance had spies planted everywhere.

We climbed the spiral staircase to a private terrace, away from prying ears. A pair of lanterns dimly lit the sweet-scented, vine-engulfed balustrade. I rested my forearms on it, watching the lake surrounded by mountainous forest and appreciating the silence.

"I'm glad to be back. I was freezing my ass off up there," I said, referring to my recent journey to the western highlands of Dunamun.

Kanis leaned on the balustrade, too, his hawkish eyes scanning the forest.

A shadow moving across the pine trees caught my eye. "Did you see that?"

"Yes ..."

"What do you think it was?"

"I'm not sure. It could've been a deer."

"Earlier, I saw a spy at the edge of the forest, just outside the palace."

Kanis ran a hand through his tawny hair. "Something has been brewing while you were away. One of the army's companies has been acting strangely. Several weapons went missing from the artillery chamber."

"They took them," I gathered.

Kanis knew every whisper, every word uttered in the streets thanks to the web of little spies I had weaved across Sol City. I thought of the pack of youngsters who had once pickpocketed me. We had kept them fed and cared for in exchange for their eavesdropping and messaging services since then. "Yes, the brats confirmed it. The question is: what are they going to do with them?"

I drew back. "Galbreg would've notified me." The General had once been my mentor, almost like a father, and he treated me like a son. But he was ruthless. I had forged the Alliance to bring him under my control, to stop the mindless killing. He received funds from the secret Alliance, and his troops were ours to command.

"My point exactly. Why didn't he?"

I sighed. Galbreg and I had continued working together, but things had soured between us when the Alliance stepped in. "I'll ask."

"What will you tell him of your visit to the west?"

"If he acts soon, the Houses of Dunamun will join the Alliance, and the Sun Empire will be finally ours." My letters to Kanis were encrypted in a code only he could decipher, but I had omitted this crucial information in case the Emperor intercepted them.

"Galbreg needs to stop stalling."

I nodded, pressing my lips together. My urgency to meet with the General grew. If he did not act within days, the Alliance would be forced to seek control over the army without Galbreg.

"And what about Saphyr?"

I turned to glare at the crowd below. All of Saphyr's suitors downstairs had been handpicked by her father, the Emperor. He had ensured I was not on the list of eligible bachelors. In exchange for a decent dowry, the chosen one would gain not only the future title of Emperor but also the beautiful Crown Princess as his wife. But Saphyr was so much more than that. She could outbrave any man.

My fingers drummed on the veranda rail. Kanis and I had watched her bloom from a scruffy girl who slept through our private tutoring and nagged me to do her homework into a graceful beauty.

"Who does the Emperor expect her to marry?" I snarled.

"Anybody with enough coin to satiate his needs. He must be truly desperate." Kanis threw me a quick side-glance. "So, will you give it a try?"

I scoffed. "All the coffers of my House would never satisfy his greed. And, even if she wanted me, the Emperor would never allow it. We're a threat to him already. Give us the Empire, and my father will swallow him up."

"First, you have not asked her. Second, you are correct." Kanis chuckled. "Colthus would gobble him up on a whim."

I frowned at the thought of my father. He was the reason I had originally turned to Galbreg for mentorship, to fill his void. I crossed my arms over my chest. "If Galbreg would throw the coup already, she would no longer need to marry."

"Are you certain he will spare her if he does?"

"He has promised not to touch her or her family, only the Emperor and his underlings." I reassured myself. The problem lay with how to depose the Emperor without killing him, and how to spare Saphyr from an arranged marriage while convincing her I was doing everything for her as well as caring for her subjects, the people of the Sun. "We have not even seen each other for so long."

"I guess planning to overthrow her father poses an issue." Kanis snickered.

His words stung. I had not told Saphyr about my plan nor about the secret Alliance. She despised her father more than I despised mine, so I assumed she would not mind as long as I guaranteed her family's safety. Her younger sister and her mother posed no threat. And Saphyr would never betray me, even if I betrayed her.

"It's already a mess. Might as well take her in the process."

"She must agree to it first," I muttered between my teeth.

Stone stairs gave way to walls of gold-flecked polished marble as I ascended the staircase. The secret hallway led me further into the back wing of the palace, where sovereign affairs were conducted. Galbreg was probably already waiting for me.

It was empty; everyone was at the party. The General's study sat beside the lavish throne room. I entered, not bothering to knock on the mahogany doors.

Clouds dimmed the moonlight streaming through the crystal ceiling. The massive hearth barely lit the room, although a tall candelabra nearby cast lively shadows over the books stacked against the walls.

Galbreg sat comfortably on a winged chair, facing the fire. His hair, soft and snowy white, was tied neatly at his nape. He toyed with the end of his silky cravat as he studied the flames with cold, calculating eyes.

He had never been a General who fought at the front of the battle; he strategized and commanded troops calmly from his desk.

I perched on the chair next to his, no longer his ever-faithful shadow. "It's been a while," I said by way of greeting.

"Yes." He studied my appearance. "I'm glad to see you're back."

"They're growing impatient, Galbreg. We need you to set a date for the coup." We had discussed the strategy many times. Once he confirmed the date, the army would strike at dawn. The Emperor would be exiled, the Heads of each enemy house imprisoned, and no women or children would be hurt under any circumstance. I would not accept casualties.

"Soon."

I narrowed my eyes at him. "When? Members of the Alliance think you're not applying the funds where you should be." For Galbreg, the money was never enough. He kept pressing for more, willing to bleed the Alliance to death, which had driven me to rally more support from Dunamun.

Galbreg's face twisted with outrage. "Who?"

I remained silent. A previous mistake had taught me to withhold this type of information. I would not allow him to sever the trade and ruin the subsistence of another family.

"I've distributed part of the funds among the common people. They'll be the ones to rise, and our soldiers will stand by them. This way, we'll guarantee our legitimacy," Galbreg said.

Something was off. I remembered Kanis's warning. "Why did your company take weapons from the artillery chamber without authorization?"

He stared at me from under furrowed brows. "My army is mine to command."

I held his stare.

"My dearest Corvus, don't you trust me?" He smiled softly with a kindness that had always escaped my father. The type of kindness that had driven me to constantly seek his approval, but not anymore.

I pressed my lips into a tight line, forcing the bitter *"No!"* to stay inside my mouth. My jaw clenched at the things I had done for him over the years, never failing him. He had forged me as his sword, despite my youth.

Clearing my throat, I reminded myself why we needed each other. The Crystal Palace was a vivid reminder of the Emperor's rule: a beautiful, lavish palace encapsulated in a fragile, selfish bubble. It was not meant to last, and we would be the ones to break it.

"Just make it happen," I growled. The Alliance had designated Galbreg their puppet emperor under my advice because I did not desire the immense responsibility. I admired and trusted his skills, so it surprised me he did not wish to move sooner and occupy the throne.

Galbreg's lips twisted in a grin. "It'll happen … in due time." He stood and sauntered out of the study.

I hoped Kanis was wrong. Galbreg could be cruel and headstrong, but he cared for the people. If anyone could end the corrupt rule of the Empire and feed its people, it was Galbreg. I felt certain he would never betray me. Still, I could not avoid the feeling we were making a terrible mistake.

I marched back through the empty hallway to the spiraled staircase, the sour taste of failure filling my mouth. Galbreg had not given me a date, although I refused to consider what that meant just yet. Instead, I focused on the second issue at hand. At least, I might be able to provide an immediate solution for it.

It was almost midnight. I spied on the crowd through an opening in the wall, disguised by a painting on the other side, but Saphyr was nowhere in sight. The stone wall cooled my forehead, and I shut my eyes, sighing.

"Look up, Corvus," Kanis whispered in my ear, making me wince.

"At least make a noise when you—"

"Shh!" He held a finger against his mouth, a drink in his hand. Then the hall went silent, and he fixed his eyes above us, a concerned look on his face.

The vision of the slender figure atop the cascading stairs felt like a punch to my gut. Saphyr glowed under a crown of solid gold spikes designed to mimic sun rays. A crimson dress bared her shoulders and hugged her creamy skin in clean-cut lines. A deep cleft in the fabric between her breasts guided my eyes down to a second split that revealed one slim leg almost from her hip bone.

"For the love of God, what does she think she's wearing?" I managed between clenched teeth. The muscles of her thigh stretched out down the first step, scandalizing the women who had never worn dresses with leg slits nor low necklines. The sight of her drew ferocious gazes from the men. My chest burned.

"Seraphine Catherina Stella, Crown Princess of the Empire of the S-Sun," the herald stuttered, his gaze fixed on her leg.

My jaw hurt, and I contained my desire to knock him down. Saphyr was not fond of her full name. She preferred the short nickname Kanis and I had given her.

I started forward, but Kanis's restraining hand stopped me.

"Take this instead." He offered his glass of uske, and I downed the fiery drink without a thought. "Do you think she picked out that dress herself?"

My gaze trailed her slow descent in ludicrously high shoes. She normally preferred simple, elegant dresses. Her father, or one of his advisors, had probably chosen it. Saphyr's trained emotionless expression did not hint whether she felt uncomfortable or not. I was certain she hated it.

"I'm not sure we're even celebrating her birthday anymore," Kanis said. "They have thrown her into a pit filled with beasts."

He was right. My blood simmered as I studied her admirers below. Men ogled her as if she were a haunch after a long hunt.

The crowd parted in a circle, and Saphyr glided toward the center for her first dance.

"For God's sake! You can't allow her to marry an old fart like that, Corvus!"

The old man kissing her hand almost made me spit out the uske. He could be her grandfather.

"To hell with the Emperor," I hissed.

Kanis, the stairway, and the courtiers became nothing but blurs as I bolted out from the hidden staircase. Saphyr's eyes widened as I pushed through the crowd toward her.

The man immediately stepped away, his gaze lowered.

I flashed a presumptuous smile and offered my hand to Saphyr. "Happy birthday, Saphyr," I breathed.

"You came." A smile lit up her honeyed eyes and made the loose golden locks framing her face bounce.

"You look …" I hesitated, searching for the right word.

"Different," she stated, taking my hand.

I smiled softly in agreement and bowed to her. "Princess …" I guided her toward the center of the floor as the orchestra resumed playing. The stares of her jealous suitors, especially the old man's, would have set me on fire if they could. Ignoring them, I focused on her. I was not on her father's list of suitors, but no one dared cross me.

Luckily for me, our private tutor had forced Kanis and me to take turns dancing with Saphyr during the hideous protocol lessons of our youth.

"Did you choose the dress?" I asked, as our palms joined, and I pulled her closer.

"Let's say it was the least scandalous one," she whispered.

Fire crawled through my veins. Kanis was right; I could not allow the Emperor to whore her out. Saphyr looked stunning, but not like herself.

"Come with me." I led her through the crowd, toward the stairway door. Some courtiers stared, while others whispered. Then, fireworks boomed just as the music changed, and the Court's attention drifted to the sparkling sky. I pictured Kanis setting the fireworks off on the terrace and smiled, thankful.

The undercover guard opened the concealed door again, and we hurried inside the narrow stone stairway. Kanis was undoubtedly gone.

Saphyr arranged her gown nervously. I stood a step above her, giving her more space. She looked strikingly different to my memory of her, her not-so-gracious appearance after competing in horse races when we were much younger. I missed those days, when nothing but cheating our way out of a boring lesson mattered. Now, everything had changed. She had been kept away from me, and she was now to marry.

"Saphyr, why are you going along with this?"

"What option do I have?" She raised an eyebrow.

"You're the Crown Princess of the Sun Empire. You should not be sold like cattle!"

"Tell that to my father. The coffers have run out. He is desperate."

"Clearly. But he doesn't care about you. He is not even coming today, is he? If it were not for your father ... if it were not for the circumstances, would you still marry any of them?"

"Who wants to marry someone they don't know, Corvus? Don't be ridiculous. I'd rather marry someone I love, but upholding the Crown is more important." Her gaze dropped to the floor. "You know how this damn Court works."

"You owe them nothing," I said. "You're not an asset to be sold. You're priceless, Saphyr. No wealth could possibly buy your slavery."

"Well, I have no alternative! I'm doing the best I can." Her eyes gleamed with tears.

"I'm sorry. I didn't mean to ..." I wished I could smack myself for being so imprudent. "Saphyr," I insisted, grabbing her by the shoulders. "Look at me, Saphyr ..." My throat tightened with despair as her forehead fell to my chest. Gently, I pulled her chin up. "Saphyr, look at me."

Her amber eyes met mine, and I swallowed. "Perhaps, you and I, perhaps we could ..."

Her gaze dropped to my stuttering mouth, and with one glance at her parted lips, I forgot to keep breathing. Time froze, her breathing the only sound. Saphyr glanced up, drawing me in, and I delicately brushed her soft lips with mine for the first time.

A piercing scream interrupted us, chilling my bones.

And chaos erupted within the Crystal Palace.

Chapter 2

Chaos

"We must go. Now!" Kanis shouted.

Before I could even understand what was happening, he was next to us, his dagger gleaming in the dark.

"Galbreg," Kanis spat, in answer to my silent question. "His soldiers have infiltrated the palace. They vastly outnumber the Royal Guards."

"He would have told me if it was happening tonight!" I stiffened, recalling our recent conversation. Besides, we had planned for the coup to occur at dawn. Saphyr threw me a confused glance, but I averted my gaze to Kanis.

"It doesn't matter anymore. We must go—now!"

The sound of crystal walls shattering was followed by more screams. A *thud* on the wooden door behind Saphyr sent us hurtling up the stairs. Kanis guided Saphyr to the terrace while I unsheathed my long dagger and guarded her back.

Out on the terrace, hell unleashed below us. Armed soldiers shoved through the open doors to the hall, where courtiers trampled each other, desperate to escape.

Kanis and I looked at each other, eyes wide, clearly both arriving at the same conclusion. We had to navigate to the back of the palace through the secret hallway. It was that or fight our way through one of those exits. The servants' corridors were probably already teeming with terrified civilians.

We rushed back to the stairway, and I flung open the door. A sudden crash echoed off the stone walls; the soldiers had smashed the door downstairs. "Up! They're up on the terrace. Hurry!" they commanded.

I slammed the door shut. "The pots, quickly!"

We swiftly piled the heavy potted plants to block the door and buy us time.

"Corvus!" Someone else had made it to the terrace too. I spun around, holding up the long dagger.

"Brenen," I said gravely, recognizing Galbreg's son. He walked to us, as if gliding, his swinging silver hair reflecting the moonlight.

"My father has gone mad." His serious tone matched the austerity in his eyes. "You should hurry. Use this to escape the balcony." A bundle of thick rope tumbled from his hands to the ground. "A carriage awaits you by the lake."

"Why should we trust you?" Kanis bared his teeth.

"You are aware that my father and I despise each other."

We evaluated him. Galbreg loathed his idle, hedonistic son. I had never considered Brenen a threat, although I did not particularly like him.

"Should I let them enter, then?" Brenen pointed at the door.

I did not trust him, but we had little choice. *Why has Galbreg sent in his soldiers tonight without warning me first? And why are they targeting us?*

I would not allow anything to happen to Saphyr.

"Save her. I'll stall them as long as I can," Brenen said, the longsword in his hand glistening lightly.

I kept my dagger up, pointing it at his throat.

Kanis was already knotting the rope to the balustrade, as Saphyr gaped at us.

"I can't jump out of the building in this!" She gestured desperately to her dress.

"Take off your shoes," I instructed, trying to instill calm and logic. "Your outer skirt, as well."

Brenen's gaze was impenetrable. I could usually detect people's emotions, but he seemed devoid of them.

From the corner of my eye, I spied Saphyr shaking off her shoes and unlacing the back of her dress, letting the outer skirt drop to the floor. The red petticoat beneath was much lighter and more manageable. Brenen turned indifferently toward the door, his sword hanging low in his hand, and I rushed to Saphyr.

"That slit in your dress will come in handy now," I said jokingly. She chuckled as I efficiently tied the rope around first her waist and then mine.

She gasped. "Are we going together?"

"Yes, climb up," I said, kneeling before her, offering her my back.

Her fingers trembled as she climbed on my shoulders. I looked down, an empty feeling lodging in the pit of my stomach. A fall of this height would leave one or two broken bones.

"Is it tight?" Kanis asked.

I tested the rope wrapped around my hand. "Yes."

"Jump. I'll go right after you."

It took all my concentration and strength to swing one leg out over the veranda, and then the other. Saphyr silenced a squeal as she swayed on my back.

"Hold tight," I suggested softly. "Close your eyes."

She nestled her head into my neck as I pushed us off the veranda and slowly crawled down the marble column, gripping the rope. My body ached with the effort of keeping the balance. By the time we reached the floor, my hands were burning.

The clash of swords upstairs kept Kanis occupied, so I put my fingers between my teeth and let out a prolonged whistle. Within seconds, Kanis jumped agilely over the veranda and shimmied down the rope, one foot wrapped around it to slow his descent.

The grounds were empty of guards, who had all rushed inside already, but the entrance thronged with people running away.

The carriage was waiting by the lake, as Brenen had promised.

"Princess!" The royal coachman waved.

I grabbed Saphyr's arm, unsure.

"It's fine. I know him," she said, jumping into the carriage.

"Only her," the coachman said, as Kanis and I approached.

"I don't think so," I said bitterly, as if the pathetic coachman had been inside to protect her.

"I'll be fine," Saphyr assured us from the window. "He'll take me to the safehouse."

Before I could argue, she shut the door and the guard set the horses galloping at full speed through a path into the woods.

As the carriage disappeared, I wished we had remained by her side.

"Has she always been this stubborn?" I asked Kanis.

"We must head home. Make sure everyone is fine."

I glanced around in search of horses or a carriage. Terrified people still fled the palace, and soldiers bolted through the portico.

A dark carriage rattled over the gravel path, catching my attention.

"Oh, for heaven's sake! Colthus and mother!" I swore as Kanis and I sprinted toward the carriage.

"No!" I shouted at the coachman, waving my hands in wide circles. "Turn around! *Turn around!*"

The coachman, seeing the courtiers and soldiers fleeing the palace, forced the horses into a dramatic turn.

Kanis and I jumped on the carriage's high sides in the nick of time. We glanced back at the eerie sight of the Crystal Palace plunged into chaos.

A hunch told me this was just the beginning. The palace soon vanished into the darkness as we rolled along the main path that curled through the mountains.

"Corvus, I must check on my parents as well," Kanis said.

"Were they in attendance?"

"Thank God, no. But if Galbreg has thrown a coup, I should go to them."

"Stop!" I ordered the coachman, and the carriage halted.

We went to the horses, and I untied one as Kanis untied its companion, putting the traces away.

"What are you doing?" Kanis asked.

"I'm going after her."

"But she's fine. That was the royal carriage."

"I have to be sure." Now that I knew my parents were fine, I had to follow my instinct to help Saphyr, even it was illogical.

The remaining four horses whinnied, remaining hitched to the carriage.

"I can't go with you." Kanis frowned. "I must return home."

I swallowed. "I'll be fine."

"Madman!" Kanis gave me a firm hug and mounted his horse. Steeling myself, I jumped on mine.

"Corvus!" My mother's head popped through the carriage window. "What on Earth is going on?"

My horse's hooves clattered against the stone as I guided it toward her and took her gloved hand in mine through the window.

"Mother, a coup. Galbreg has gone rogue."

She gasped, and I heard my father shuffle from inside.

"Please, go straight home," I begged her. "I must check on Saphyr, but then I'll meet you there." I was certain Galbreg's target was the throne, not my family.

Mother pursed her lips but nodded. "God bless you, my son."

"You too, Mother."

She fingered her necklace anxiously as Kanis and I wheeled our horses around.

"Ha!" The coachman sent the carriage racing down the road at the same time Kanis and I barreled into a narrow path in the woods, taking advantage of the moonlight. This night was endless. I hoped Saphyr was safe.

An icy breeze slashed my cheeks as we galloped down the mountain path. Anything beyond the bushes and trees was blurry, submerged into darkness. Kanis eventually disappeared, diverging onto a track toward his home. I followed the trail back to the woods surrounding the palace until it merged onto the one Saphyr's carriage had taken.

It was hard to see in the forest's obscurity, but the horse was familiar with the path and did not deviate.

I slowed after entering the main road again, but Saphyr's carriage had vanished. Riding farther down the path, hoping I might still catch her, it seemed Kanis was right: this was a waste of time. Maybe Saphyr had already arrived at the royal safehouse by now.

A glimpse of gold in the distance caught my breath. Saphyr's carriage lay abandoned on the path. I galloped to it, noticing the door was still open. My hands trembled as I halted the horse and prepared for the worst. "Saphyr?" I whispered into the shadows as I dismounted.

An owl answered, making me wince. *Where has she gone? Where is her coachman?* I took my glove off and stroked her velvet seat. *Still warm.* My feet stumbled upon something, and I crouched down, feeling with the tips of my fingers until I found her crown, thrown on the ground. My throat tightened. *God, please let her still be alive.*

Suddenly, the clouds parted, and moonlight unveiled the forest. I blinked in this new clarity, absorbing the surroundings. Something crimson twinkled in the underbrush. Reaching for it, I rubbed the scrap of thin fabric between my fingers. Her dress.

"Oh no ..." The path was still empty, but fresh footprints were stamped on the earth leading away from the carriage. It looked like she had ventured into the forest alone. I tied the horse to the carriage and followed the dainty footprints, hoping I was not too late.

The underbrush soon gave way to tall pine trees spread far apart, giving her ample room to walk or run. *How far has she gone?* I inspected a bare clearing between the tree trunks. It extended into the darkness, but there was no sight of her. A ruffle of feathers sent my heart racing. Glancing up, I saw a raven flapping through the forest canopy, dropping a black feather. Perhaps it would see her. Following, I searched for her.

"Saphyr?" I whispered into a forest clearing. Only the silence answered. A gust of wind rattled the crowns of the trees. I raised my arms to protect myself from the shower of pine needles.

A growl behind me, followed by a sword slashing the wind, sent me diving forward. If I had not rolled just in time, I would have been run through. A soldier snarled, showing his teeth, his eyes bulging with rage. He raised his sword again, and I fumbled to unsheathe my dagger.

Clouds wreathed the moon again, and the forest sank into darkness. Blinded, I stilled, listening for the soldier's steps but hearing nothing.

Crouching, I dug my hand into the ground and took a fistful of dirt. The moon shone again, and I hurled the dirt toward his eyes. The soldier shrieked, desperately rubbing them with one hand while his sword swung aimlessly on the other. His neck lay exposed, and the dagger pulsed in my hand. I raised it, but the soldier's wide bloodshot eyes begged me for mercy. For the split-second I hesitated, the soldier sprang back and grinned maliciously, holding up his sword.

I planted my feet on the ground and took a defensive stance when a blur of red fabric bolted from the trees from behind the soldier. The soldier let out another shriek, kneeling and clutching his leg as Saphyr slashed the back of his thigh with her own dagger.

I gaped at Saphyr's furious eyes, lit by a ray of moonlight, and immediately wrapped my fingers around her cold wrist, pulling her away from the soldier's reach. Intertwining her trembling fingers in mine, while still holding the dagger in my other hand, I rushed her in the direction I had come, leaving the injured soldier behind.

After we reached the stone road and found it still empty, I exhaled with relief. "Hop up." I helped her mount my horse. Then I untied it and swung my leg over the horse's back behind her. "Hold tight," I instructed as I pressed my heels into the horse's sides and sent it barreling away down the forest path, back to my home.

We galloped on until we arrived at the House of Alba. Saphyr and I had barely escaped certain death, yet I still refused to accept Galbreg's betrayal. I had threatened to withdraw the Alliance's support if he touched a hair on her head. He had called me a fool, assuring me that surviving members of the Royal Family would threaten the legitimacy of our rule. But I refused to be a murderer, so he had given me his word.

I kept watch around us in case we were being followed, but we were clear. My parent's dark carriage still stood at the entrance, and I sighed my relief.

Saphyr and I dismounted and dashed up the steps to the arched bridge in front of the manor, the water rushing under it and down the mountain.

Finally, feeling somewhat safe, I turned in the middle of the bridge and engulfed Saphyr in my arms. "I'm so sorry," I murmured against her hair. "I should never have let you go alone."

Saphyr gripped my coat with both hands, burying her head in my chest. "I'm alive thanks to you. If you had not come and distracted him, he … he probably would have …" Saphyr's voice quivered, unable to finish the sentence.

My mouth dried, and I could not swallow. I pressed her tighter against me. "On the contrary, thank *you* for saving *me*. Never again put yourself in danger for me or anyone else like that."

She pressed her mouth in a fine line. "I couldn't let him hurt you."

I sighed, both admiring and feeling anxious about her bout of fearless courage. Saphyr would always do whatever she pleased. "What happened to the coachman?" My teeth bared at the thought of him. "Wasn't he supposed to protect you?"

"He ran as soon as we were ambushed. Some soldiers went after him, so I ran into the forest."

"I'll lock him up myself," I said between clenched teeth.

"No, I don't blame him. We both panicked."

I took a deep sigh. Now was not the moment to argue with her, but the damn coachman had been ordered to protect her with his life. "For a moment, I thought—" Unable to say it, I shuddered. I had expected the worst. "Thank God you're alive."

"Thank you for coming for me."

Relief washed over me.

"Sire! Sire!"

"What is it?" I spun toward Thali, my mother's handmaiden, dashing out from the manor.

"It's absolutely dreadful. Your poor mother, Sire. Or actually, your f-father," she stuttered.

Screams erupted from the manor. Raw, visceral screams. My mother's. *"No! Bring him back to me."*

Saphyr gaped at me, and my spine shrank inside my skin. "What's happening?" I demanded.

"Your … your father, Sire." Pure fear filled Thali's eyes. "Their carriage was ambushed, and he was abducted. Your mother drove the carriage here by herself."

My insides twisted, making me feel nauseous.

"She … she is fine, physically. She was not harmed. But she is not herself, Sire. She keeps howling for your father."

"Who did it?" I barked. "Who took him?" Galbreg's aim should have been to take the throne. Galbreg was not that stupid. If he thought he could threaten me, he would still have to face the wrath of the Alliance.

"C-common thieves, it seems, my lord. But your mother believes they were actually sent by the army."

"Galbreg." My vision tunneled with rage, and I ground my jaw. "I must go, Saphyr."

"I'll take care of your mother," she said.

"I want more guards stationed around the manor," I commanded the handmaiden before turning and sprinting back to my horse. Galbreg was about to feel the wrath of the same sword he had so carefully honed.

CHAPTER 3
TREASON

Treason—the word roared in my head, silencing any other thoughts. *Treason of the highest kind.* Galbreg had betrayed me.

My footsteps reverberated through the marble hallway, my personal guard following me closely. The stone columns flew past us as we marched through Galbreg's house.

I had enough guards to outnumber Galbreg's, who let us inside without a word. I had expected them to at least put up a fight. Even if the Emperor did not allow the Houses to have private armies, we had a considerable amount of guards at our disposal. And I knew Galbreg's house and his guards' stations like my own.

I stormed through the dark-mahogany doors of his grand study, leaving my guards outside.

As if expecting me, Galbreg looked up from his desk. White curls framed his icy stare. "Corvus, what a pleasure. Please have a seat."

I returned his conceited smile and continued standing. "You have indeed been busy, Galbreg."

The General raised one brow.

"Where is my father?"

Perhaps I was a fool for stating my anger so blatantly; perhaps it made me look inexperienced in the delicate art of cynical diplomacy. But I was too livid to care.

"Oh?"

He would not admit to anything, not without adequate pressure. The corner of my mouth curved up in a sneer. "Have you seen your son lately, Galbreg?"

Galbreg sat upright.

Now I had his attention. "He paid us a visit tonight, after you left. After your company, armed with the missing weapons, invaded the Crystal Palace." I leaned my weight against the chair.

"Well, I'm glad you have been in touch with him," Galbreg said with a spiteful smile.

I was well aware he despised his son, using him only as his personal Court spy. Brenen had become a favorite among the Houses, but he had been selling information about them to Galbreg.

"Oh yes, Brenen was very helpful. He threw us a rope so we could jump off the terrace and escape," I added nonchalantly, letting the statement simmer. Let Galbreg wonder if his kin had betrayed him as he had betrayed me. "You gave me your word." I stared into his silver-blue eyes, remembering our argument about ensuring a bloodless dethronement.

Once a cloudless sky, his eyes now reminded me of a frosty morning: treacherous and conniving. I stiffened, unleashing myself, unable to believe that my beloved mentor was now my enemy. "You promised you wouldn't touch her! The Emperor wasn't there, so who were you after? On the very night of Saphyr's birthday, you planned to murder her!"

His gaze narrowed. "And her little sister could come and cut your throat twenty years from now because you let her live. The entire royal line must end for a new rule to flourish, yet you insist on letting them all live." As the High General, Galbreg had gotten his hands dirty to keep the Sun Empire united. But I had wished to shed light on the Empire without spilling any more blood.

"I thought that we had an agreement," I snarled. "Yet you didn't expect your precious Brenen would betray you. Well, you've failed."

Galbreg studied me with furrowed brows. "Have I?"

I had admired him once. He had claimed to defend the poor, the feeble. Yet all he had done was endlessly press me for funds while he failed to establish a new monarchy. We had agreed to initiate a new reign under his name to serve the people. Lies! All that would have happened is that the riches switched hands.

"I trusted you," I growled, remorse lacing my words. "I fulfilled my end of the bargain, and this is how you repay me? I've done all you asked for and more." Deep down, my gut had always warned me he was a selfish

23

man, yet I had ignored it. We had let our guard down, choosing to believe he cared, that he was doing this for the betterment of the people at the cost of some wrongdoing—all nothing but lies.

Galbreg kept frowning and said nothing.

"Where is my father?"

"I don't know."

"Where is he?" I banged a fist on his desk.

He did not budge. "I don't know," he repeated. "And that's the truth."

I pressed my lips together. For a second, I almost believed him, clinging to the refusal of his betrayal. But the memory of his company storming the palace and of the soldier slashing at my back in the forest was too fresh.

"You've chosen war, Galbreg," I concluded coldly, considering taking his life at once. Why wait, when I could close the short distance between us and stab him in the heart? *No, I am not a murderer.*

"Too weak for this world," my father's words echoed in my head. The shuffling sounds of my personal guard outside reminded me I had come here to detain Galbreg until he confessed my father's whereabouts.

"I hope it was worth it, for I'll make you regret it—every bit of it," I promised.

CHAPTER 4

ASHES

Everything stood in silence, as if waiting alongside me. The crickets, the distant cascades, the wind—the usual nightly mountain sounds fell quiet.

Leaning on the stone rail of my chamber's terrace, I studied the shadows nestled at the foot of the mountains. Far in the distance, the Dark Forest also stood eerily still. I wondered if the raven flying over the Crystal Palace had come from there, just like many of the fairytales. Movement on the other side caught my attention, and I observed the guards on the steps and the bridges below.

After I had confronted Galbreg, the next morning the thieves had requested an astronomical ransom in exchange for my father's life. It was ironic that right after I told Saphyr no one could put a price on her head, one had been put on my father's.

Lords from nearly every House paraded their secretaries and officials into my mother's study. The meetings, short or long, brought coffers filled with gold and jewels. Tonight, I could already glimpse heavy boxes and chests being transported up the steps to the main hall.

Galbreg insisted he was innocent and would not budge. That did not alter the fact that he had tried to murder Saphyr.

Moonlight illuminated the archways of my chamber. I would normally enjoy such a quiet evening, surrounded by nothing but the mountains and the sky. But tonight, even the stars were absent. Clouds and mist drifted past the mountain peaks surrounding my home.

I felt suffocated—lacking the air to breathe. For three days, we had been doing the impossible to retrieve my father and return him safely.

A knock on my door startled me. I had been too distracted with spying on the main building. My round chamber was surrounded by a cliff, from which water flowed freely into an abyss, watering the bushes that covered the rugged terrain below. The only way in was up an exhaustive set of stairs that ended on an arched bridge leading to my chamber. I unlocked the door and pulled open the wooden panels.

A small, cloaked figure stood before me. The hood fell away to reveal Saphyr's golden locks, which tumbled free over her emerald cloak and around her exquisite face. She bore an anxious expression.

"Saphyr!" I engulfed her in my arms and pressed my nose to her silken hair, inhaling its scent of summer nectarines. It filled me, made me feel whole again. *To think I had almost lost her forever.*

She clenched fistfuls of my robe and nuzzled her cheek against my collarbone.

Swiftly, I pulled her inside and closed the door. "What are you doing here? How did you get in?"

"My father came to meet with your mother. I disguised myself as a maid and came to see you."

"The Emperor is here?" I clenched my jaw and glanced at the endless procession of boxes being carried to the manor.

"We're going to rescue your father, Corvus," Saphyr said, locking her gaze on mine. Her hand threaded through strands of my obsidian hair.

Oh, the irony of my mother joining forces with the oblivious Emperor to rescue my father. My chest tightened with despair.

"Let yourself breathe," Saphyr ordered, tracing her hand over my chest under the opening of my robe. Her skin felt cold and refreshing against mine.

"The Emperor is not fond of my father," I whispered, without explaining I had been conspiring to dethrone her father all this time.

"My father owes your mother. She is calling in debts, is she not? That includes those from the Royal Family. After the attack on the palace, well … my father is making amends with certain Houses. He realizes how weak he has become."

Too late, I thought. Even if Galbreg had failed, I would find a way to exile her father.

"I captured Galbreg. He will confess soon." My chest tightened.

"Brenen sent several coffers of his own with the Emperor's tonight."
Saphyr bit her lower lip.

"Brenen?" I took a step back. It was one thing to accept payment from
the Royal Family for what was owed, but another to accept unrequested
help from Galbreg's son.

Saphyr nodded. "What exactly happened at the Crystal Palace?
Nobody answers my questions!" Her hand closed in a fist. "They've kept
me locked up all this time."

My teeth clenched. Even it was for her own safety, I disliked her being
held captive. "Galbreg threw a coup." I stared over at the mountains. "By
the time the Royal Guards arrived, the Crystal Palace was empty. A few
courtiers were hurt, but nobody died. It seems like they were after someone
in particular." I eyed her tentatively.

"He wanted me dead, didn't he?" She dropped her gaze to the floor,
her face somber. "Why?"

"As the Crown Princess, you're a threat to him and to his legitimacy
should he take the throne. The company that raided the Crystal Palace was
his."

"Yes, I remember Kanis mentioning it. I also remember the guards
shouting that *we* were upstairs on the terrace. It seems no coincidence that
his soldiers tried to murder me on my birthday, and thieves then abducted
your father."

"There is no such thing as coincidence," I asserted. "Galbreg is behind
my father's abduction, although he won't admit it yet."

"I'm so sorry you were there," Saphyr said. "You never attend Court
celebrations. It's my fault you suffered this."

"No! It would have been more dangerous if you were in the main hall,
rather than hidden in the staircase with me. And if I had not gone after your
carriage ..." I let my words trail off. "It was all meticulously planned," I
admitted bitterly.

"You snatched me from the claws of that old man." Saphyr grinned,
trying to lighten the mood.

I cupped her cheeks, my hands tingling. We had been apart for so long,
yet it felt like just yesterday that we had laughed as we chased each other
through the palace's hallways. "Saphyr, I just want you to know that ... the

offer I made, on the staircase, it stills stands … if you choose to take it." I swallowed. "If, by some miracle, my family recovers from this, or even if it doesn't, I can take care of you—if you want me, that is." Perhaps, with the wealth of my family gone, she would not want me anymore.

"Thank you." She smiled shyly.

Knocks sounded on my door again, and Saphyr's eyes widened. "I shouldn't be here," she whispered.

"Wait here," I instructed before going to the door and cautiously opening it.

A maiden in a white tunic stood, hands clasped before her. "Your presence is requested at the dining hall, Sire."

"Very well."

She turned and left, and I shut the door and returned to Saphyr, eyeing her maid's disguise. "How long can you stay?"

"As long as my father remains."

"I'll send someone for you when I see he's about to leave."

Saphyr nodded. I felt the urge to embrace her again, fearing she would disappear, but I contained it. "I'll be right back," I assured her.

I traded my black robe for a long dark coat before leaving my chamber. Saphyr turned away, facing the mountains, and I smiled at her small gesture of privacy.

White arches lit with brass plates of fire marked the path toward the manor.

Glancing back at my domed chamber, I saw Saphyr leaning on the stone railing, as I had been before she arrived, engulfed by the mist. The other half of my chamber's archways remained secluded, hidden by gracefully curved stone walls that reflected the fluid motion of the water rushing loudly below.

I continued my descent to another arched bridge that opened toward the main building. I did not recognize the guards standing on either side; they were probably the Emperor's.

More fog engulfed the main building, which spread out like a spider with arches of different heights, all with sinuous lines bending and turning back on themselves. Its elaborate architecture blended naturally with the surrounding mountains and cascades.

Soft light coming from the entrance beckoned a warm welcome to visitors. Entering, I then veered left to the main hall. Fire emanated from stone plates embedded in the walls, illuminating the small group that congregated around a chair overlooking the valley.

My mother stood next to them and turned at my approach. Dark circles ringed her eyes, making her look ashen and tired. She met me and offered her hand. I took it with a heavy heart, wishing I could be of more help. Perhaps the thieves should have taken me instead, saving my mother the suffering of losing my father.

"Your father is here," she said.

I froze. The people surrounding the chair looked at me with surprise, and perhaps even contempt, as they exited the hall. I could almost hear their thoughts—*the son who had let his father face probable death.*

I squared my shoulders as they passed. At the sight of my father, I held my breath. A huge purple stain blemished his left cheek. Grayish bags sat under his eyes, and white bandages wrapped his right arm. I assumed there were more bruises covering his body. Someone must have beaten him during interrogation.

"He is fine, more or less. No broken bones, and no deep gashes. Just a few scrapes and bruises," my mother said.

I gazed into my father's eyes with regret and sadness. The gleam in his eyes suggested he had witnessed awful things he would not reveal. "I'm sorry," I said.

He seemed surprised. "I'm happy to be back."

I could not tell if he placed some blame on me, but all I cared about was that he was alive, well, and back with us.

"Did you pay for his rescue, Mother?"

"Yes, dear. As you've probably noticed, I had to call in some debts owed to us, and I incurred a few new ones."

"How did they know how much to ask for?"

"Don't worry, Son." She glanced at my father. "In due time, we'll be able to pay them back."

My father shifted uncomfortably in his chair. I expected that the thieves had probably beaten the figure out of him during his interrogation.

"Is the Emperor still here?"

"How did you know?" My mother frowned. I remembered Saphyr, still waiting in my chambers, and swallowed.

"I saw the coffers traveling up the stairs, and guards I did not recognize. I assumed …"

"Ah, yes. The last batch will be delivered tonight."

"To the thieves?" I tried to contain a frown.

"Yes, we're planting a bait. See if we can link them to Galbreg or find out who's behind this."

Or just kill them, no questions asked, I thought, blinded by rage. My father locked his gaze on mine, and I was certain he shared the sentiment.

Hurried steps reverberated across the hall.

"My liege!" The guard was almost out of breath. "They shot it through the main gate." He kneeled and extended an arrow to my father, who took it, frowning at the rolled parchment attached to it with a thin red ribbon.

"The nerve!" My mother seethed.

My father unrolled the parchment, and his face paled.

"What is it?" She snatched it and read the message. Her gaze flew to me as her mouth fell open.

"What?" I demanded impatiently.

My parents observed each other silently.

"What?" I controlled the urge to tear the message from her hands.

"Corvus …" My mother hesitated, and I noticed her hands trembled.

"Out with it, Mother!"

"You must leave at once." My father sighed.

Time stopped. "Leave?" *Is Father taking vengeance on me?* "Leave where?"

"The Empire."

"Leave the *what*? I'm not leaving anywhere."

"They've placed a price on your head, too," my father explained bluntly. "They are asking for a further one-third of the bounty price, or they'll kill you."

My mother sobbed and threw her arms around me.

What on Earth is going on? "Mother, I won't leave you."

"Nor do I want you to leave," she said between sobs. "But what are we to do, Corvus?"

"Go after them! We have Galbreg. He doesn't have leverage against us now that Father is here. The Alliance will back us!"

"Houses from the Alliance have also been targeted, Corvus. In the past three days, many heads of the Houses have been abducted. We have all been stripped of our wealth. They're hunting us down, and we have no armies to protect ourselves with. We're at their mercy."

All I had worked for, all my power, gone in a single night. Galbreg had decimated me, coming after Saphyr, my family, and the Alliance. I stared at the long arrow on my father's lap, and fire blazed in my veins.

Galbreg would not kill me, but he wanted to exile me, just as I had planned for the Emperor.

"Who shot it?" I shouted at the guard.

"We don't know for certain. It came from the mountains. It pierced the door right next to my head."

"The Royal Guards are also here, for God's sake! How could this get past all of you?"

"We've sent scouting companies into the woods. Hopefully, we'll find them."

"You still haven't found the band of supposed *thieves* that abducted my father! And now we're held hostage in our own lands?" I balled my fists, then inhaled deeply to contain myself.

The guard remained silent, his gaze on the floor.

"Allow me to fight," I beseeched my father. "I'll find a way to gather more men."

"There is no use, Son," he replied wearily. "These are not mere thieves. We presume them to be connected to the Royal Guard."

"How? The army barged into the palace, not the Royal Guard."

"The Emperor told us spies infiltrated his guard. Things have been amiss for a while," he explained. "This stems from a much more serious matter that we can't handle."

We all remained silent for a moment, assessing the sudden weight of this news. If we had been able to wield a private army, even an unlawful and expensive one, we could have prevented all of this.

"But we already have Galbreg," I insisted. "Who else could be behind it?"

"We don't know," my mother whispered. "But you are at risk, so you must leave until we find out."

"I can take care of myself."

"I'd rather you didn't sleep here tonight, Son."

"But, Mother, I—

"This arrow landed near his head," she roared, pointing at the guard. "They could come and take you tonight. Don't you understand? You're at risk, even here."

The moments that followed elapsed slowly. I watched as they decided where I would be taken, what I would take, and who I would go with. They would not allow me a say in any of it.

No. I would fight. I would seek the Houses still standing from the Alliance and ... My mother locked eyes with me. Her worry put a knot in my throat. If I died, it would kill her. Clenching my teeth, I imagined myself beating the truth out of Galbreg with my bare hands, but my father's words reminded me the issue ran deeper. It was not something I could solve immediately. I needed time and more resources.

Suddenly realizing what I had to do, I hugged my mother fiercely, not knowing when I would see her again. Then I kneeled before my father and muttered an apology. At least he was alive.
"Please take good care of her." Then I stood, turned around, and left the hall.

Galbreg had turned me into nothing but a useless, helpless tool to threaten my family with. If I was to be kicked out of my home, out of my family, and to disappear, it would be on my terms. And if I had just lost everything, I vowed I would return powerful enough to recover it all—and then some.

I startled Saphyr when I stormed through the wooden doors of my chamber. She dashed to me, sensing my indignation.

"I must go ... tonight. To Oldterra." I took her by the arms and stared deep into her eyes. "They've now set a price on my head, and we have nothing left. I have to leave the Empire."

Saphyr's eyes widened. I had expected her to burst into tears or fire off a series of questions, but, to my surprise, she remained calm.

"I'll come with you."

A wave of relief crashed over me. I had prepared for her to reject me and stay behind with her family, which I would have understood. After all, she was the Crown Princess. But my heart wholly hoped she would choose me instead. I could not bear the idea of anything separating us again.

"Thank you." I swallowed.

"With one condition," she countered.

Anything. Anything she wanted.

"We leave for my sister's home in Isverden."

Her decision of going to the glacial lands of the north surprised me. The only place I had left was Oldterra, my mother's birthplace in the east, an ocean away. But if Saphyr wished to flee north, I'd be on my own with no blood relatives or known allies to rely on.

"She will take care of us. Trust me."

I nodded, putting my plan of going to Oldterra aside. "I trust you. We'll head there, but first, we must visit Kanis. I must also send word of this decision to my parents later. If I tell them now, they'll nail me inside a box and ship me off to wherever they please tonight."

She chuckled nervously.

Turning to observe my chamber for one last time, unsure of when, if ever, I would return, I saw that the mist had lifted and the moon glistened over the range beyond. I would miss these tranquil views daily, so beautiful at dawn and nightfall. But what I would miss the most, besides my mother, lay quietly sleeping on the veranda.

The fluffy white ball unfurled from the ground, its ears popping up at the thump of my approaching steps.

"Come here, Snowball," I instructed, my voice trembling. The white wolf stood and rubbed its head against my thigh. Kneeling, I ran my fingers through his thick fur. The noble beast had been with me since it was a pup, there for me during the best and worst days. Now, I could not take him with me. It would be too exhausting a journey for Snowball's old paws. I knew Mother would take proper care of him, but that did not alleviate the feeling that I was abandoning my dearest friend.

"Please forgive me." My voice faltered. "Be a good boy. I'll be back as soon as I can."

Who knew how long it would take? Months? Years? What if Snowball died from sadness and a feeling of abandonment?

"I'm sorry," I whispered again as he tried to comfort me by sniffing my neck.

A warm hand squeezed my shoulder kindly. "Everything will be fine," Saphyr murmured, knowing how much I cared for him.

I squeezed him in a last hug, unable to take my eyes off him as we threw on our cloaks. The wolf stood on the terrace, watching us silently. With a lump in my throat, I slung on my satchel and shut the door to my chamber.

As Saphyr and I hurried down the steep steps, a howl echoed through the mountains, cleaving my heart into pieces—Snowball howling to the moon, accusing his traitorous owner. I knew my heart would never again be complete.

CHAPTER 5
FORGING FATE

The fire crackled vividly in the forest clearing. Kanis leaned on a tree, peeling an apple with his dagger. The past few hours had passed numbly. I had followed the steps, putting one foot in front of the other—an empty carcass, an automaton moving by itself.

Overnight, I had been stripped of everything. My family, my wealth, my home, even my wolf. I had only a blade, a satchel containing food and water, and barely enough coin to pay my way along the path into exile.

Luckily, Saphyr and Kanis were with me, the two friends I cherished most apart from Snowball. For that, I was grateful, yet I had never felt so alone in the world, so forsaken. My childhood, and everything I had known, was left behind. I was an exile. One day, the world lay at my feet; the next, I had nothing. Had I deserved it?

I lay on the grass, inhaling the pure mountain air and staring into the night sky. At least I was alive. Being so high in the mountains made me feel like I could stretch my fingers to the stars and touch them, or perhaps take one. I imagined how that would feel, the sheer power of it. Would an all-powerful being materialize, perhaps angry to be torn down to the hellish world of men?

I peeked at Saphyr, who sat leaning against the tree trunk, her eyes closed. I must truly have been mad to have taken the Crown Princess of the Empire with me on such a perilous journey through the woods and down the mountains. Her father would be furious when he awoke to find her chamber empty. As would mine. At least mine would not send a unit of guards after us, given the handwritten note I had ensured he would receive in the morning.

I pondered what the Royal Guards would do if they found the princess with us. They would not dare kill the successor to the House of Alba and the fifth son to the House of Phoebus. Then, I remembered they may have been the ones behind all this chaos, and I cursed them under my breath.

"Said something, Milord?" Kanis mocked me.

I huffed. "At least I don't have to mourn a title I never had." Our wealth had accumulated by generations of hard work, not by a noble title.

"A title means nothing," Saphyr said, her head resting against the tree trunk as she observed the fire.

I sighed, thinking she probably felt rather miserable herself. Running away to avoid being sold into marriage by her own father after escaping murder—the Crown Princess of our Empire. *Yes, I guess a title means nothing.*

"How long will it take?" I asked Kanis. "To get to the port?" Our horses neighed anxiously, and I knew the path down the mountain could be treacherous, especially as we were traveling an abandoned trail rather than the wider main path.

"Four hours, more or less, depending on how fast we move."

"We'll probably have until dawn before the Royal Guards come after us," I replied, eyeing Saphyr. She did not react. Kanis nodded.

"There's a full moon. We should head down tonight instead of waiting for them to come at dawn," Kanis suggested.

Saphyr said nothing. We were mostly concerned about her. We had no issues riding the horses at night, but with comfortable carriages at her disposal all the time, it was not often that she chose to ride on horseback.

"Should we try?" I asked her.

"Yes," she said, returning from her thoughts and blinking twice.

Kanis and I exchanged worried looks. I subtly signaled for him to come to me as Saphyr sighed deeply and closed her eyes again.

"She seems tired, and so do you." Kanis sighed himself and lay down with his head next to mine. We both stared at the sky.

"The past few days have been a complete nightmare."

"I guess I'm lucky my family is fine."

"Between me losing everything and Saphyr almost being enslaved in marriage and killed, yes, you are most definitely lucky." Silence stole all conversation for a few seconds.

"We will find more allies in Isverden and send word to Oldterra. They'll come to our aid." I tried to reassure myself, but the free-falling sensation in my stomach suggested otherwise.

"We should focus on our survival. We must first reach Isverden."

"Are you certain you want to accompany us?" I asked Kanis for the fifth time that day.

After Saphyr and I had left my chamber, we stole a pair of horses from the stable and rode to Kanis's home. He had been surprised to see us but quickly decided to join us after hearing what had happened. Once we had made all the necessary arrangements, we set off down the mountain with his guidance.

"The good part about having four older brothers is that I won't be missed, Corvus. They'll take care of everything, so stop worrying about it."

"I can't thank you enough," I said, deeply moved by his friendship and unwavering loyalty. "I want you to know I'd have done the same for you."

"I know." His tone told me he was smiling. In the dark, I smiled back, grateful.

"We're brothers," he assured me, catching my train of thought, as he so often did.

I searched for his wrist and squeezed it tightly.

"Everything will be fine," he drawled, as if to calm a nagging child.

"I sure hope so."

We rested for a few more minutes before we roused Saphyr, mounted our horses, and resumed our journey. Kanis led the way down the path, Saphyr rode between us, and I guarded her back.

She had let her hood down, and her hair shone in the starlight. She had been alone for so long, trapped in the hellish Court where so many tried to rip each other's flesh to gain her father's favor. We were both wary of others, never knowing whether they were trustworthy or were after our wealth and power. In so many ways, we were the same—trapped by the fate of our families.

Although they had forced us to leave everything behind, a subtle feeling of freedom and hope hung in the air. It was time to forge our own destinies, free of the will of others.

Saphyr half-turned back to me, as if the weight of my gaze had tugged her to me. Her beauty was unparalleled, unlike that of any other woman I had ever seen. Her skin was dewy in the moonbeams, and her curls shone where they caressed her cheeks. Her peachy lips were scarily inviting. A gust of wind brought a breath of her fragrance, and my stomach fluttered, remembering the seconds we had shared before the attack.

Breathless, I wondered what the future held for us. Suddenly, I felt hopeful. A future with her was something I had imagined only in my wildest dreams, and, I realized, was what I had been fighting for all this time. At least now we had the opportunity to be together, even if we had been forced to leave. Everything came at a price. But I would cling to this small hope. I would hold fast to it while I could.

We rode in silence for two hours. Deep silence gripped the forest. Most of its creatures were asleep, not even the crickets chanted. Twice I had almost fallen asleep, but I held on tightly, so I would not fall off the horse.

In the hour before sunrise, I could see Saphyr nodding off occasionally. I covered my mouth and made an owl call, letting Kanis know we needed to find shelter and sleep for an hour or two.

Soon, we stopped at a small cave. I offered my hand to Saphyr to help her dismount. Taking it, she then swung her leg backward, but having miscalculated the distance to the floor, she lost her balance. I swept her up, my arm encircling her torso, and helped her stand. I could feel her heart beating rapidly beneath my palm.

"Thank you," she said, her almond eyes blinking with surprise.

I felt a warm flush color the skin of my face and neck, and my fingers tingled at the warmth of her touch. I was still getting used to it.

"Ladies first." Kanis held one arm toward the cave.

I let my hands lose their grip, and Saphyr walked along the narrow path bordering the cliff and entered the cave.

"I'll guard for an hour. You sleep, and then we'll switch," Kanis said, signaling me to follow Saphyr, and I did.

The rocky opening was small, but it protected us from the wind and had enough space for the three of us, should Kanis join us. The horses remained tied to a stand of trees close to the cave.

Saphyr sat against the rock wall. A clear mantle of stars illuminated the silhouette of the mountains and the valley of Sol City below. I could even see the sea farther away, where I knew a ship awaited us at the port.

I was exhausted. My thighs were sore from riding, and my head was full of anxious and useless thoughts. I needed to rest. I shucked off my cloak and laid it on the floor. Thankfully, it was large enough to cover the floor space. Then I slumped against the cool stone wall and invited Saphyr to lie down on the cloak.

"Only if we share," she said.

My brows shot up at her decisiveness. I had figured she would be too uncomfortable to sleep next to me. "Very well." Too tired to argue, I lay down facing her. Saphyr tossed her cloak over us to shield us from the bitter mountain wind.

"Thank you," I said, wondering whether she would have done the same for Kanis.

My eyelids felt heavy; they itched, begging me to close them. "Goodnight," I whispered, and something warm enclosed my hand before I plummeted into sleep.

I woke abruptly, jolting up as if a cord had tried to pull my heart out. Pink-orange sunbeams lazily bathed the mountains, but the valley below was still drenched in purple shadows. The birds already sang. Saphyr slept soundly next to me.

I stood carefully, ensuring my cloak stayed in place over her. The mushy earth muffled my steps. I found Kanis sitting against the outside cave wall, his dagger moving swiftly in his hands, carving a bear out of wood.

"Awake so early? You barely slept."

"I want to get to the city," I said. "I don't feel particularly safe here knowing there could be bastards lurking around in the woods, searching for us."

Kanis looked up through the clearing to the tight line of trees delineating the forest. "Let her rest. You can ride with her, so she can nod off while we head down the mountain. We'll tie the other horse to mine."

I nodded, taking a seat next to him. He continued to carve the figurine. "Kanis, I want to practice my close combat skills. I want to learn how to injure quickly without killing, so I won't hesitate again."

His eyebrows shot up, but then he quickly nodded in understanding. "We'll begin training as soon as we reach a safe place," he promised.

"I want to learn how to shoot a crossbow too." Never again would I be threatened without being able to fight back and defend those around me.

"Look, even if you knew a few specialized moves, and with or without stronger weapons, you wouldn't have been able to neutralize the thieves who abducted your father."

"You don't know that," I said. "At least I would've done a better job of defending myself and protecting Saphyr from the soldier in the woods."

"You probably would've got yourself killed." He sighed.

"If I had stayed with my parents, they wouldn't have taken my father." My heart throbbed at the memory of my mother's desperate cries.

"You wouldn't have *had* a mother nor a father left by the end of your attempt. Stop blaming yourself."

I lowered my gaze.

"Corvus, you've lost everything. But you're not the only one. Take Saphyr ... she was put on the market by her own father. This had been brewing for a while, and you know it."

"Does that mean we deserved it?"

"No! It means it could've been worse. You could've died, Corvus. At least you're both alive. They could've abducted you instead of your father. The oldest from the House of Vilmir didn't have your luck, you know? He had his ear chopped off and was left naked in the middle of the main road. He, too, lost everything. Some of the heads of the Alliance were murdered in their own houses. Your life, Corvus, is worth so much more than anything. It's irreplaceable."

"Who?" I asked, unable to swallow.

"Dolmir and Gellis."

My face turned ashen, but I kept silent, reflecting over my friend's words. The Houses of Dolmir and Gellis had been involved in some questionable business deals before joining the Alliance, but that did not justify their deaths. I stared into the sky, wondering if the souls of the two old men had ascended to the divine realm or if they had completely ceased to exist. My chest ached at the thought of it—death.

"Corvus?"

I flinched. "Yes. I—"

I knew Galbreg had been riling up the people to use them against the Emperor. But I refused to accept that the Heads and sons of wealthy families would become the targets of violence and hatred. We were being hunted down; our coffers turned over. The hard work of many generations, and all the benefits it had provided to many others, was now jeered at, thrown out. We had to consider ourselves lucky they had spared our lives.

"How did it come to this, Kanis? We were only trying to help them by establishing a new rule, one that would not hoard the wealth but keep the Empire financially stable for the benefit of all. Even if I failed, we—"

"Galbreg must be behind it. The General turning against the Emperor and the Houses of the Alliance. The soldiers we've funded and fed to protect the Empire are now chasing our tails. Galbreg has gained the support of the people by giving them free food and promising them free housing and more wealth. Who will say no to that?"

"But *we* provide for them. We give them work with fair pay, let them work our lands, reap the harvest, and live comfortably on our land with their families. We even offer them our protection from foreign kingdoms. What's so bad about it that they're willing to annihilate us and take what's ours by right?"

"Galbreg has promised them all of that in exchange for nothing, Corvus. He has promised them our lands, our coffers, our food to reward their support. Most of them are happy to lie around all day with their bellies full and warm, without having to lift a single finger."

"When did you learn of this?" I asked, angry. Had I known of Galbreg's misdeeds, I would have stopped him much sooner.

"The brats sent the word right after your father was taken. We were fooled."

"He'll end up usurping the throne anyway—only now he won't have the Alliance telling him what to do. Handouts won't last forever. The crops will die without care, and then who will protect the people from outside forces?"

"The people don't know that, Corvus. They just see us as privileged bastards. We should be dead, for all they care, and our belongings, theirs. It doesn't matter how hard we worked, nor the humble origins of some of the Houses. Instead of giving them the opportunity to grow by working hard and collaborating with us, Galbreg has planted hatred and jealousy in their hearts." Kanis ran a hand through his hair, his eyes wide. "These people don't know how to keep an Empire alive, nor what it takes to keep them safe. They only see us as the bastards who've put them to work in order to feed ourselves."

"Galbreg will throw them a bone to keep them docile and horde our wealth for himself," I said bitterly.

"You know he will." Kanis huffed, his stare piercing the wooden miniature bear.

"Unless we stop him." Saphyr stood at the cave opening, the dawn at her back. The three of us knew it was only a matter of time before Galbreg escaped, and our families would be in real danger again.

Kanis and I silently exchanged looks. It was pointless. We had nothing to offer, nor could we win the empire back alone. What could I possibly do when I had already lost?

"We must stop him," she insisted.

I sighed, looking away. Let Kanis talk some sense to her.

"Saphyr, believe me, I understand you. But there's nothing we can do by fighting blindly in the dark. We don't know who's helping him. It's too late. We can't change anything."

"So, you're telling me, I'm supposed to let my father and his Court die at the hands of Galbreg?" She stood before Kanis and looked down on him with the strength and grace of a future empress.

"The father who almost auctioned you off to God knows which old creep offered the most money for you? I think the answer is very clear. This is a new start for you. A life of your own with someone who actually cares about you and who can protect you—even if penniless." Kanis pointed at me with his chin.

I looked away; my jaw clenched. *Always so helpful,* I thought, standing, and walking to the horses. Saphyr had not given me an answer, and I did not intend to pressure her.

"The best we can do right now, Saphyr, is go to Sol City and board the ship that's waiting for us. I've contacted Delphino; he'll have everything ready."

I thought of the admiral who commanded the naval fleet. He had also grown up with us. To my dislike, he also liked Saphyr. At least we had him on our side.

Kanis stood, and we saddled the horses. He tied Saphyr's to his mare, which remained standing quietly in the same place.

I took the reins of mine and guided it toward her. "Come," I said softly. "Ride with me. It'll make the journey easier on you."

She ignored my open palm and put her feet up the stirrup. Grabbing the pommel with both hands, she then swung herself up onto the strong black stallion.

I let out another sigh as I swung myself up behind her, sensing it would be one silent ride. Saphyr's hood already covered her hair and body. Her warmth felt odd against my forearms. I tried to leave as much space between us as I could when I grabbed the reins.

Kanis led the way into the forest. Saphyr's white mare trotted behind him, a tight rope ensuring she wouldn't stray off the path.

Sunlight finally made its way through the crown of the forest, setting the morning dew sparkling on grass sprinkled with delicate white and purple wildflowers. I had half expected the sky to be mired in gray clouds and endless thunder. Instead, it was serene, ironically perfect for a morning stroll.

The lack of sleep hit me again after a while, my eyes burning with the need to close. Thankfully, we faced no upheaval throughout our journey. Kanis and I finally relaxed when we entered the city's stone archway.

The *trot-trot* of our horses' hooves echoed through the empty streets. Saphyr had nodded off against my chest, and I had welcomed her warmth in the morning's chill. But the clatter of hooves on the cobblestone woke her.

"We're almost there," I murmured.

She straightened up and remained silent as we ventured into Sol City.

CHAPTER 6
NEW BEGINNINGS

The merriment had continued nonstop for hours—a cozy inn, abundant drinks and food, and a generous fire. We sat close to the welcoming hearth. Kanis sat sprawled in a wing chair, clutching a tall tankard of ale, and grinning at the drunkards shouting rambunctious lyrics to a fiddle, bagpipe, and lute melody. Taking up the jug on the table, I poured my third glass of mead. It was a pleasant change from the hell of the last two days. I had to admit it was refreshing to be clad in clean attire after a warm bath. We had slept most of the day when we had arrived, and Saphyr had not ventured from her room since.

"Do you think she is all right?" I slurred.

"I'm sure sheesh fine," Kanis drawled back.

Glancing at our empty bowls of beef stew, I wondered whether she had eaten. *Has she slept at all? Is she still asleep?*

The piper's fat fingers moved swiftly over the pipe while his other hand pressed against the bag.

She can't possibly be asleep with all this noise. I studied the men who still lingered, mostly all drunk or distracted by conversations and music. *What if one of them hopes to find a warm bed in the rooms upstairs? What if Saphyr has left her door unlocked?*

A long swig of mead helped me recover my breath. "That's it. I'm going to check on her."

Kanis gave me a bored, reproving look. "As you please." He made a dismissive gesture, and his gaze returned to the musicians.

I nodded as I stood. The inn suddenly lurched sideways, lopsided, and I clutched the back of my friend's wing chair. I was unaccustomed to drinking so much. Kanis seemed fine, even with double the drinks in him.

Summoning what sobriety I could, I walked in a relatively straight line through a sea of pipe-smoke to the staircase.

Upstairs, the camphor of wooden walls and the floor masked the stench of ale and liqueur wafting up from downstairs. The hallway was empty, silent. I passed the room I shared with Kanis and paused at Saphyr's door, pressing my forehead against the doorframe. The air felt cold and dry as I inhaled deeply through my mouth.

"Saphyr…?" I tapped twice.

Nothing. Perhaps she was asleep after all. I knocked again. Silence. I was about to leave when I heard the lock dislodge gently. The door opened a few inches.

"Saphyr?" I tried again, pressing my palm to the door to push it open. "Are you here?"

The room was in darkness. Embers gleamed ruby where a final log died in the grate. A lone candle next to the bed provided the only light. Saphyr sat on the bed, her curls falling loose down her back.

"Are you all right?" I asked, standing by the doorframe.

"Yes …"

"Did you eat?"

"Yes."

"Sleep?"

"Yes. Why have you come, Corvus?"

Her bluntness hit me like a slap.

"I wanted to make sure you were safe. I'll be on my way now."

"Wait …"

I tilted my head, curious.

"… stay."

I glanced behind me, doubting that she was indeed speaking to me. But the hallway was empty.

I stepped in, gingerly closing the door behind me.

I moved across the room to the window, gazing out over the port below. Waves crashed against the boulders that protected the streets from their deluge. Our ship rocked at its moorings, illuminated by a crescent moon. I exhaled, remembering we were to embark in the morning.

"Presumably, my father's guards could not track us."

"Not that we are aware of. They're probably still descending the mountains, following our tracks. We moved faster, skipping a night's sleep." I covered my yawn with one hand.

Terracotta roofs spread down to the water of the Tagus River, which flowed down the mountain to part the city until it freed itself at the sea. Several palatial houses nestled in the skirts of the mountains, their torches aglow.

"It is a beautiful city." Saphyr came to stand next to me, modestly pulling close the shawl that covered her nightgown.

"I'm sorry I come unannounced at midnight. It wasn't proper," I muttered.

"It's fine." She looked amused by my apology. "I couldn't sleep anyway—not with the drunks shouting their lungs out downstairs."

I huffed out a laugh. "I figured. Kanis insisted that a few drinks take the edge off."

Saphyr evaluated me, concern darkening her eyes.

"That's the ship ..." I pointed out the vessel. "The one that'll take us to Isverden."

"I know." She sighed.

"Are we doing the right thing, Saphyr?"

"Are there any other options, Corvus?"

The ocean glittered far off on the horizon, where the waves met the sky. "If I could, I'd have helped my family fight and helped the other Houses take back their peace."

"Look at us—the Crown Princess and the Empire's wealthiest heir running for their lives and their freedom. Kanis is brave to join us. This journey wasn't forced upon him."

"He has a kind soul, and I'm thankful. I am proud to call Kanis my brother, although we don't share the same blood."

Saphyr nodded silently. "Isverden will help. Do you worry they'll guess where we've fled to?"

"Not even your sister knows we're traveling her way," I soothed her, but the thought made me uncomfortable. "Once we're on that ship, no one will be able to trace our location. Delphino will keep our identities hidden, insist he is transporting no one but a few ambassadors. And we have barely shown our faces to the public. I'm more worried about you … Your beauty is renowned throughout the Empire." I eyed her with a soft smile.

Her lips curved into a smile, but she looked away at the bobbing ship. "I've hardly ever left the Crystal Palace. No one will recognize me down here."

Gazing at the mist-covered mountaintops, I wondered about my parents. How had they reacted to my note? Mother might never forgive me for the change of plans, but at least no one could now blackmail them by using me. I shook off the guilt that whispered I was abandoning them.

"We must trust that we're doing right. There's nothing else we can do," Saphyr said.

"All will be fine." I sighed. "We should rest. We must wake early." The mead had kicked in, and I wished to throw myself into oblivion.

Saphyr took my wrist and guided me to her bed.

My eyes widened.

"You sleep *over* the covers. I'll sleep under," she clarified, tucking herself under the bedsheets.

Grinning, I kicked my boots off, all thoughts receding as I sank into the softness of the mattress and airy pillows. "Thank you," I breathed, quietly admitting to myself that I otherwise would have fallen asleep on her doorstep to ensure her safety. *Never let Kanis invite you for a drink again*, I made a mental note.

I jolted awake, my skin prickling as a man's shadow passed across me in the darkness. Without a thought, my hand shot out and I gripped his neck, squeezing tight as my other hand grasped for the dagger on my thigh.

"Relax, you dimwit. It's me!"

I blinked the haziness away, and Kanis's face came into view.

"For God's sake …" I rasped out.

The sun was not up.

"Come on, drag your drunken ass back to our room. I can't believe you fell asleep here."

"How did you get in?"

"You left the door unlocked, smartass."

"Bloody hell!" I clutched my head, wobbling to my feet with my friend's help. "I'm never letting you get me drunk again."

"Yeah, sure!" Kanis huffed, supporting me with his shoulder.

Saphyr giggled and rolled over.

I made sure to lock her door behind us and we headed back to our room, where we both collapsed onto our beds until the first rays of sun lit our faces.

By day, the inn was a pale shadow of its nightly vigor. Blinding light shone through the round windows, bathing the chairs, tables, and walls. Saphyr lifted a steaming pot of black tea and poured me a second cup.

"You look miserable." Kanis laughed.

"Bastard," I drawled, straightening up from the table. We had already almost finished the basket of bread and cheese.

"No sugar, thank you," I said, as she poured cream into the dark liquid. I took a sip. The bitter drink helped settle my stomach and focus.

Few people buzzed about their business on the streets, and we had to depart. Miserably, I cloaked and readied myself to leave. Saphyr had braided her hair, twisting it into a tight crown upon her head. Her porcelain skin glowed in the sunlight as I held the door open for her. She nodded appreciatively, her dark-emerald skirt swishing as she swept out onto the cobblestone street. She led the way to the dock; Kanis and I walking together behind her.

A sweet aroma rose from freshly baked pastries, tempting me to postpone our hasty departure to enjoy them with a third cup of tea. Crisp sea air filled my lungs, and seagulls chirped along the esplanade and hovered over the harbor, hunting for scraps.

I gazed one last time at the smoking chimneys of the townhouses and their balconies adorned with flowerpots. The citizens were still at home, enjoying breakfast before a hard day's work.

Bells chimed in the distance, marking a new hour as we reached the ship on the dock. We were on time. The boy who had brought fresh clothes for us to the inn last night stood waiting. Our steps clanked on the wood, drowned by the splash of water against stone.

"We're ready, Milord." He bowed to Kanis.

I looked away, hoping he would not recognize me. Saphyr had not removed her hood and peered at him from its shadows.

"Take me to the Admiral." Kanis nodded to the boy.

Saphyr and I waited on the deck while Kanis made final arrangements. Before long, Delphino welcomed us aboard and showed us to our cabins.

He was happy to see us, and we shared in whispers the events of the past days. Lines furrowed the young Admiral's forehead, and his dark gaze studied Saphyr with concern. She had assured him we would strategize once we arrived in Isverden, but Delphino did not seem convinced. He offered to help in any way he could, as the interests of his family, Dellmar House, were at stake. We shook hands, and he excused himself to the captain's cabin.

Saphyr, Kanis, and I moved up to the stern to watch Sol City fade from view. The valley city, kissed by the sea at its feet, made for a picturesque view as the ship sailed through the turquoise waters. Kanis tapped my forearm, signaling to dolphins racing alongside us, leaping over the ship's wake. I pointed them out to Saphyr.

"Beautiful," she breathed. "Almost as if they're saying goodbye." Her voice quavered. The melancholy I had pushed to the bottom of my stomach rose like bile, and I had to fight to keep it anchored.

"Think of it as a long journey, not a goodbye for good. We'll return soon," Kanis suggested.

The question none of us could answer was "*When?*"

Saphyr turned and descended the stairs into her cabin.

"This is absurd," I said, watching the city disappear on the horizon.

"Life is absurd," Kanis agreed.

Fortunately, the boat's rocking did not sicken me, but the unstable floor made Kanis's stomach churn.

"I can't wait to leave this godforsaken ship." He leaned against the deck rail of the creaking wooden vessel, emptying the contents of his dinner into the waves crashing below.

The three sails above us flapped ferociously in the wind, ferrying us at full speed through the open ocean. Saphyr rarely ventured outside her cabin, aware that her presence made the crew nervous—some nonsense regarding women bringing misfortune to sea voyages.

I pondered how she was faring in her isolation. After dinner, the crew sang tales on deck to the rhythm of their lutes. The night was still clear, with just a dash of orange and purple twilight, although the first stars glittered. God had blessed us with wonderful weather and a clear sky to guide us to Isverden during the night.

Sailors banging on the uske barrels that served as percussion drowned out Kanis's curses as he wiped his mouth with the back of his wrist. The wind that had propelled us at full speed all day suddenly dropped, slowing the vessel considerably and flattening the ocean before us, stilling the crashing waves.

I shut my eyes, inhaling a full breath of sea air. Strangely, the water called to me. I inspected its surface. Apart from the dolphins, we had seen no sea creatures since leaving Sol City, so a sparkle in the water caught my attention. *Another dolphin,* I thought, but the creature that emerged twisted my guts as I recognized the back of a woman's head full of golden curls.

"Saphyr!" I shouted, but the drumming drowned out my shout. "Saphyr!" I shouted again, desperately. How had she fallen in? I shucked off my boots and placed a hand on the rail. She kept moving in and out of the water. She would drown.

"Corvus!" Kanis's hand stopped me. "What are you doing?"

"She'll drown!" I pointed, exasperated.

Kanis's eyes widened. "What on—!"

Not catching his last word, I pushed myself over the rail and dived into the water. It was excruciatingly cold. I emerged looking for Saphyr, but I was unable to see her. Back at the ship, Kanis was already diving in after me, a rope attached to his torso. But it was not the sight of him jumping nor the freezing water temperature that chilled my bones. It was Saphyr, wearing her nightgown, staring white-faced at us from the deck.

If Saphyr was on the deck, who had I seen in the water? As if to mock my stupidity, something curled around my feet and yanked me under the waves. I kicked and thrashed with all my might until I shot up to the surface and desperately filled my lungs with air. I shot a terrified glance to Kanis, who had also realized Saphyr was not in the water. Suddenly, it was me who was drowning. The rope tied to Kanis's torso became our only hope.

I tried swimming toward him, but whatever had curled around my feet was now encircling my waist and hauling me down again. In despair, I knew I could not fight for long. Kanis gaped at me as, in a split second, we were both dragged underwater.

Dim rays cutting the water's surface muddled the already blurry waters. *What kind of creature is this? What a ridiculous end—to find death while running from it.*

My hazy vision of Kanis gave me hope. I reached a hand to him, but I found a golden-haired woman instead, her tresses floating around her. Past her waist, two long fishtails replaced her feet.

I kicked furiously again, gasping for air as her hands curled around my neck. *Has death finally come to take me?* I thought as everything went dark.

CHAPTER 7

SIRENIBUS

The first sound I heard was the crackling of a fire. The second sound was the opposite of the first: a bubbling murmur of water enveloping everything around me, including the fire. My confusion did not allow me to discern my location as I slowly opened my eyes.

Kanis lay unconscious on the floor, strands of bronze hair covering his eyes. I tried to stand, but everything was drifting and hazy. My head begged me to remain asleep, but my gut ordered me to stand and flee. And so, I stood, slowly, trying to determine what had happened. I recalled us being dragged underwater by a strange creature. I immediately touched my neck, where I had felt those cold, uncanny fingers. Two parallel scrapes lined each side of my neck. Whatever it was, it had claws.

"Kanis …" My voice was hoarse, and my mouth tasted of salt. Behind Kanis, a hearth spat greenish sparks and tongues of jade flame blazed almost to the ceiling. Made of polished limestone, the hearth was flanked by intricately spiraled columns. Atop it, a sculpted mythical creature watched over us: a siren, long hair obscuring her breasts. She sat on her twisted legs, a fishtail instead of feet in each hand. A shiver chilled my spine and made the hairs on the back of my neck bristle.

Emerald light rippled around the room and the muffled sound of water invited me to turn to inspect it, but I froze, rooted to the spot like a tree. I did not wish to confirm my suspicions of this place we were in.

My gaze followed the sculptures adorning the fireplace and vaulted ceiling: undulating seaweed, corals, fishes, and other sea creatures. As I turned, I examined the length of the columns to the floor—there was no floor. Water formed a glassy panel between the columns and the place where the floor would have been. I stood staring through the watery window, for a moment forgetting to breathe.

A vast underwater city opened up beneath our feet, allowing us a bird's-eye view. Human-like creatures swam about, accompanied by all kinds of fishes, some even riding dolphins and sharks, one hand gripping their fins.

Sirens! I took a step back, rubbing my eyes. A white palace loomed from the submerged city's center, enveloped by a swirling, conch-like protective structure. Several other globes with glowing oval windows, very much like ours, floated around the palace.

"Where on Earth are we?" Kanis approached from behind me, finally awake.

We were alone.

Then it hit me: I had lost her. Saphyr was not here. I covered my eyes, condemning myself. I had thrown myself out of a moving ship, plunged into a freezing ocean, willing to die to save her; yet, here I was, still alive in a strange place, but without her. And she alone in a ship full of drunken sailors.

"Oh God." I paced. "What have I done, Kanis?"

"Are you seeing this?" Kanis crouched, sticking his finger through the floor's watery surface.

"Saphyr," I muttered.

Kanis stood again and his lips formed a tight line. "I thought it was her, too," he said. He must have seen the misery in my eyes because he added, "We both saw her in the water … and then on the ship."

"None of this makes sense." I extended my arms, gesturing around the room. "We should've drowned. Whatever pulled us underwater knew it and probably wanted us to."

"Yet we didn't. We're alive. Perhaps it lured us into the water not to die but to be brought here."

"Brought *where*?" I growled. "We've never heard of an underwater kingdom, nor the possibility that humans could breathe underwater, let alone build an entire civilization here."

Kanis's jaw tightened, and he looked puzzled as he studied the room. "This was premeditated, Corvus. A trap."

He was right, and it bothered me. I was always used to being in control of my surroundings, but we were in fact, trapped. There were no doors anywhere, only a fireplace and a window to the marine city. "By *whom*? Sirens do not exist—are not *supposed* to exist."

"I'm not being any sea monster's supper."

"I'm flattered, human. But your bony flesh doesn't suit us."

My guts knotted at the silvery, high-pitched voice. I clenched my teeth as I turned to face the creature.

Kanis squared his shoulders, stepping before me to confront the newcomer. "Who are you?"

"Your worst nightmare." She sneered as she walked, with feline grace, from the fireplace. Her smooth skin shimmered and rippled with the water's reflection. Platinum blonde hair fell straight to her hips and provided a contrast to her cold blue eyes. She reminded me of Brenen, although her hair had a hint of lavender.

She wore a loose sleeveless tunic, tied at her waist and then falling freely in an undulating pewter shimmer, something akin to fish scales. I stiffened, understanding that she was the creature that had pulled me under the water.

"You," I spat, unconsciously touching the two slits she had slashed in my neck.

Suddenly, her silvery hair levitated, and a golden light shone from her eyes. I inhaled sharply at the sight of soft golden curls, porcelain skin, and hazel eyes.

Saphyr suddenly looked back at me with a cold smirk.

"Yes, me," she hissed, clearly pleased with the effect.

"Enough!" I growled.

The monster wearing Saphyr's skin paced the room.

"What do you want?" Kanis asked.

"You'll soon find out." Green flames spouted up like two curtains of water, and she slid in through them. Kanis and I immediately followed her through the tall columns of the fireplace.

We entered a hallway of polished stone with an enclosed colonnade on the right. The left-hand side was completely open, and sea creatures swam freely. What opened this tunnel of air in the ocean? I felt compelled to pierce the screen of water and touch a fish. The shapeshifting siren, back in her own skin, led the way to the heart of the city, toward the palace.

It was beyond absurd, seeming nothing but a nightmare, and I hoped I would wake up soon. To my right, Kanis appeared to share the sentiment.

Not even the myths of Sol had depicted such a thing as an underwater city, only sirens seducing mariners, or sea monsters sinking ships during a thunderstorm. They had been nothing but children's tales. How had they become our reality? Had we drowned? Was this the underworld?

The creature sauntering before us had purposely taken Saphyr's form to lure us into the depths. What kind of power did humans trapped deep below the surface have against this otherworldly being? Against this world? I touched the spot on my thigh where my dagger would have been and swallowed hard. It was gone. We were at their mercy.

We strode through the underwater tunnel and entered through a tall door of polished emerald.

The siren led us to a larger round chamber with a surprisingly cozy atmosphere. The wooden floor creaked as we approached a crescent-shaped couch upholstered in cherry velour. Fishes swirled outside the oval windows, flashes of color in the deep ocean blue.

The siren sat on the center of the couch and crossed her legs. "Welcome." She extended her arms. "Sit."

I was unsure if it was a suggestion or an order. Kanis and I sat together at the furthest end of the couch.

"Where are we?" Kanis's stare was hard.

"This is Sirenibus, the realm of the sirens."

We had gathered as much, absurd as it sounded.

"We've never heard of such realm, my lady." Kanis smiled mockingly.

"Of course you haven't. And you never would have, had I not brought you here." She smirked back coldly.

"Against our will," Kanis added, showing his teeth. He was probing her, needling her, trying to figure out how much he could push her.

"Ah, yes. Nothing like the damsel in distress pretense. I can't tell you how many sailors have literally fallen into our waiting, watery arms for that one." She sneered. "But I must admit, not that many future emperors trying to rescue the future Empress."

I seethed at her mocking tone.

"Well, you've got yourself the wrong lads, siren," I said, feigning indifference. "Neither of us is a future emperor." It was not a lie. Saphyr had not yet accepted my offer. She had no need, no longer gripped by the controlling talons of her father.

"Oh, is that so? Then what were you three doing sailing to Isverden, Ambassador Corvus?"

She was toying with us. I eyed Kanis, hoping my eyes signaled my suspicions. *She must have spies on land.*

"Very well. I'm no longer an heir. My fortune was stolen. The Crown Princess has abdicated her throne. We aren't even betrothed. What could you possibly want from us?" It was a risk, showing our hand. There seemed no point in lying, but we had nothing else to offer. She could lose her interest and have us drowned immediately or, preferably, released.

"Stolen? Yes. Retrievable? Absolutely. Abdicated? Well ..." She huffed. "You cannot run away from your blood. The Crown Princess is the legitimate heir, no matter where she hides. And whoever she marries shall be Emperor. Isn't that what you had in mind?"

I ground my teeth. "What does it have to do with you or your realm?"

She studied us carefully. "You, Corvus, are to be the new Emperor of the Sun Empire."

This time, I was the one to huff. "What do you call yourself, siren?"

"You need not know my name, nor who I am. All you must know is that my word means your demise. What I say, you do. If I ask you to jump, you ask how high." She flashed her teeth in a dangerous smile. "Is that clear?"

Kanis and I stilled. If, by some miracle, I became the Emperor, I would be nobody's puppet.

The siren held our stares, her smile widening. My throat hurt, and a deep thirst hit me. She glanced at my hand, and I noticed, horrified, that my skin had wilted as if I had aged eighty years.

"Do you understand, my sweet Corvus? Or is death something you seek?"

"I understand," I answered, seething. And just like that, my hand rehydrated back to normal, and my throat stopped aching. *Bloody magical creatures!* She had been ready to desiccate me with next to no effort.

"What is it you want from us?" I clenched my teeth.

"Rulers of the Sun Empire who are loyal to the Sirenibus realm." She shrugged. "It's that simple. Consider this our first diplomatic meeting."

"Is the current Emperor aware of your existence?"

"Not all rulers need to know we exist. But you can be certain of one thing: we have always intervened if the balance is broken in the human realm, such as now." Her eyes narrowed. "Keeping the peace is all we're interested in."

"And how do you plan to keep the peace by making me the new ruler? There's turmoil within our Court. The High General hunts down dissenting Houses. The Emperor himself has emptied almost all the Royal Treasury."

"We'll provide you with the funds to gather an army and win back the throne. I'll guide you throughout the process. All you'll need is Saphyr, my dear Corvus. Earning the title of Emperor by right and keeping the royal lineage will guarantee you the support of the other Houses, not only of the Alliance."

My eyebrows shot up at her mention of the Alliance.

"You say it as if everything will be done at the stroke of a pen," Kanis said taciturnly.

"It would not be the first time that has occurred—that I can guarantee. Humans have fought countless wars above us throughout the years. This will be nothing but the establishment of a new rule."

"For how long have you been watching? Interfering?"

"Thousands of years. You're nothing but a speck in our timeline," she concluded.

Guards escorted us to new chambers within the palace. The waterwalls in its outer rooms offered views of the palace grounds far beneath the ocean. Colorful fishes wove in and out of equally vivid corals. If not for the strange and dangerous circumstances, I would have found our chambers magnificent, relaxing even. The architects of Sirenibus had spared no expense in design and construction.

Kanis and I engaged in a heated debate as soon as the guards had locked us in our chamber.

"Yes, I asked her to marry—not for her title, but to save her from a terrible destiny!" I replied, exasperated by Kanis's intense, questioning gaze.

"Well, this is our chance. Magical creatures have appeared out of nowhere to help recover your home, help Saphyr keep her title, and restore peace to the Houses! Why would you refuse? You even get to marry her."

"She has not decided yet. And I cannot tolerate everyone's fixation on my private affairs. It's none of your business, none of this siren's business. Whether or not we return, I don't want it to be by the grace of a new world we know nothing of. If we agree to their help, we'll be indebted to them, Kanis. I do not want to be a puppet Emperor."

"They have said nothing about you being a puppet! They're simply financing a private army to march against Galbreg, in return for a peaceful diplomatic relationship."

"Are you kidding? Diplomatic relationship? Did you believe her?" I laughed. "She's after more than *keeping the peace*. There's more to this than she is showing. She insists they've been intervening for millennia, yet she looks no older than us." I paced the confined space. "These … beings … are in the midst of the ocean between the Sun Empire and Isverden. Humankind has heard just whispers of their existence, which we've foolishly turned into children's tales. Do you seriously believe all they want is *peace*? How does it benefit them? Why not take their army to land themselves and conquer the Sun Empire? What's stopping them? We are at a disadvantage. We wouldn't even have known they existed if they hadn't lured us here."

"You need to sit down." Kanis rolled his eyes. "You're jumping to conclusions. We have a good offer on the table. We may not know exactly what these sirens want, but it wouldn't be any different if Isverden financed us. They would've wanted a permanent chance at the Sun Empire's riches and our blind loyalty and support in their political dealings, too. They would have stuck their noses in our Court, perhaps even more so. These unknown creatures, why would they pose a threat to us on the land?"

"I'm sure they'll find a way." I scoffed. "Did you see her power? She almost sucked the life out of me in seconds. And what about that underwater tunnel? They seem to thrive underwater and on land. They parade in human form within these walls, so there goes the chance of hiding or fighting them with an armada. We wouldn't be able to take them on the water with Delphino's fleet; it is their *realm*. They own it."

Kanis remained silent for a while, and I sat, thinking. "We should discover more about them, their exact powers, and then make a decision," he suggested.

"We need to get out of here." I sighed. "I don't trust them, and dealing with them may result in a life of burden or a swift death. I want neither."

"What makes you think they won't come after us again if we escape?" Kanis scoffed.

"Weren't you the one who just said we'd be safe on land?" I reminded him.

"Then I take it you want to make Isverden your permanent home? Assuming we're miraculously able to make it out of here and hide there, we wouldn't be able to set a foot back in the sea to return home, according to your theory."

I let out an irritated breath and leaned back in the green velvet chair.

"They'll forget about us as soon as Galbreg is freed from prison and takes the throne. They'll bother him instead," I said, staring at the vaulted ceiling.

"And how do you aim to protect your House while Galbreg remains in power?" Kanis scrutinized me, one eyebrow raised.

I had no answer. We had to take responsibility for this, but I wished we could move on with our lives.

Kanis seemed to read my thoughts. His entire household was at stake, at risk of being overthrown by Galbreg. He frowned and crossed his arms. "At the very least, you owe it to your parents," he hissed. "If not to me and Saphyr."

I bolted upright, taking two steps toward him.

"I owe nothing to *anyone!*" I emphasized the last word with a pointed finger. Then I turned my back on him and strode out of the sitting room.

The bathroom was underground, accessible only from the spiral stairway in our chambers. A pool of bubbling water cut into the limestone floor, surrounded by more marble columns. The bath felt ancient, as if it had been healing weary bodies for ages. Candles scattered throughout the floor lit the room. I undressed and slowly submerged myself in the water, which flowed in from an opening in the wall and out through another, constantly flowing and forever scorching.

A basket of dried flowers, herbs, and mineral salts rested on the floor. I shook its contents into the water, and the steam rose with the scent of lavender, sandalwood, jasmine, and other fragrances I did not recognize. *The sirens probably have trade deals with humans*, I thought, *unless they have their own farms hidden to our eyes.*

Closing my eyes, I sank into the water. I counted the appearance of the sirens as both a blessing and a curse. I feared what they were capable of, but I knew they could be useful allies to regain our power. My mind went blank, my thoughts lulled by the steaming water and the calming fragrance.

Kanis had a point: we had little choice. We either accepted the sirens' help or became their enemies. They would not let us leave now that we were aware of their existence. I had to make them think we had accepted their offer and then shrug off their power over us later. This was a mess. But we needed to find Saphyr.

The siren queen, or so I assumed, had requested our presence at dinner. It would be the perfect occasion to draw information from others. I had so many questions. What sort of creatures were they exactly? Where had they come from? Why did they hide underwater? Few of them would likely want to provide me with any answers. Who would provide tactical information to two human strangers?

I was unsure how long we would remain in Sirenibus. But I was determined to make our time here count.

CHAPTER 8
MERCY

The table was a work of art. The plates were meticulously arranged in an elegant display. Even if I was not inclined to taste much of it, I had to admit that the display looked striking. Glistening cuts of raw fish were arranged in colorful swirls, piles of viscous greenery were sprinkled with seeds, and whole grilled fish sat next to smaller fried ones bent over wooden skewers.

It was not the cuisine we were used to. I would have traded these plates for a simple platter of fish and chips any day. I glanced at Kanis's untouched plate, and my lip curled into a grin.

A silvery light that reflected to my left reminded me of her presence, making me tense. The platinum-haired siren sat at the head of the long table. She emptied the amber liquid in her crystal glass, and a boy with crimson hair sprouting from his head in unruly curls rushed to refill it.

Tall, languid sirens, clearly unnerved by our presence, filled the room. They all wore loose tunics that revealed silvery scales on their arms and shoulders. Only hushed voices, tinkling silverware, and the sounds of bubbling water reached our ears. Another extensive waterwall overlooked marine creatures swimming through colorful corals.

"It's not poisoned." The siren pointed to the food. "Help yourselves." She slid several raw fish fillets onto her plate.

I took one of the small, skewered fish, and Kanis reached for the green seaweed salad.

A memory suddenly flashed into my mind: *Eat no fairy food, and drink no fairy wine, unless you wish to be forever trapped.* My mother, cautioning me during a bedtime story. I huffed. Well, Mother, it was that or starvation. As I sank my teeth into the crispy fried fish, I realized I had underestimated how famished I was.

A crisp white wine helped me wash down the grease of the fish. Sitting back, I watched a pair of tan and white seals perform in the water, almost dancing with one another, their white whiskers nearly touching. Following my gaze with emerald eyes, the servant boy gave a barely perceptible sigh and his shoulders slumped.

"More wine!" The siren clicked her fingers.

"Yes, Ma'am." She was clearly in charge. The other sirens did not dare address her unless she addressed them first. Her name and title still evaded us. In the safety of our chambers, Kanis and I had resorted to referring to her as the Nightmare Queen.

"So, you have accepted our offer?" she asked, sipping her wine indifferently.

"Yes, we have," I answered dryly.

"Wonderful! I will make you boys ready for war."

"Splendid," I retorted, masking my bitterness.

"Very well then." The Nightmare Queen stood, and the sirens with her. Kanis and I rose too, somewhat reluctantly, as she swept from the hall without another word.

Slowly, the other sirens left the table, some alone and some in groups. They did not spare a glance for us and showed not the slightest interest. Perhaps they had been instructed to ignore us. Or they had no interest in humans. I sighed, downing the last of my wine.

With the dining hall emptied, Kanis and I were left to our own devices. I glanced around. Only the crimson-haired boy remained. He still stared longingly at fish through the waterwall. The playful seals were long gone.

I went to him, casually pacing alongside the window. "Hungry, boy?"

He glanced at me with an expression more akin to hatred than sadness. "No, Sire."

"Then what's the matter?"

"I long for the sea." His gaze dropped to the floor.

"Well, go for a swim. Aren't you a siren?"

"I'm a selkie and a servant, Sire. A prisoner here, much like yourself."

He captured my interest. I peered around us. Kanis nodded behind me. We were still alone.

"How exactly are they holding you a prisoner? You can step right out of this room and swim away." I touched the rippling wall of water with my index finger to make a point. It was cold, and my wet finger reeked of fish when I pulled it back. The waterwalls, with no protective glass, divided everything in Sirenibus Palace.

"She has stolen my skin."

"The Nightmare Queen?"

He chuckled. "No, well … I mean, yes. Her name is Morgana, Queen of Sirenibus, Ruler of the Seas." He trembled at his own words.

"What sort of skin are you talking about?" I asked, inspecting his milky skin.

"My seal skin. The sirens call us selkies, Milord, to differentiate themselves from us 'lowly sea animals.'" He stared at his hands.

I looked up, surprised, recalling the dancing seals in my head, understanding. "I thought the sirens could transform into any sea animals at will."

"Not really, Milord. They can adapt their human-like bodies to swim and breathe underwater, but they cannot completely transform into animals."

"I see." I caressed my chin. So, sirens could shift into a human body but not an animal one. And selkies could shift into seals. "You're a selkie, so how did you end up here?"

I regretted asking as two tears welled and then dropped from the boy's eyes.

"My damned hair color, I'm sure, Milord. It called to her as I swam with the other selkies. All my friends have darker tones. I'm the only one cursed with this ruddy hair."

I inspected his hair, furrowing my brow. Sure, it was like seeing fire in the water. I could appreciate its uniqueness, but I did not understand why it would matter. "I think it's a rather handsome color. It makes you quite unique."

He nodded appreciatively, clearing his tears with the back of his hand.

I doubted it was the reason Morgana had made him her slave, unless she had a thing for collecting rare "valuables."

"What's your name?"

"Ean, Sire."

"It's a pleasure to meet you, Ean. You may call me Corvus."

He nodded with a soft smile.

"Ean, let me ask you something,' I said, taking a liking to the boy. "Where's the kitchen? I'd like some tea and sweets tomorrow afternoon."

Ean eyed me curiously. "I can bring some to your chamber tomorrow, Milord."

"Ah, will you? That's very kind. And if I wake at midnight and find myself with a growling stomach? Where might I find a glass of milk?"

The boy chuckled. "I'm not sure what milk is, Milord, or if we have anything similar, but I'll show you where the kitchen is in case such a thing happens."

"Excellent!"

Kanis stood, and we followed the boy through a black marble corridor, lit by golden veins running through it, until he signaled to a wooden door. Spices and coal wafted from it, a stark contrast to the crisp maritime scent of the palace.

"Here's the kitchen."

"Wonderful, thank you. I'll see you tomorrow afternoon, Ean." I winked at him.

He smiled back, bowed politely, and left. I observed him with an uncomfortable sensation in my belly. He wanted to be free to return to his world, yet Morgana kept us all trapped here.

Kanis and I nodded to each other. We had used the excuse of finding the kitchen to memorize more passages and doors within the palace. We retired to a room that appeared to be a library, next to the dining hall. The doors were the only ones that had been open during our reconnaissance mission.

The room was almost as large as the hall. Morgana sat in a chair, rolling a tawny liquid within the glass in her hand.

"That took you long enough." She pointed to a crystal decanter filled with liquor. "Help yourselves."

"Thank you," Kanis replied, ignoring the bottle.

We both paced the room, studying the artifacts and artwork scattered throughout: a golden globe with oceanic maps, a purple fluorescent coral undulating with lights, a thick ancient book titled *The Age of Pisces*, the massive jaw of a shark, and a golden harpoon.

A gold-embroidered crest hung on the central wall. It depicted a trident with two fishes over it, one above the other as if passing each other on their way. Under the crest were the words:

SI VIS PACEM, PARA BELLUM

"If you want peace, prepare for war," she said, noticing where our attention had landed.

"Very fitting," I said bitterly, narrowing my eyes. "It is peace, after all, that you're after."

She smirked. These were dangerous beings. I knew they posed a threat to humankind if they came freely out into the world. Yes, we had swords and bows, but weapons would never be enough to hold them back if they possessed the same powers as their queen.

"Do sirens all have the power to manipulate water?" I asked disinterestedly as if we were chatting about the weather.

"No," she replied easily. And I exhaled in relief. They were only able to shift into humans. Only their queen could dehydrate people to death at will. I wondered what else they could do.

"But you are able to shift into sirens at will?" It was something obvious to me, but I wanted to get her talking. A gigantic manta ray swam by the waterwall, its elongated tail flowing behind.

"Yes, we choose how to adapt to the water. It is up to us to have one or two tails, or even tentacles." She eyed me with a twisted smile.

My stomach folded over itself in disgust. "Marvelous." I turned to her. "How about shapeshifting into other people?" I remembered how she had resembled Saphyr.

Her lip curled into a cruel smile, but she held my stare. "Scared, human?"

I sniffed, looking away.

Kanis studied her with a wrinkled brow. She had tried to hide it, but her defensive stance indicated that she alone could shapeshift into human form.

Realizing she had given too much away, she waved her hand, dismissing us. "Rest during this time, while I begin preparations."

I pursed my lips and turned toward the door.

I awoke after midnight and found myself unable to fall back to sleep. My gaze rested on the kaleidoscopic coral reef visible through the waterwall in our chamber. The sea came alive at night—a myriad of teal, amethyst, and emerald lights. As I watched, fishes scattered when a school of sharks appeared, hunting the weak. To think it was this terror that kept the corals alive. If not for the sharks, the fish would nibble the corals to death and eventually die themselves. Their very fear of death sustained them. The cycle of life and death, ever-present and strangely necessary.

"What are you doing?" Kanis asked. He poured us both a glass of the tawny fluid Ean had left us, the same drink Morgana had enjoyed earlier. I took a sip, letting its sweetness burn through my chest.

"What's keeping you awake?" Kanis insisted.

I sighed. "Doesn't it bother you?"

"What?"

"Not having an answer to any of this." I signaled to the sharks and the few sirens still gliding through the darkness. "Death? Why do these creatures exist? And why do humans?"

Kanis exhaled. "Are you afraid of it? Death?"

I swallowed, the memory of Dolmir and Gellis springing to mind. "There is no certainty, Kanis. No one lives to tell us what happens afterward. Do we cease to exist?"

"People are wicked of their own volition. It's written in the sacred scriptures that the souls of the good will survive death, and the wicked will perish. Don't you believe so?"

A sudden movement through the water caught my attention. A shark sank its teeth into a slow fish, shaking it sideways before driving it down into the pit of darkness. "It's hard."

"Stop trying to fit the sea into a teapot. Don't try to understand it. As intelligent as you are, all of this goes beyond us."

I frowned at him.

Kanis sighed. "The scriptures also say God came down as one of us, descended into the depths of hell, and conquered death for us all. He didn't need to, but He did—for us. You can opt to believe death doesn't matter, which makes life meaningless, or you can choose to believe we live on through this winter and join God in his eternal spring."

"What else do you suggest?"

"Pray."

"I don't know, Kanis. What exactly do you gain by praying?"

"Sometimes it is not about what you gain but about what you lose, among other things."

"And what's that?"

"The fear of death."

I thought of how I had lost it all, and my throat closed. "If I talk to Him, will He reply?"

"In unexpected ways," Kanis said. "God is more powerful than death. If He is with you, nothing will be against you."

I fixed my gaze on my hands with all ten fingers stretched under the ghastly light. My heart beat rapidly. To imagine that my soul escaped my body after death was an outlandish thought. "I just hope there is more to this."

Kanis grabbed my wrist, smiling kindly. "There is."

CHAPTER 9
MIRAGE

My sparring and physical training sessions with Kanis began before sunrise in our sitting room, and Ean brought breakfast after each session. I enjoyed trying to beat the crap out of Kanis every day. It was calming for the mind. Although I did not always win, I was getting better at it. We practiced with the fireplace pokers, since we had no actual swords, but I looked forward to practicing with a crossbow once I got my hands on one.

A tap on the door interrupted us. My temple pounded with a headache; the sleepless nights were catching up to me.

Ean appeared through the door, pushing a trolley. I welcomed him and took a seat across from Kanis.

He poured us two cups of black tea and set watery porridge and dried fruit on a table. Kanis and I dropped our pokers and focused on Ean. Apparently, there were other water creatures in this realm. Selkies and sirens were just two of the human-like species that roamed the seas. And Sirenibus was only one of the six realms. Some creatures he described, I immediately recognized, but the others I had never heard of.

I could not believe my ears, but Ean talked about it with such normalcy. I guessed I would not believe Ean was truly a selkie until I watched him transform before my eyes—like Morgana had done.

I wondered where she kept Ean's seal skin. I imagined how furious her expression would be if she found out Ean's seal skin was missing, and the thought made me smile.

After we finished eating, Ean excused himself. "I'll see you tomorrow, Sire," he promised. He seemed as fascinated by stories of our world as we were by his.

The day quickly went by. We usually dined together in our chambers, but tonight we were to dine in the main hall again. I supposed Morgana would be there; what I did not expect was to see Morgana wearing Saphyr's skin.

"Good evening," I greeted her nonchalantly as I sat opposite. Kanis also greeted her, choosing a seat next to me, as usual.

Saphyr gaped at me. I scowled back. Seeing a mirage of Saphyr here, after I worried every day about her whereabouts and wellbeing, was unpleasant, to say the least. I downed half of my wine in one gulp and served myself to what Ean had explained was seaweed salad; it was good, crunchy rather than slimy as I had expected.

Kanis also seemed uncomfortable in Morgana's presence.

Ignoring her, we both continued to eat.

"Won't you eat, dear?"

I looked up to see Morgana entering the hall. I spun back to Saphyr, staring incredulously. Her eyes blazed with cold outrage. Something was not right. From what we had gathered, none of the sirens apart from Morgana could shift into other people. Saphyr gazed at me with glassy eyes. I was reminded of my fingers catching her tears on the hidden stairway of the Crystal Palace. Was she …? I looked to Kanis, but he seemed as confused as I was.

"Why are you two dimwits ignoring me?" Saphyr demanded.

"Is this another illusion?" Kanis snarled to Morgana.

Saphyr scowled indignantly. "What do you mean?"

Morgana settled back into her chair, clearly amused.

"Explain yourself," I growled at Morgana, who simply sniggered.

"I thought you two had drowned!" Saphyr gazed at her hands.

I froze, uncertain of whether she was real. Only a personal question would unmask an impostor. And only a particular one came to mind.

"Saphyr," I whispered across the table. Her amber eyes twinkled as they met mine. "Do you remember my … offer at the Crystal Palace?"

"You mean … when you kissed me?" she whispered back, subtly blushing.

I winced, not expecting her to be so explicit.

The knife in Kanis's hand clanked loudly onto his plate. I shut my eyes.

Morgana roared with laughter.

Saphyr! It was her. I could not believe my eyes. She remembered it! I could see it in her eyes and in the way she bit her lips. I stood, suddenly fuming. The sirens gave me disapproving looks, but I could not care less.

"I assume you'd like to talk in private," Morgana said. "You two may go back to his chambers."

Saphyr stood and prepared to follow me. Kanis also stood.

"I said *them*. You may finish your supper." Morgana pointed at Kanis, whose eyes blazed at her.

A guard escorted us to the chambers that Kanis and I shared. After we entered, I carefully shut the door and turned to Saphyr. She was observing the fluorescent corals under the night light.

"How long have you been here?"

It terrified me that Morgana might have kept her concealed from us.

"That same night you two jumped into the ocean," she said, hugging her arms.

"It's all right." I pulled her into an embrace. "We're together now." I gently placed my chin atop her head. "You must've been so scared, being here alone."

"At the beginning, I was," she said. "But Morgana has been hospitable."

I pulled back with a scowl, studying her. "Morgana? Morgana, the Nightmare Queen of the Seas? Are we talking about the same creature?"

"You shouldn't call her that." Saphyr laughed. "She's quite decent once you spend some time with her."

I huffed, remembering she had almost dried me dead the first time we met. "I insist you must be talking about a different person. Be very careful around her. Do not trust her. Has she asked something from you?"

"No, not really. We've talked about the events that led us here and a bit about this world."

"She is not who she seems. These creatures are dangerous. They're not to be trusted."

"What do you mean? She saved me when I was drowning. When I jumped in after you two."

"You did what?"

71

"You were drowning!"

"So, you thought you'd jump and drown as well?" It upset me to think she had been so careless with her life when we had risked ours to save her.

She crossed her arms, scowling. "I tied a rope around my waist! I'm not *that* stupid."

I could not stifle a chuckle. "Kanis did the same thing, you know?"

"I didn't know that. I came out after I heard you shouting my name. I thought you had just fallen overboard drunk, or something, and needed my help."

I pressed my palm against my forehead. "Has your friend Morgana told you why we jumped into the water in the first place?"

Saphyr glared at me.

"She took your form and made us think *you* were drowning, to lure us into the water. What do you think of her now?"

She winced. "She took my *form*? Are you certain?"

I nodded. "She cannot be trusted."

Saphyr put her hand to her head and began to pace.

"Saphyr, sit down," I suggested.

She let herself drop on the velvet chaise across the hearth, from which emerald fire sparkled reflections over the room. I sat next to her and told her about everything Kanis and I had witnessed here and about Morgana's offer.

"It doesn't seem like we have much choice." She sighed.

"If we choose to go along with her plan, Saphyr, I'd like you to know that you won't be forced into marriage with me unless it's what you want." I felt like an idiot saying it, but it was important she knew. We had barely turned our friendship into something else, only to be thrown headfirst into marriage. I would have much to discuss with her; her father's future was a conversation I dreaded.

"It's fine." Saphyr gazed into the fire. She wore a loose pewter tunic, similar to the ones the other sirens favored. The exposed skin of her cleavage flushed pink. "I envisioned a future together after we escaped."

I swallowed. So she had given it some thought after all. Warmth radiated through my body, and I beamed at her.

"I haven't said yes yet." She smiled back playfully.

"Of course." I nodded, my throat dry.

She let her long hair slide over her shoulder. The heat from the hearth burned stronger, and we stayed silent for a moment.

"Do you remember the first day we met? How many years has it been?" I reminisced.

She laughed. "Too many, that's for certain."

I grinned. "It surprised us to hear the Crown Princess would join our private classes at the manor."

"You had the best tutors." She shrugged. "My father wanted the best education for me."

"I must admit that we had expected you'd be a bit more—

"Princess-like?"

I chuckled. "I suppose so. But you were a welcome surprise. Your unruliness definitely brightened up my school days."

"Remember when I stole Kanis's hidden mead, and we ditched class and drank it all in the field? It was one of my favorite days."

"Oh, my favorite was seeing his face when he caught us with his empty flask."

"He was just jealous we drank it all without him." Saphyr and I laughed together, and then we fell silent again.

"Why did you come to the Crystal Palace that night?" she asked. "You always avoided those gatherings."

"I know." I sighed. "I couldn't bear knowing your father planned to offer your hand in marriage on your birthday. I had determined that … if marriage were the only choice, then I'd offer you the opportunity of a marriage where you could still be free, even if your father disapproved of me. You know I would never dare force you to do anything you didn't want to."

"I know," she said, placing a hand on her heart. "I admit I was scared." Her voice trembled. "I spent the most miserable days before my birthday thinking about what sort of man I'd be forced to marry. I imagined the most horrific scenarios. Being trapped in a loveless marriage for a lifetime. Having a complete stranger force himself upon me. Having to carry his children …" She shuddered. "If the wellbeing of my family hadn't depended on my marriage, I'd have run away. But there wasn't much I could do. I was desperate. I'd have taken your offer on a whim if it weren't that my father would never have accepted you. He fears losing his power so much; he'd never allow your family control the Empire."

"I admire your love for your family, but I still think you shouldn't marry anyone for their wealth—that includes me."

"And you shouldn't marry anyone for their title," she countered.

"Touché." I grinned. The moments we spent together during our journey provoked a thought. "Saphyr, if we ran away and lived off the work of our labors in a cottage in the mountains, would you still marry me?"

"Perhaps." She smiled coquettishly. "It's too soon to tell. Would you?"

"The night I found your carriage abandoned in the woods, I thought I had lost you forever," I confessed grimly. "So, yes, even if we had nothing, no titles nor wealth, I'd still marry you."

Her eyes gleamed. "I almost lost you forever when you were nearly killed by that soldier. Maybe that's why I foolishly jumped into the water after you," she joked lightly.

"I guess we're both fools," I teased.

Fools who could not stand being apart. That was more than a start. I studied her closely, noticing minor changes I had not seen before. A few more freckles sprinkled on her nose. Her face sharper, less round. I let my gaze travel down her slender neck and then had to stop myself, turning my gaze to the hearth instead. *To think I had wanted to take things slower.*

A soft hand on my knee sent pure fire surging up to redden my face.

"I guess we'll have to deal with my father later," she joked again, and I felt the color drain from my ashen face. She did not realize the full meaning of her words. I felt like a cur.

Saphyr looked up from her curled lashes, her eyes flickering reflected fire.

Then someone loudly cleared their throat. We had been so enthralled with each other that we had not heard Kanis enter.

"Am I interrupting?" He marched in, arms crossed.

I closed my eyes, drawing in a deep sigh that made Saphyr giggle.

"Saphyr, I'm thrilled to see you," Kanis said. "Are you all right?"

"Yes, I'm happy to find you're both alive," she replied warmly.

Kanis nodded, and his face hardened. "Corvus will bring me up to speed, but you must leave now. A guard is waiting outside to walk you to your chamber."

Saphyr stood, and my muscles tensed. I did not want her to leave, and she seemed frustrated by it too.

"I suppose I have to go." Saphyr sighed.

I considered offering to accompany her, but Kanis planted himself before me. The two guards posted at our door would not let me follow her in any case.

"I'll find you," I promised.

She beamed as she turned and left.

When I looked up, Kanis's arms were still crossed. "What?"

"I had to sit through an unbearably unpleasant supper with Morgana while you two lovingly reunited." He sighed.

I crossed my arms and glanced at him sidelong.

"I've been meaning to ask you. What did she say when you first asked her to marry you?" Curiosity gleamed in his eyes.

I winced as I remembered the stuttering words that had rolled out of my mouth. It had to have been the clumsiest proposal of all times. "Nothing."

Kanis's eyebrows shot up. "Nothing?"

"My point exactly," I said, and clamped shut my jaw.

"And what did you say?"

"I—I kissed her."

Kanis burst out laughing. "A proposal before a first kiss. I don't blame her for keeping quiet."

I frowned.

"And what about just now? She didn't seem particularly upset."

"We talked about it again and, well, she didn't seem against it," I confessed, unable to hide a wide grin.

Kanis grinned back at me. "About time, if you ask me. You two have been making eyes at each other for far too long. Finally, one of you had the guts to come through."

"You think so?"

"I think she has been interested in you for longer than you think. You were too idiotic to notice it before."

I sagged against the couch. *Was it true? If only the Emperor had not kept us apart.*

"Cheer up." Kanis patted my shoulder. "I'll head to bed. I'm exhausted."

I thought of Saphyr, heading back to her chambers somewhere in this palace, and smiled. At least we were in the same place together again.

Steaming bathwater flowed through the ancient pool. The herbs and flowers were different today, with more of a sweet, zesty scent. I inhaled the fragrant vapors with my eyes closed, tilting my head and leaning my back against the pool's lip. The image of Saphyr floated in my mind, her skin gleaming under the light of the hearth. I sighed heavily, remembering the fire her touch had ignited in me.

A sudden touch on my chest brought me back. I enclosed the wrist swiftly with my hand and stared up at Saphyr's widened eyes above mine. "Saphyr?" I frowned. "What are you doing here?"

"I hid until the guard left."

It seemed odd. Why would the guard leave without her?

"I didn't want to leave." She shrugged. "Besides, we never finished our conversation."

I sat upright and turned to face her, the water lapping my stomach.

To my surprise, Saphyr calmly walked around and descended the steps into the pool, closing the distance between us. Her pewter tunic floated about her waist, the current pulling it behind her. She stood before me, placing her wet hands atop my chest.

"What are you doing?"

"What do you think I'm doing?"

I gazed into her eyes, baffled. This was unexpected. We had barely kissed on her birthday. I looked her over. She was exquisite, but she lacked her usual graceful manner.

Grasping her wrists, I pulled her hands to my chest. I leaned close and nuzzled her neck but instead of summer nectarines I smelled powerful jasmine.

I brought my mouth to her ear, stopping short of brushing it with my lips, and hissed with barely controlled rage, "Out!" I let her wrists go and took a step back.

A snigger formed on her lips. Then, in a flash of light, Morgana's blue eyes watched me, flickering with amusement.

"I can wear any skin you want," she purred.

"Out! Now!"

"Your loss." She shrugged as she stepped from the pool.

Kanis bolted out of the stairway, gaping at Morgana as she passed him, her wet tunic sticking to her legs.

She smirked and winked before disappearing up the steps.

Kanis raised an eyebrow. His clothes were disheveled, as if he had just stepped out of bed. "Care to explain?"

I punched the water furiously. "She came to me disguised as Saphyr."

"Did anything happen?"

"Thankfully not. Saphyr wouldn't act like that. I caught her before she completely fooled me."

"That would've been a nightmare." Kanis whistled. "Imagine explaining to Saphyr what you did with another woman thinking it was her." He shook his head. "What did she want?"

"Probably to spy on us or to get more information out of me." I seethed.

"You think she wanted to know whether we're planning on betraying her?"

"I don't know how that'd be possible. Her damn guards always surround us; we can barely speak in private."

"How long do you think she'll keep us imprisoned?"

"I don't know. But at least she finally unveiled Saphyr to us, although she kept her secluded from the first day."

"They took her as well?" Kanis sounded confused.

"She jumped after us, with a rope tied to her waist."

Kanis roared with laughter. "Well, she's one of us all right! Quite proud of her myself. That takes some guts. Now, these sirens are crafty! They took all of us in the same night."

"Exactly." I ran a finger through my hair. "Look at what she just did. How can we possibly trust her? I'm getting us out of here."

CHAPTER 10
A LITTLE GRATITUDE

The following morning, Morgana called for me, and the guards led me to her private study. Wood panels covered its walls. A polished mahogany desk stood in the room with several scrolls scattered on top. I was tempted to crane over to read them, but I instead trailed a finger over the black feather standing next to the inkpot.

Something else caught my attention. A fiery, mottled fur was draped over the desk chair. Its hairs were short, but in total, the fur was over a yard long. It was the color of dark syrup with touches of crimson. The reflection of the waterwall behind flickered on it, calling strangely to me. When I touched it, the memory of Ean looking longingly at the dancing seals came to me. *His seal skin!*

Footsteps alerted me to Morgana entering the room.

"Sit!" She signaled to the velvet chair across from her desk. Then she pulled her chair out, her claws digging into the seal skin, and sat.

Keeping quiet, she stared, evaluating me. I stared back at her. Was she always this shameless? After what she had tried to do last night, she acted as though nothing had happened.

"Preparations are almost ready for you to leave," she said finally. "We've readied a base for you at the Stella Islands. There, you'll gather forces to confront the Empire and restore the power of the Houses."

"And how will we do that? As you already know, I detained Galbreg. Either he has already escaped, or his entire army must be back under the Emperor's power by now."

"You'll find that things have changed."

I raised an eyebrow. "How so?"

"You'll be given the details after you arrive," she said curtly.

"Why did you lie about Saphyr and keep her from us?" I asked bluntly.

Morgana raised an eyebrow. "She's lovely. Maybe I wanted to keep her for myself." She grinned, flashing her fangs.

"Well, how about keeping your hands to yourself?" I sneered back at her. "You're not welcome in my chambers, in your own skin or not."

"Must I remind you that those are *my* chambers, not *yours*?" Her eyes twinkled with mischief. "Corvus, I believe you'll be a fantastic leader. The Empire will be lucky to have you. A reluctant, intelligent Emperor, *faithful* to his people and lacking a thirst for wealth, and handsome at that. Quite the combination. I think I've made the right choice."

"I don't think you're talking about me. If that's what you think I am, get yourself a different emperor," I replied indifferently.

"You don't seem to know yourself," she mused.

"You don't know me."

Her eyes sparkled strangely. She always seemed to know more than what she let on. I studied her, her mystic beauty bordering on dangerous, the way her silver hair cascaded in long strands over her slender body. Her long, nude claws drummed the smooth desk in a flowing motion. And her glacial blue eyes swirled with faint lavender hues, an obvious reminder of her otherworldly nature.

"How old are you?" I asked, unable to contain my curiosity.

"Older," she replied, smiling.

"How did you become the ruler here?"

Morgana tilted her head. "The sirens chose me. Just like I've chosen you."

"Were you also chosen because of your family's wealth and power?"

She pursed her lips. "Well, even if you had it at some point, that wealth is now gone. But as you can see, it's not wealth that we seek." She gestured toward the lavishness of Sirenibus Palace. "I was chosen for my power, which instills admiration and fear." She grinned. "Just like I've chosen you for your character, your essence. It was you who created the Alliance, wasn't it? You were already planning to overthrow the Emperor and establish a new rule, weren't you? What I don't understand is why you planned to put Galbreg on the throne instead of yourself. No wonder he betrayed you all! I believe you have potential, Corvus. You need only rid yourself of your naivety."

"You're mistaken," I snarled. "But you can be certain of one thing: I don't trust you, and I believe you're hiding something."

"If that's what you choose to believe …" She studied the back of her nails.

I had to admit her confidence was alluring. Her power and ability to go about as she pleased lured me. To a degree, I had experienced the freedom and respect that came with being the sole heir to the House of Alba, and Galbreg's right hand. But I had forever been under the shadow of my father and his control.

To earn freedom, by my own power and ability, was something I deeply yearned for. I had thought I would live under my father's shadow forever, but seeing how Morgana had made a name for herself was enthralling. She answered to no one.

I supposed I was not that reluctant after all, if this journey meant gaining enough power to create my freedom.

After the guards led me back to our chambers, I sneaked out again, hidden inside Ean's tea trolley. The trolley's side curtains were thick enough to conceal me; its trays now lay abandoned back in my chamber.

I tightened my grip on the cart's iron frame, and we moved through marble corridors until the clinking silverware atop me ceased, and I heard tapping on a door. Ean pushed the cart again before we came to a complete stop. The burgundy curtains of the trolley opened to reveal a head full of springy crimson curls and two gleaming emerald eyes.

"We're here, Sire," he whispered.

"Thank you," I replied, crawling out of the tea trolley to straighten out. Saphyr stood before me, her hands covering her mouth. I strode toward her with a sly grin.

Ean silently took up the trays he had left earlier and placed them inside the cart. "You'll only have a few minutes," he warned me as he set off for the kitchen.

"Hello," Saphyr said with a dazzling smile.

"Hi."

"You've found me."

"I keep my promises."

She blushed. "I don't think I've seen that boy before."

"He helped me find you. He's a selkie, meaning a seal. Morgana took his skin. She's holding him here as her servant."

"How awful!" She gasped.

"I saw it earlier, his skin. Morgana has it draped over her office chair. I have a mind of taking it from her and returning Ean his freedom."

"How does it look?"

"It's the color of syrup but with a reddish hue. About a yard long."

"Like his hair?" she asked, surprised.

"Darker."

"Hmm, I have some furs here. Some next to the hearth, a few by the bed. Perhaps we can find one to exchange for his. Maybe she won't notice."

"Oh, she eventually will. It has a particular sheen to it. But, it might buy Ean enough time to flee."

"Come." Saphyr motioned for me, and I followed her as she showed the furs to me.

"I think this one is the most similar. Why do you have these here?"

She shrugged. "I get cold at night, so Morgana offered them to me from her private collection."

I frowned at the furs, wondering if they had belonged to selkies or regular seals. "I've devised an escape plan, Saphyr. I don't know if it'll work, but we'll try."

Her eyes grew round in surprise. "But what about her offer to help us?"

"I don't trust her."

"It won't be easy. Even if we reach the surface, how will we return to land?"

"Trust me, we'll make it. We won't bow to her. And I most certainly won't become her puppet."

A soft beat on the door alerted us, and I hid behind a door.

"It's me, Sire," Ean said after entering and closing the door. "The guards are still outside, but Morgana's maid has fetched her food in the kitchen. She must be on her way to Morgana's chambers now."

"Good," I said.

Saphyr tilted her head to the side, pursing her lips.

"Ean, we've found a skin similar enough to serve as a distraction after we take yours."

Ean's eyes glimmered with excitement. I had already explained my plan during our conversations over tea. "This should buy us some more time than we originally planned." I extended the russet fur, and he studied it.

"It's not exactly the same, but it'll do."

"That's what I thought." We grinned at each other. "Get ready. We're getting out of here today, on our own terms."

No guards were posted at the doors of Morgana's studio—a big mistake. Ean took the stolen key from his pocket and dug it into the lock. I held my breath, watching from a slit between the velvet curtains of the tea trolley. The lock clicked, and the door swung open. We entered quietly, but the studio was empty.

I unfurled out of the trolley, which Ean immediately abandoned. He rushed to his skin as soon as he saw it.

"You were right, Sire! It's my skin!"

"Perfect." I grinned.

"Are you ready?" Ean asked, a new tone of confidence and excitement replacing his gloomy demeanor.

"Absolutely." I would risk it. If everything went well and our plan worked, we would be gone by tonight.

"Sire," Ean hesitated, and I feared he might flee now that he already had his seal skin.

"Yes?"

"Since you've been able to buy time, I'd like to show you a special place I discovered while living here, as part of my gratitude to you."

"Sure." I frowned, puzzled.

"It's accessible from the kitchens. They should now be empty, as lunchtime is over. Shall we?"

It was risky and outside of the plan, but I followed my instinct and trusted Ean. If he thought it was important for me to see this place, then I would.

I traveled inside the tea trolley again. Under different circumstances, I would have thought it hilarious—almost like a child's game, hiding in a tea trolley pushed by a palace serving boy. It was absurd. Luckily, Ean made it seem effortless, as if the cart was not heavy at all, as if an adult human was not traveling inside it.

We rattled across the corridor and entered the kitchen's wooden door. Within, it smelled fishy, and it was hot, but no burners were on. Just as Ean had said, the place was empty. No cooks or servants were in sight.

I rolled out of the trolley, and Ean signaled for me to enter a cellar. Inside, he immediately rolled away a barrel. Behind the barrel, a small wooden door was set in the wall at about the same height as Ean's head. A large, thick fishing net covered the door.

He looked at me, noticing my confusion. "I don't know who else has discovered this, or why it's here. Nobody touches these barrels, as they contain ancient, expensive wine belonging to the queen."

I frowned, remembering the secret passages and hidden chambers of the Crystal Palace. All palaces seemed to have such secrets in common, and the sirens' palace was no exemption. "How did you come to discover it?"

"By mistake. I once thought these barrels contained the pickled seaweed."

I grimaced.

Ean unlocked the door, picked up a lantern from the floor, and threw the massive fishing net on the floor. A dark, narrow hallway lay opposite.

I crouched down and followed him into the hallway. After minutes, the path seemed endless.

"It'll open up soon," Ean said.

Ahead, a purple light illuminated the hallway, which became less dark with every step. When the purple turned into pink with cerulean ripples of light, we stepped into a cavern and the lantern was no longer necessary.

The gravel floor crunched underneath my steps as I stopped in front of a pool of clear water that filled the cave. It sparkled turquoise, and in its center, above a bed of earth that rose over the water, was an enormous tree standing tall and strong, its glowing blue roots submerged in the water. It grew up and up, to no visible end. Its leaves glowed in a fascinating crimson, and some fluttered down and floated over the pool.

"What's a tree doing here?" I marveled.

"I'm not sure, Sire. I've heard whispers of an enchanted tree hidden in Sirenibus. It must be this one."

"What powers does it have?"

"I wish I knew." Ean sighed.

I came closer, inspecting the roots. The pool's floor was composed of countless perfectly round white gemstones.

"Are these ... pearls?"

"Siren's tears, Sire."

I huffed, amazed. "Is the water enchanted?"

"No. I've touched it before. Nothing happens."

I dropped a stone into the pool, but it just sank to the bottom. Taking a chance, I plunged my hand into the water, plucking out a smooth pearl about the size of my thumb. I examined it against the tree's amethyst glow. The pearl's iridescence confirmed its nature.

"A pool filled with blue pearls," I breathed. Then I remembered Morgana's promise of providing enough funds to buy an army. No wonder. These could buy thousands of armies. "Why are they just lying here?"

"What do you mean, Sire?"

"They're invaluable. Pearls of this size and quality are incredibly prized in our world."

To my surprise, Ean chuckled. "They're just siren's tears, Sire. All the sirens in Sirenibus make them when they cry. They hold little value to us."

I laughed, unable to believe my ears. "If that's the case, then I'm sure they won't be missed." I filled my pockets with handfuls of pearls, Ean helping me by turning his brown jacket into a sack.

Then, a crimson leaf floated toward us. It gleamed so beautifully that I picked it up and held it between my fingers. It was silky, but it suddenly turned solid within my fingers, as if made of iron. The rest of the leaves floated further away, in their natural state over the water. I put the solid leaf in my pocket and set out to return to our chambers.

CHAPTER 11
THE STELLA ISLANDS

Back in our chambers, Kanis could not believe his eyes when I showed him the treasure I had hidden in my pockets.

"Where did you get them?" His face beamed as he stared at the sack of blue pearls.

"Siren's tears—they're worthless here apparently."

"How ironic, a lavish palace built out of sorrow." He scoffed. "Who knew?"

"I wonder how often the sirens use these pearls on land. If they're endlessly wealthy, why would they need a puppet emperor? They could do it themselves."

Kanis frowned. "Perhaps because wealth can't purchase time or power?"

"The sirens live forever, Sire," Ean added.

I cocked my head. "There must be something else to it."

"Well, I'm glad you found these." Kanis held a fistful of shimmering blue pearls against the light.

"Indeed, I wouldn't have found them if it weren't for my dear friend Ean here." I patted his shoulder proudly.

Ean blushed and smiled.

"Well, we're ready to leave this place now, and with more than an army in our pockets," I said.

"You'll be thrice as wealthy when we get home," Kanis added.

"Exactly." I could barely contain my excitement. "And able to fight on our own. We won't belong to anybody."

"Hopefully, the sirens won't miss a few of their tears. If so, they can always drop a few more on our departure." He smirked. "They have an entire cave filled with them, after all. We'll take these as payment for our imprisonment here."

I nodded.

"I guess one siren's sorrow is another man's treasure."

"Literally!" I snorted. "Let's get out of here. Saphyr! Are you ready?"

"Almost!" she shouted from the bedroom. Ean had brought her to us within his trolley.

"Are you sure they'll come to our aid, Ean?"

"Yes, Sire. They've returned my message. Three of them will come."

"I can't tell you how much we owe you." I squeezed his shoulder.

"Not at all, Sire. If anything, it is I who am indebted to you for helping me regain my freedom."

My heart swelled. *Freedom.* "Will I ever see you again?"

Ean smiled. "Drop seven tears of a woman into the sea and have her call my name. I will show wherever you are."

I nodded, my throat sore. Then I hugged him, and Kanis after me.

Ean grinned and took out his seal skin, wrapping it around him. Before our eyes, his crimson curls extended to fuse with his fur, and his face and limbs shifted. A young seal shook its head and legs and then dived with a splash through the wall of water in our chambers. He shot up and down the water's flow with endless joy, reminding me of how Snowball used to dart up and down the mountains in pure bliss whenever I let him out of my chamber back home.

Suddenly, the main door to the chamber snapped open, jogging me out of the memory. We barely had time to look at each other when a female siren stormed into the sitting room and glowered at us. I recognized her as one of our earlier guards, slender, tall, and powerful.

For a moment, I was worried the siren would dehydrate us unconscious, but oddly enough, she instead sang a hauntingly beautiful melody in a silvery voice. I tried to frown, but I could not. Kanis's mouth hung open like he could not close it. He did not blink either, and then I realized that neither could I. We were enchanted by her singing, unable to move.

I guessed that was a good thing, because otherwise I would have smiled as Saphyr crept up behind the siren, silent as a cat. She had changed into our clothes and seemed utterly unfazed by the uncanny singing.

Her hand shot up and squeezed firmly behind the siren's neck until the siren dropped, like a dead weight, on the floor.

Kanis and I blinked rapidly and stretched our necks and shoulders, coming out of the trance.

"Thank you," I said.

"Is she dead?" Kanis massaged his neck.

"Of course not!" Saphyr frowned. "She's only asleep."

"Where did you learn that?" I gaped.

"Teach me," Kanis said.

"Our royal captain of the guard taught me some self-defense."

"Self-defense, indeed." I scoffed, eyeing the siren, who was completely out. "Well, it's time to go before this gets any worse."

Kanis strapped to his back a fireplace poker and his satchel filled with blue pearls, and I did the same with mine.

Saphyr finished tucking my long white shirt under her belt.

"Boots off?" Kanis asked, looking through the water at the long distance between us and the surface.

"Yes," I said. "Now, all we need do is hold our breaths for less than a minute and swim straight up. Try to stay together. Let's go."

Saphyr slid her fingers between mine, and we jumped into the wall of water just like Ean had done before.

The water was freezing, even with the afternoon sun rays penetrating the cerulean surface. Everything was blurry, the sounds muffled, but I could still distinguish Kanis and Saphyr at my side. Fat, silvery fishes swam around us, observing us large-eyed. The smaller fishes immediately skittered into the colorful corals.

We propelled our bodies through the water, pulling, kicking, and repeating.

We were close; the water had brightened, and the sky was visible through the surface. But then the water stifled a scream. I immediately looked right and saw a horrified Saphyr being pulled down by another siren.

Her claws dug into Saphyr's legs, and her fangs gleamed savagely. Spiny, fiery fins shot from her elbows and her long tail.

Kanis thrust his fireplace poker into the side of the siren, but she wheeled quickly, and he barely scratched her. I clung to Saphyr's arms, trying to kick the savage creature away.

Another muffled screech vibrated through the water. This time, it came from the siren. She let go of Saphyr as two young seals gnawed at her tail. Another crimson seal materialized, nudging Saphyr up to the surface.

I felt incredibly grateful as Kanis and I pulled and kicked upwards, finally breaking the surface and gasping for air. As the salty ocean air filled my lungs, I spotted Saphyr hugging Ean through the waves.

Nothing was visible in the distance but an endless ocean and a bright sky through which a single blackbird glided.

Kanis and I swam over to Saphyr and Ean as three majestic birds glided in from the horizon. The creatures, the stuff of myths until Ean had assured us they were real, were far larger and more imposing than I had imagined. The griffins screeched, spying us on the water with their eagle-like eyes. Then they tucked in their wings and plummeted toward us, plunging beneath the surface with barely a splash.

Saphyr, Kanis and I readied ourselves as the guardians of earth and sky emerged from the water. I held my breath as I met the stern silver eyes of the largest one. The white feathers of its neck glistened as it signaled me. I swallowed, remembering Ean's words. They were ten times stronger than a lion and a hundred times stronger than an eagle. *Griffins*.

Carefully, I slid one leg over its strong back, securing my hands around its neck. Kanis and Saphyr did the same, and without a word, the creatures spread their wings and we shot up to the sky.

We were exhausted by the time we reached the Stella Islands, slightly east of Sol City. Our hands and thighs ached from clinging to the griffins for so many long hours. We just made it by sunset, landing on the empty beach and falling to all fours the moment our feet touched sand. When I glanced up, the griffins were already gone.

"We've made it." I gasped, my voice raspy.

Kanis and Saphyr lay on their backs, breathing heavily.

I stood, with effort, and helped them get up.

Kanis, Saphyr and I hurried up the stone stairs carved into the rocky cliff and into the well-lit city. Whitewashed houses were stacked against each other on the mountain, overlooking the sea. We dragged ourselves to the first inn we could find by the beach road. The innkeeper stared at our wet clothes and overall disheveled state and almost refused entry until Kanis promised her three times the cost of the stay. Then she led us to a sizeable room with two beds, and we all dropped into total oblivion.

The following morning, Kanis bought an entire Doric-columned, marble-hewn hilltop house with a single blue pearl. Shallow water pools surrounded the impressive pavilion out front, and the back opened to unbroken views of the shimmering sea far below. Olive trees and scented bushes were sprinkled throughout, calming the mind. The capital city of the Stella Islands lay at our feet.

We rested for a couple of days, enjoying the views from the cool, shadowed terrace. My skin, more golden than red now, no longer burned to the touch. It had been a pain putting clothes over our sunburned backs, so Kanis and I had taken to parading around the pavilion half-naked, with only tunics wrapping our hips. Thankfully, Saphyr did not mind. She had been loosely covering herself with airy white tunics that plunged at her cleavage and left her arms bare, similar to those worn in Sirenibus. Her skin had also taken on a bronze sheen.

I glanced at Kanis, who was sprawled on a couch next to mine, his gaze fixed on the magnificent sunset, splashing in oranges and yellows over the cerulean sea and sky.

"I think I'll visit the city tomorrow. I feel rested enough," I said.

"We'll go together."

"Morgana said things had changed. I'd like to find out what she meant."

"I'm curious about something ..." Kanis turned and studied me.

"Shoot."

"Did you consider taking the pearls and fleeing? Perhaps to build a new life in Isverden?"

I tilted my head and stroked my chin. At one point, I had wished to give up, but it was my duty to fight to protect my family and the rest of the people. I was exhausted, tired of feeling like everything was my responsibility. I had thought, *Why not leave the fight to others?* "I'm not sure. It just didn't feel right to leave them behind." I thought of my family, his and Saphyr's.

He kept silent.

I guessed Galbreg's betrayal had given me the right to say that I had already fought and lost, allowing me to move on.

"You could've sent part of the pearls to your family and Saphyr's and still have left with her."

He had a point. With that number of pearls, I could have ensured their safety and funded their journey out of the Empire.

"Have I made a mistake? We still have time to change our plans."

We bot chuckled, knowing we would not.

"I don't know if I'd ever be at peace unless everyone I knew had also left the Empire, given the circumstances. Do you really think Saphyr would leave her family behind?"

"Hasn't she already?"

"She didn't have much choice. She didn't see it as something permanent."

"Regardless, I don't think you should tie your life to others. Everyone is responsible for their own fate."

I raised an eyebrow at him. "That was not what you told me in Sirenibus. If I'm not mistaken, you said it was my *destiny*." I rolled my eyes at the word. "My destiny to fight for the people, given my birthplace, even if that made me a martyr."

Kanis pressed his lips together. "I think you have the right to choose. I also think you deserve happiness. The freedom of others ends where yours begins. It's not like you haven't tried to help them already."

I gave him an incredulous look. "Are you having second thoughts about this?"

He sighed. "No, I just have a bad feeling about it. Maybe we should let the people fend for themselves, even if they're being fooled by Galbreg. They won't believe us now. It's hard to fight for those who are inclined to destroy us."

"Not all of them are like that. I'll fight not because it's my duty or what I was born into, which was not my choice, but because it's what I choose. It's the right thing to do for the Empire."

"Is it?"

"You said it yourself. We have the best chance of making a difference."

Kanis groaned. "You, out of all people, should know not to take my words so seriously."

I frowned. "We'll finish what we started. We're not cowards. And we're not bound by destiny. After seeing Morgana, I realized that I, too, had the power to bend life to my will, to not only fight for other people's freedom but also for my own."

Kanis flashed a smile. "You're as stubborn as a mule, and I like it."

"Rumors had spread of a wealthy prince from Oldterra arriving in the islands, but it's just you three. I'm happy to find you're all alive." The admiral's dark eyes gleamed as Saphyr entered the main pavilion, beautifully clad in a silky white dress.

"Good evening, Delphino," she greeted him with a singsong voice that made me frown. "I heard you found each other at the market today."

"Yes, Your Royal Highness. After losing you three in the ocean, we had been patrolling the sea, anchoring at every nearby port to look for you."

"Have you told my father?"

Delphino looked down, ashamed. "No, Milady. He'd have had my head before I found you."

"Very well. It's best if he doesn't find me," she suggested.

Delphino nodded, obviously understanding the message. "What happened to you?"

"Sirens abducted us," I said bluntly.

Delphino raised his eyebrows and then let out a loud laugh. "I think I've heard that one before," he joked.

"I'm sure you have," I replied icily.

Kanis, Saphyr and I glanced at each other in confirmation. We knew nobody would believe us.

"I fell," Saphyr lied. "And they jumped after me."

Delphino's features hardened. "Why didn't you warn us before you jumped? We would've stopped the ship until you climbed aboard."

"You were too busy singing your lungs out to hear us shout. She would have drowned if we'd waited a second longer," I replied, sliding my hands into my pockets.

Delphino frowned, and his jaw tightened. "What happened afterward?"

"We were fortunate enough to be rescued by a ship on its way to the Stella Islands. Hence, we're here." Kanis also casually lied, gesturing to the surrounding pavilion with his open hand.

I clenched my jaw at the memory of us clinging to the griffins as they glided over the ocean for hours on end.

"I must admit it was a dreadful experience. I thought I'd drown without ever seeing you or anybody else again." Saphyr put the back of her hand to her forehead rather dramatically.

I narrowed my eyes at her. Kanis's lips curled up in a small smile.

"I'm so sorry, Milady." Delphino kneeled and clasped Saphyr's hand between his. "Please forgive me. It was my responsibility to keep you safe. If there's anything I can do to make amends, please say the word."

I huffed in disbelief at Saphyr's act, looking away.

Kanis beamed at her.

"Well, I'd like to sail back to Sol City as soon as possible. We must see Galbreg."

Delphino's head jolted up in obvious confusion. "But, Milady, Galbreg is here."

Chapter 12
On Pride

The night settled in as Delphino recounted all the events we had missed since jumping into the open ocean.

Just as we had predicted, Galbreg had escaped. He had fled to the Stella Islands, where he had presumably been gathering what was left of his army to attack the Emperor again.

"Take me to him," I commanded.

Delphino raised his eyebrows. "You wish to see Galbreg?"

"He'll agree to see me."

"What will you do to him?" Saphyr inquired.

"Nothing. I'll negotiate his passage out of the Empire."

"You'll only make him more powerful. He'll take the money and grow stronger," Kanis said.

"Then what do you suggest: kill him?" I countered.

They remained silent. We were not murderers.

"There's something else you should know." Delphino cleared his throat uncomfortably.

"Speak." I raised an eyebrow.

"His son, Brenen, betrayed him."

"We already knew that much," I said, bored.

"Yes, but Brenen also sent his father's soldiers to the Crystal Palace behind his father's back." Delphino threw a quick glance at Saphyr.

Kanis and I held our breath and silently locked eyes.

"Are you certain of this?" Kanis asked.

"Yes. We overheard Galbreg's soldiers talking about it down on the docks at night."

"That changes everything," Saphyr said.

"Brenen set up his own father, knowing you'd detain him." Delphino jutted his chin at me.

Anger seethed up my spine and burned my cheeks. *So, Brenen dared to use me in his scheme.* "Is he also behind the abduction of my father?" I remembered Brenen had sent coffers to my mother to help pay my father's hefty ransom.

"Presumably so. He conspired with the Legate, Galbreg's second in command. The Legate wishes to become the new General."

"And Brenen Emperor," Kanis concluded.

Clever bastard. Brenen had set up his father, hoping I would kill him myself to take over the army. He had meticulously planned the raid on the palace, creating the chaos before showing up as the savior. He had allowed us to escape only to get rid of Saphyr so his thieves could steal the wealth of the Empire's most powerful House.

Knowing I would take his head, he then put a bounty on mine, forcing me to leave and take Saphyr with me. He had neutralized his three biggest threats at once, leaving the path to the throne open.

Brenen had gained military force, power, and wealth, all in a single night. All that I had lost. And he had fooled us all.

"My father ..." Saphyr's voice trembled. "How is he?"

"Brenen made him believe Galbreg threw a failed coup," Delphino explained.

"He doesn't even know he's at risk." Saphyr gaped, her worried eyes fixed on the polished wooden table.

"It's only a matter of time before Brenen overthrows the Royal Family," I said. "With the Emperor dead, the Crown Princess missing, and no army to defend the Royal Family, it'll be easy for him to crown himself the new emperor. The people will believe him a hero. The righteous son of the treacherous General, stepping in to fill the void. No one will know he set up his own father and took the Crown by force."

Saphyr's face paled. "I can't believe he tricked us," she spat. "The bastard even threw us a rope! He arranged a carriage for me out of the mess *he* created—if only to send me to a sure death!" She banged her fist on the table, rattling the glass cups and silverware.

Kanis and I exchanged looks again. This had fallen on us like a bucket of icy water. I knew Brenen despised his father, but I never suspected he was so crookedly ambitious to pit himself against all Galbreg's might.

"I'm surprised he didn't send someone to kill you too, Corvus. It'd be easier," Kanis weighed in.

"He probably expected me to return in my father's carriage. He would've taken care of me then," I said grimly.

Delphino cleared his throat uncomfortably. "So, do you still wish to see Galbreg?"

I fixed my eyes on him, considering the situation and the potential outcomes. Our places had switched. We had to get to Brenen before he took the throne and possibly murdered Saphyr's family. "We'll have to deal with Brenen first."

"How do you two plan on taking Brenen?" Delphino mocked us. "He now controls most of the army. The rest has pledged fealty to Galbreg and are spread throughout the islands, awaiting his command."

"Enough funds to buy an army ..." Kanis tapped his fingers on the table pensively. "We can buy off Galbreg's soldiers right here in the islands. Then we march them against Brenen."

"Galbreg's army won't be bought. They'll remain loyal to him for as long as he lives," Delphino said.

"Then we'll gather soldiers from the desert," Kanis suggested.

"They don't have enough men."

"Then gather mercenaries from Oldterra."

"They won't get here on time," I growled.

"Then what?" Kanis's white knuckles struck the table.

"We have the money, but we don't have the time. And time can't be bought. The only way is to ally ourselves with Galbreg again, get him on side."

"No." Kanis shook his head. "We can't trust him, even if it was Brenen who set him up."

I remembered what Kanis had discovered through the brats after the attack on the palace. "I need to find where his loyalties lie and make him believe we're on his side."

"He won't tell you the truth," Kanis growled, glancing to the dark sea lit by moonlight.

"There's no other way," I insisted.

Pride was nothing but a currency—pride in exchange for power or survival. Although we had secured the funds, we still had to swallow our pride and join forces with the lesser evil.

I had come alone, without telling Kanis or Saphyr. They would have stopped me, and time was scarce—we had no choice.

Torches illuminated the narrow passageways down the mountain. White houses clustered against each other guided us down the stairs to the sea. Our cloaks swished against the corner of a house as we veered right, a wider road opening before us. During the daytime, it would have thronged with people running errands, but in the wee hours of the morning, it was deserted.

Two men stood smoking outside the tavern. Its name, carved into a tree trunk that hung above the door, signaled we had found the right place. Delphino dropped his hood and nodded to the men, who must have recognized him, as they nodded in return and guided us inside. Several others were drinking and playing cards on upside-down wooden crates. A few eyed us as we climbed the creaking staircase to the second floor. We stopped before the last door upon which one man knocked, and another opened it from inside.

"They're here," he announced.

"Send him in," came a voice.

The man held the door open, and I crossed the threshold as Delphino remained outside. The door clicked shut just as Galbreg glanced up from the parchment on his desk.

His icy blue eyes sparkled. "Ah, just like the last time we met." He sneered. "Have you come to unlawfully apprehend me again, Corvus?" He sat back, smiling warily.

I returned his scowl and settled in a chair across from him. I had come to negotiate. "I believe this time the guards outside the door are yours, not mine, or should I call them *traitors* now?" I said, taking pleasure in watching Galbreg's smile freeze. "Why are you hiding here, Galbreg? Did my father release you?"

Galbreg's cheeks turned red.

"Have you run away with half the army after your failed coup?" I pushed harder.

"*You* had no reason to detain me," he muttered between clenched teeth.

"Did your son help you flee?" I drummed my fingers on his desk. "Here I was thinking he had *betrayed you*." I emphasized the final two words.

"Why are you here?" His eyes narrowed.

"To help you, of course. Were you not set up and betrayed by your own blood?"

He pressed his lips into a flat line.

"I'll help you get rid of Brenen."

"And what, exactly, do you have to gain from it?"

"I wish to recover what's mine." I sighed falsely. "Here we are, two exiles hiding on the Stella Islands. Why shouldn't we help each other reclaim our rightful lands and assets? I'll recover the wealth of my family, and you, your position." I had blatantly omitted mentioning that I had recovered my wealth tenfold with the sirens' tears. He did not need to know that.

Galbreg angled his body away from me. "I don't need you. I have part of my army. You have nothing." He pointed to the guards outside the door.

"I have something that will guarantee you direct access to the Emperor, so you can prove your own son set up the coup. Then, you can beg for his mercy in exchange for your son, who, as we speak, is probably whispering in the Emperor's ears, telling him how proud he is to have saved the Empire from his cunning, traitorous father."

"Why should I trust you?"

"Why should I trust *you*?" I countered with a mocking smile. I would lure the Emperor out with the pretense of having found Saphyr, requiring Galbreg's troops to standby in case Brenen showed up. Then we would convince the Emperor to capture Brenen, or do it ourselves. I was unsure what I would do about Galbreg afterward, but I certainly would not let him occupy the throne. I doubted I could ever trust him again.

"Fair enough." He returned the smile.

"I'll open the gates of the Crystal Palace once again for you. Everything can be restored," I lied. "As you know, if you dare breathe just a little closer to Sol City, Brenen will instruct the Emperor to send the rest of the army against you. You'll lose many men. Why risk that when you can negotiate with the Emperor through me?" I raised my palms innocently, as if stating the obvious.

Galbreg remained silent for a moment, a frown on his face as he considered my words. "I'll think about it," he grumbled. "But if I choose to go ahead, it'll have to be soon."

"I'll get everything ready." I smiled, standing. "Send word through Delphino." I sauntered from the room, my hands in my pockets.

I felt Galbreg's gaze trail me until the door shut.

Delphino joined me wordlessly as we strode from the tavern into the cold, dark streets. We turned through various passages until we found a rundown inn. Before we entered, I glimpsed the two men hidden in the shadows at the edge of the street. They had been following us, and I hoped they had not noticed we knew. I needed them to report to Galbreg that we were staying in an inn and not in the lavish pavilion on top of the city, where the Crown Princess slept.

Chapter 13
Before the Storm

I poured water over the mesh and into a mug filled to the brim with cut apricots and slices of ginger. The steam drifted from the kitchen's round wooden table into the open garden, where I sat marveling at the cloudless morning and at the sunshine streaming into gardens dotted with lavender and olive trees.

Footsteps entering the dining area made me look up and greet a silent Kanis. He wore brown leather pants, and the lacing of his shirt was untied at the front. Ruffled hair could not cover a mulberry bruise on his neck, which made his disheveled state even more noticeable. I was clearly not the only one who sneaked out during the night.

"Where were you?" I asked.

"Where were *you?*" He snatched a tangerine from the fruit bowl on the dining table.

I frowned as he sauntered toward me and took a seat at the table. Sighing, I poured a second cup of tea. Kanis calmly peeled his tangerine, offering me a wedge as I pushed the second cup over to him.

"Is she awake?" he asked, taking a sip, guessing I had made the tea for her.

"Not yet."

"I'm not surprised. She was distressed last night. I left her asleep."

I studied him.

"I woke to her sobbing at midnight. You were not in your room, so I drank with her until she fell asleep. Then I left to find you. Of course, you were nowhere to be found. Yet … here you are"—he made a melodramatic flourish in my direction—"drinking tea." He took another sip.

I felt an unsettling anger.

"Where were you, Corvus?" Kanis asked calmly, his attention back on the tangerine.

I held back a bark. Kanis's predilection for drinking, women, and fighting was notorious. He enjoyed life, and I enjoyed it with him, letting him push my boundaries into such things but never beyond my limits. It infuriated me to think his boisterous tendencies were now rubbing off on Saphyr.

"She is the Crown Princess—you must not forget that," I said coldly.

"She is your friend! Our friend! And you abandoned her last night when she needed you. She was worried sick about her moronic father, her mother, and the rest of her family. She's anxious that Brenen might convince the Emperor to marry off her little sister, although she is not yet of age. Where were you while she cried her eyes out at this very same table?" Kanis tapped the tabletop with his fingers. "You have no right to chastise me for trying to console her."

My vision tunneled with anger. "I left to guarantee us a chance at recovering the Empire," I snarled.

"You went to see Galbreg, didn't you? Even though I told you not to."

"I did what needed to be done. Galbreg will help us capture Brenen."

"Do you honestly think he'll kill his own son?" Kanis crossed his arms over his chest.

"Of course not! I offered him an alternative—an audience with the Emperor will allow him to expose Brenen and recover his title. If the Emperor believes us and jails Brenen, it'll all be over. We will not spill a single drop of blood."

"Reinstate Galbreg as General?"

"Absolutely not! We must make him think we're on the same side again until we can gain control of the throne."

Kanis sighed. "Why not just bring Saphyr back, saying you saved her? Marry her, take the throne, and then rid yourself of Galbreg."

"Must I remind you that the Emperor hates me? He won't let me marry her."

"So, exiling her father is still on the table?"

I swallowed, nodding. The Sun Empire could not keep crumbling under the Emperor's hands, and I would never let him steal Saphyr away from me again.

"How do you plan on getting Galbreg an audience with the Emperor?"

At that moment, Saphyr trudged in, a silk robe covering her filmy nightgown. Her hair was loose and tousled.

Kanis huffed. "Well, good morning, Your Royal Highness."

"I feel like crap, thank you for asking," she replied, taking a seat at the table. "Oh, perfect." She took the cup of tea I offered her. "Thank you." Saphyr smiled at me. "What's all the fuss about between you two?" She eyed us and took another sip.

I stared at Kanis, daring him to say a word.

"She's all yours!" He sighed, standing and striding away.

Saphyr bit her lower lip, looking curious. "What's gotten into him?" She pointed at him with her head as he disappeared into the hallway.

"Do you still have your Royal Seal?"

"Why, yes." She put her hand to her neck and pulled out a pendant that featured a tiny golden tube; it dangled together with another curious item: a carved wooden bear, much like the one Kanis had been whittling as we descended into Sol City.

I pointed to the figurine. "What's that?"

"Kanis gave it to me last night." She shrugged.

I stared at it coldly, pushing away my jealousy before it made Saphyr feel awkward.

"He said it'd bring me good luck." Her gaze dropped to the table, and I worried that the memory would bring back her anxiety.

"We'll write to your father, asking him to meet us under the premise that we've rescued you. Galbreg and I will convince him that Brenen took you, which will unveil him as a traitor."

Saphyr raised her eyebrows. "Where will this meeting take place?"

I glanced at the hallway, certain that Kanis was eavesdropping.

"At the prairie across the Dark Forest."

Saphyr inhaled and straightened her back in the chair. "At the foot of the mountains back home?"

"Yes," I replied.

"What about my sister, my mother? My father?"

I winced at the latter. She still cared for him, even though he had tried to marry her off. I made a mental promise to tell her the truth about my plans to exile him once we captured Brenen.

"Galbreg's unit will hide within the Dark Forest in case Brenen joins the Emperor. The mountains will be at their back, so they'll have nowhere to run."

"It's a trap," she said.

"Yes, for Brenen. And, if Brenen doesn't come, we'll at least be able to talk with your father."

"Why should my father come down the mountain?"

I pointed at the golden tube hanging from her necklace.

"You'll write asking him to meet you there and sign it with your Royal Seal. There are still companies in the mountains scouting for you. He'll be pleased to learn of your whereabouts and will come for you."

Saphyr shuddered.

"We won't let him take you. You'll remain here, in the islands. It's unsafe for you to return to the palace. Only Galbreg and I will attend the prairie."

"I don't know about this, Corvus. My father will expect to see me. He will be furious to have been cheated."

"I'll have Galbreg's army watching my back." My stomach clenched in the knowledge that I could not fully trust Galbreg nor the Emperor. It would be best to gather a squad of my own to accompany me on the mission.

"What will you tell him if he inquires about me?"

I met her concerned eyes with a serious gaze. "I don't know yet."

I hoped the Emperor would be too distracted with processing the truth about Brenen to consider what to do about his daughter.

"Maybe you can tell him I will meet him at the palace after he has sorted all of this out?"

"Very well. Will you actually go back?"

"No … Not unless you do. I don't know. If my family is fine, I don't need to go back."

I sighed, nodding. Times were uncertain. If Brenen showed up, we would have to take him down by force. A clash of armies, of brethren who used to fight alongside each other, and all over a traitor.

"It's best if you wait for me here. Don't go out. Avoid bringing attention to yourself, and you'll be fine."

Saphyr nervously rearranged her robe over her chest.

I pushed the letter I had already prepared over the table.

"You'll return soon," she assured herself as she pulled the tube out of its cap. The Royal Seal gleamed with red ink in the sunlight. Saphyr took the parchment from the table and a bloody drop of ink splashed at the bottom. She then pressed the seal next to it and signed it with her name and title. "There." She returned the cap and put the seal back around her neck.

I stared at the letter with her signature and seal and felt a twinge of sadness. There was nothing I could do. I would risk myself, put everything on the table for her sake, and for the sake of the Empire.

"Thank you," I said, as I rolled the parchment and tucked it in my pocket. As I did, I felt the leaf from the siren's secret tree, which I had kept in there since. The image of the brown bear figurine dangling from Saphyr's neck sprang to mind. I decided it was probably a good idea to do the same and attach the leaf to a chain of my own.

Saphyr nodded, the sun gilding her hair as she stood to return to her chamber.

Sighing, I stood too and headed out the door to the city, where Delphino waited.

"He will settle his unit in the woods surrounding the prairie and wait for the Emperor to descend from the mountains." Delphino confirmed Galbreg's decision.

I had neglected to tell him that the Emperor would believe he was going to meet his daughter, not the General, but I would take care of that at the prairie. Now, all we had to do was await the palace's response to Saphyr's letter. I was certain the Emperor would agree.

After sending the letter on its way last night, Delphino and I spent the night moving from inn to inn, recruiting back-up from the sons of the Stella Islands. A dozen, all the sons of tradesmen—the blacksmith, the carpenter, the farmer, and even the baker—joined us. I asked each why they would fight for me. Most were close to losing their family trade. The Emperor had imposed too many taxes, had shut down their commerce, had made sustaining their families impossible. I offered each a hefty pay.

Although their force would be minute compared to a trained army of Galbreg's men, or those soldiers still commanded by the Emperor, they would at least grant me some protection should Galbreg turn his back on me.

I sighed, tossing another pebble into the waves. A night and a day had passed, and below us, the sea was as conflicted as my sleepless mind. I gazed at a bloody sunset, gray clouds skidding across it to announce an incoming storm.

I clasped the leaf that now dangled from a leather cord around my neck. The sunset gave it a lustrous sheen, akin to gold.

I tried to imagine how Morgana had reacted after she discovered our escape. My eyes screened the water, expecting a head of wet silver hair to emerge from the ferocious waves, but the sea seemed as empty of angry sirens as the village had been. There was not a glimpse of Morgana nor any whispers of sirens in the Stella Islands. Then I remembered how they could transform their tails into legs, and I swallowed. Perhaps they were hiding in the village, disguised as humans at this very moment, searching for us. I shuddered and pushed the thought away, concentrating instead on a nook enclosed in the rugged cliffs to the village.

Suddenly, I glimpsed Kanis stomping down the stairs onto the beach. The memory of us dragging our sore, sunburned bodies out of the beach and up the stairs hit me. Not long ago, we had escaped the sirens, and now I was leading us into yet more danger. This time, I would not risk Kanis and Saphyr. This threat, I would face alone.

Kanis picked his way over the boulders, waves splashing against his feet on both sides. He crouched down next to me, and I studied him silently as he focused on the crimson setting sun, his lips face taut and compressed. I waited for him to utter the first words.

"You've chosen to go to *that* prairie to meet the Emperor?"

I nodded.

"Do you forget what surrounds it? The reason everyone avoids those lands? The reason they were buried in oblivion in our world?"

I nodded again, unsure of anything anymore. "Fairytales ..." I responded, and cleared my throat, feeling it close with uncertainty.

"Just like sirens were fairytales?" Kanis countered.

"We've heard not a whisper of them in the islands. And the prairie is the perfect place to ambush Brenen. I suspect he'll join the Emperor on the journey down the mountain. If a battle is to be held, there is no better place. Empty land means no innocent casualties."

"You honestly believe Galbreg's unit will hide inside the Dark Forest?"

"I certainly hope our soldiers don't believe in children's tales."

"And do you? Do *you* now believe in such tales?" Kanis folded his arms.

The wind kept on, mercilessly crushing waves against the rocks and spritzing salt into the air. I thought of the underwater rooms of Sirenibus, of the sirens, selkies, and God-knows-what else hidden under the murky waters.

"We don't know the extent of it. It could be just them. But whatever comes our way, we'll deal with it. Right now, we need haste. This is the best, fastest strategy. We'll use the Dark Forest to our advantage, hiding our soldiers while we meet the Emperor."

"And it matters not if I disagree, I see. You will do what you please," Kanis said bitterly.

"Do you have an alternative?"

"You won't let me devise one."

"We don't have *time* to devise one!"

"Since we met with Delphino again, you've been touring the islands at midnight, off to secret meetings with a wanted General, and doing who knows what else, keeping me on the sidelines. You used to trust me with such things." He stiffened, shifting his weight.

"You know I'd trust you with my life," I replied solemnly.

He locked his gaze on mine, as if trying to read the truth. I could see the question forming in his eyes: *Why?*

I sighed. "You're too valuable, Kanis. I will not risk losing you or Saphyr again."

"We have not spent a day apart since this journey began."

"Thankfully not. But Saphyr has. The sirens kept her hidden from us. This meeting is too dangerous for you and Saphyr. I refuse to drag you both further into this mire."

"You can't force me to stay away, however hard you try to do this on your own. I won't let you." Kanis had always protected me as if he were my older brother. I understood his unease.

"Who will stay to protect Saphyr?"

"She can protect herself," Kanis retorted, although he sounded unsure.

"You must stay with her. I'll take Delphino and several guards of my own to meet the Emperor, along with Galbreg's soldiers. I'll be fine."

Of course, I did not want to leave them, nor go on this quest alone. But I had jumped head-on into it. There was no going back now.

"Corvus, I can't leave you alone, not given your luck. First, nearly murdered, then exiled, and then abducted by sirens ... what's next? Sucked into the Dark Forest with no return? Killed by Galbreg? You'll never survive at this rate."

I grimly focused on the raging ocean. He was right. Perhaps I was a madman, but I would not run from it.

"Just promise me something," I asked Kanis.

"No," he said, glowering. "Whatever suicidal thoughts you're having right now, end them."

A brief laugh escaped my lips. "Kanis, I need you to promise me," I insisted.

Kanis crossed his arms tighter, knowing he would find no way out of this.

"If ... if something happens to me, take care of Saphyr. Do not abandon her. Never let any harm come her way."

With a frown, I remembered the bear figurine and guessed that would not be so hard for Kanis. *Had he already taken a liking to her?* After so much bickering, they had been growing closer on this journey.

"I promise …" Kanis said, only slightly grudgingly.

I nodded, feeling more at ease. It was set. Kanis would stay with Saphyr, and tomorrow night, I would march for the Dark Forest.

CHAPTER 14
BORN OF THUNDER

Saphyr strolled next to me through an otherwise empty alleyway. Flowered vines adorned its whitewashed walls until the alley ended at a short cliff above the sea.

We had been exploring the endless twisting passageways and tiny stairs of the island and had been on our way back to the pavilion before we entered this alley. Brushstrokes of pink and orange tinted the sky, and the first stars shimmered shyly over the sea.

Saphyr wrapped her thin scarf over her hair and around her neck for warmth. By day, the scarf had served as a disguise for the Crown Princess of the Empire, who was enjoying her newfound freedom. No guards followed our trail, and there were no appearances to be kept. I watched as the sea wind sucked at the tips of her curly tresses where they dangled out below the fabric.

Saphyr had been herself for the first time in years here, and I enjoyed watching her move from shop to shop, speaking to the shopkeepers, buying her own food from street vendors. When she had been distracted, I had gone inside the shop of a jeweler and had him place a delicate blue pearl in a gold ring. I had been swirling it inside my pocket during the rest of the afternoon.

My smile faded only when I remembered why I had spent the day with her—to say an uncertain goodbye.

"Saphyr?"

"Yes."

She was examining crimson flowers of a vine, and I stopped and clipped a cluster of three flowers. The look she gave me was curious, and she flushed as I slid back the scarf and placed the blooms behind her ear. How beautiful they looked against her golden hair.

I gingerly raised my hand to cup her chin, pulling her up to look at me. Her eyes sparkled beneath her lashes, and I lost myself in their amber depths.

The wind carried the fragrant scent of nectarines, and my heart leaped a beat as I drew her to me. She rested her forehead atop my chest, and I placed my chin over her silky hair, its familiar scent more arousing than ever. *If only we could live in this moment forever. If only we might never die.* The thought crept up over me like a chill settling deep in my bones.

"Saphyr, I will always be with you. Always hold me in your memory," I implored.

She gasped and tried to look up at me, but I held her tighter, feeling her tremble slightly beneath my arms. Beyond her, the raging sea threw itself against the cliffs. "If something ever happens to me, remember I will live forever in your heart."

She pulled back, frowning, ready to reproach me.

But I was quicker. Stepping forward, I kissed her. She stood still at first, surprised, but then joined me.

How would I be able to leave her? With each passing second, the thought of her absence grew harder. She would hate me to the core for what I was about to do. Yet it would be better if she hated me now for leaving, rather than hate me for leaving her alone to drown in her sorrow.

"I must leave tonight ..." I whispered in her ear.

"No!" she commanded, finally understanding.

"Please, Kanis will protect you. I will meet with your father and return."

Tears slid down her cheeks, and I wiped at them with the tip of my finger. "Everything will be fine," I reassured her, but more tears fell. My core shook with guilt. "Please do not cry, Saphyr."

I did not want to leave, but it was the only way to resume our lives. Spontaneously, I dropped on one knee. "I'll marry you," I promised her, offering her the pearl ring. "If you'll take me, that is. Then we'll never be parted."

She opened her mouth and then closed it again. Her golden eyes sparkled.

Will she reject my proposal again? My heartbeat raced with the possibility. But then her smile grew, and she nodded.

Hope. I stood and leaned in close, sliding the ring on her finger, then brushing the tip of my nose gently against hers. I would look forward to returning to her every day we were parted. Somehow, I knew she would keep me alive.

Her tears now replaced with a grin, I felt a rush of happiness. Embracing her, I lifted her into the air and swirled her around, the sweet melody of her laughter echoing around the cliffs.

She said yes! I set her back on the ground, and Saphyr leaned back against the wall, catching her breath. Her eyes glistened with joy and drying tears, and her curls had tumbled free of the scarf. Once again, I could finally breathe.

Drawn to her like a magnet, I rested my hand atop of hers and kissed her until the sky was aglow with stars.

Eventually, I left Saphyr on the steps of the pavilion. She tried to hide it, but more tears had flowed at the thought of my departure, and each broke my heart piece by piece.

Kanis was standing behind her, his face stony, his eyes flaming, and his mien furious. If not for my request that he stay to protect her, I knew he would have been on my heels. Not accompanying me to the Dark Forest was ripping him to shreds. More than anything, I knew he felt betrayed. I had sidelined him, and he was not used to it. But only circumstances had forced me to rely on Delphino more than him. As good as Delphino was, I had not liked being dependent on him either. It was as if my right arm had been excised. I had trusted no one more than Kanis, which was precisely why I had left my greatest treasure under his care: Saphyr.

As hard as it was, it gave me peace of mind that they would remain safe here in the Stella Islands. *It is one thing to die. It is quite another to watch your friends die.*

My guard and I ventured out of the islands by ship, navigating the brief span of sea westbound to the mainland before anchoring on the coast behind the mountains. Then we followed the river toward the prairie that separated the vast forest from the mountains.

The Dark Forest lived up to its name. Trees scraped the sky, entangling each other at the top to form a web of twisted branches that blocked the light. Trunks huddled impenetrably closer as we neared the forest's heart, gnarled branches forming an almost insurmountable black wall. Galbreg had set tents within the limits of the forest, where the distance between trees allowed for it. The camp was hidden enough to go unnoticed from the prairie. Scouts informed the General that the Royal Guard was already coming down the mountain. And so, we waited.

The air within the forest grew heavy, inexplicably dense amid the dry trees and fallen leaves. The mist was constant. The wind crawled across our skin like it had claws, curled between our legs, and sent shivers down our spines.

An eerie, sepulchral silence reigned. We communicated in whispers, and then only when necessary for fear of waking whatever lay dormant within. We stood silent for hours, waiting. I was not sure whether the Emperor had come in person to meet his daughter or if he had sent Brenen in his stead.

Night had almost settled, and the sky above had turned an endless gray. The wind howled through the trees, and the air felt too thick and humid to breathe. Our soldiers grew restless.

"They are here," Delphino muttered, and as I exited the tent, I silently prayed none of us would face our death.

My guard moved around me, all twelve of them tracking my every step. Forging ahead with our plan, I entered the prairie to meet the Royal Guard. Galbreg and his soldiers stayed behind, the archers positioned beyond the trees, ready to fire at his command.

If everything went according to plan, I would later signal Galbreg to approach the Emperor in the center of the prairie. The Emperor should recognize me instantly, upon which moment I would tell him the truth about Brenen.

But, to my surprise, it was Brenen who galloped into the prairie on a black horse, and not the Emperor. Brenen's platinum hair flowed freely to his waist, crowned by a circlet of entwined silver serpents; their gaping mouths joined at his forehead, a dark gem between their fangs. I detected a flash of excitement in his eyes at the sight of me.

Instead of armor, he wore a white tunic with gold pauldrons on the shoulders and forearm guards. I also wore a dark tunic and no armor, as was customary for diplomatic encounters.

I smiled. Brenen's force appeared outnumbered by Galbreg's soldiers concealed within the forest. I raised my arm and closed my fist, sending the signal to Galbreg. Time to come forward and capture his son.

"Where's the Crown Princess, Corvus?" Brenen shouted, his horse whinnying as he tugged on the reins and twisted it to a halt.

I frowned, imagining Saphyr safe and sound back at the pavilion. The chill wind made my horse restless, and it stamped beneath me. "Where's the Emperor?" I responded, stalling.

"I thought you had come to meet *me*." Brenen patted his chest.

Something was off. I tightened my horse's reins around my hand, ready to gallop to the safety of the forest along with my guard should Brenen order his soldiers forward. Galbreg's archers could guard our backs as we retreated.

"Leaving so soon?"

A sudden *swish* in the air made my hairs stand on end. Instinctively, I spun in time to see a slender arrow fly from the forest, mere inches away from my face, and *thwack* into the leg of a Royal Guard. His scream echoed through the prairie, and I froze. This was the excuse Brenen needed to attack first. Had he planted a spy among us? The guards behind Brenen shouted and galloped toward us.

I cursed under my breath as my protectors positioned themselves before me, lowering their spears. Delphino and I both raised our bows. I stared calmly down the nocked arrow I had aimed at the necks of the cavalry. I was not a murderer, but I would not die a martyr either.

A flash of light blinded us all as roaring lightning crashed from the sky and pierced the prairie. The blast deafened us momentarily and sent my horse rearing on its hind legs. I clasped my pommel as my steed careened into Delphino's, and we found ourselves both thrown onto the ground, the air knocked from our lungs.

Winded, I gasped for air and gathered the strength to stand. Still on the ground, Delphino lifted his wide-eyed stare to mine. Galbreg's soldiers should have reached us by now, but all we heard was the clash of bloodthirsty blades. Several horses had thrown their riders and fled, ignoring the frantic commands of their masters.

Delphino and I clutched the reins and mounted our horses again. The guard we had recruited in the islands had encircled us, fighting with all their might. Most were on foot, with only some still mounted atop their horses. But none had yet fallen. I roared, suddenly filled with rage.

Brenen stood calmly, exactly where he had been before. Unbothered by the battle, he grinned.

A soft buzz, like a tingling sensation, prickled the hairs on my arms.

I looked up just in time to glimpse another strike of white light rocketing from the sky. The split thread of light connected quickly through its ends, aiming for my body. I gasped, realizing it was too late. Had I been abandoned, my prayer unanswered? The light, a thousand times brighter than the first, blinded me. Every inch of my body ached. Then came the thunder.

I fell. Broken. Utterly, irretrievably broken.

The pain was jolting, excruciating—like an orb of piercing spines was pulsing out from my chest.

I lay shattered. Immobile. My mind dull and blank, my ears ringing. Smoke and ash rising from my shattered body.

They have won.

Under the gray storm, my eyes closed. Clashing weapons and screamed outrage whirled around. *Will they continue fighting until we are all dead? Or keep alive those with broken spirits—those willing to become their slaves?*

I would rather die. I would rather rot than become their instrument for pain, than let them use my power to corrupt and end others for their benefit. Selfish, disgusting creatures.

The scent of soil and blood filled my nostrils as I struggled for breath. I readied myself to relinquish life as the ground rumbled. My bones shuddered along with its powerful roar—as if God himself was shouting over the Earth. I exhaled one last time before the thunderous roar reverberated through my broken body.

And then, I inhaled death.

PART II

CHAPTER 15
RISEN

Pine trees extended infinitely, their naked branches reaching out to the void. The woods were empty, silent but for the steady beats of my heart. My fingers dabbled in the damp ground beyond a bed of dry pine needles, and I inhaled a cool breath of earthy pine.

A long black feather lay on my chest. I picked it, running a finger along its soft edge, catching glimpses of lapis lazuli and amethyst gleaming under the gray light of the forest. Flapping and the sound of a branch bent under an unfamiliar weight caught my attention. Slowly, I lifted my gaze to study the shadow of a tree. A black bird perched itself on a branch, its cobalt eyes piercing through me. A raven—the largest I had ever spied. Was it waiting for my body to rot in order to feed on the dead?

Dead. I had died on the prairie; I felt sure of it. Disoriented, I peered around the empty woods, searching for an answer. I saw not a single soul other than the bird and myself.

Strangely, I did not mind it. If this was death, I was content with it. No more war cries, no more useless plotting or ridiculous sacrifices. Finally, I was alone.

I studied my body. I had all ten fingers and was not missing any limbs. My mouth was dry, and my body ached. My legs were weak, and my clothes were singed, but there were no burns on my skin. Although ruinous, I felt strangely alive.

Alive. I immediately touched my chest, remembering my last breath on the prairie. Desperately, I tore my shirt open. The skin over my heart was perfectly smooth, practically translucent as usual, with only a faint mauve line crossing my chest above my heart and down to my right hip. Lightning had sliced through my body.

"What on Earth?" I gasped, studying the scar. *Am I truly alive?*

I tried to stand, but my wobbly legs failed me. The raven cackled at my fall. I got to my knees, my palms burning where they pressed against sharp pine needles. I glowered at the bird.

The winged beast cocked its head and stared beadily at the floor. Following its stare, I saw a crooked wooden staff lying on the ground. It was sturdy enough to help me rise, but I would have to crawl to it.

I wondered whether the raven would attack me. *I guess it no longer matters if I am already dead.* On knees and elbows, I hauled myself with great effort over the forest floor, the damp soil clinging to me as I dragged my body over it. Struggling to catch my breath, I enclosed my fingers around the rough staff at last. The entire time, the bird kept its gleaming eyes on me, as if enjoying my misery.

"Damned bird …" I cursed, gathering all my energy to drag myself up with the support of the staff, and lean my weight against a tree trunk.

A second snap of a branch alerted me, and my heart pounded as I searched the empty woodland, imagining an ungodly creature hiding beneath a tree, ready to strike. The blasted bird cawed again, and I almost lost my balance.

It made no sense. The mauve scar over my heart suggested lightning had coursed through my body, and I had somehow miraculously cheated death. But it did not explain how I had been transported from the battlefield to the Dark Forest. And I could not tell how long I had been lying there.

The raven flapped to the floor and locked its gaze with mine. All of a sudden, the forest came alive, teeming with life. Squirrels scurried up the trees, birds chirped, and rabbits hopped over the grass. I blinked several times, thinking I had lost my mind and waiting for the scene to change, but it did not. Just minutes ago, the woodland had seemed as dead as I thought I had been.

Do you now believe in such tales? Kanis's warning echoed in my head.

Stretching out its dark wings, the raven leaped above the ground and flew in circles above me before gliding off through the trees. I searched the moss growing on tree trunks, trying to determine the direction north. The raven had flown toward the prairie. I followed it, hoping to escape the forest.

After hours of stumbling along on weak legs, I finally approached a clearing. I swiped the sweat off my forehead, my hope disappearing just as easily when I saw the raven perched atop the roof of an abandoned cottage. Knowing I could continue no longer, I went in.

The place appeared to have been deserted for years. Cobwebs crawled up the windows and the inside of the empty cupboard, which I stared at, hoping food might materialize. Whoever had lived here did not seem eager to return. My upbringing had not prepared me for this. None of my skilled tutors had taught me to cook. If I wasn't dead already, I would probably starve to death, I conceded. I knew only of war strategies, trade, languages, philosophy, and art—none of which put a plate of warm food on the dusty table of a neglected cottage deep in the Dark Forest. Heck, I had not even cared to learn how to hunt. For the first time in my life, I wished I had accompanied my father on his hunting trips. What a spoiled brat I had unknowingly been.

I kicked a wooden chair over. "What is the point of surviving death only to die out of stupidity?"

Righting the chair, I slumped onto it and laughed ironically. If my mother had only known, she would have forced me to become the greatest hunter and cook the Empire had ever known.

I peered hopelessly out through the smeared window, watching the giant raven where it perched at the first line of trees. It cocked its head and then shook it almost pessimistically.

"Sure, maybe I will become your dinner after all," I said.

My eyes closed as I thought of my mother. What would she have ordered the servants to bring me? A groan escaped my lips as I imagined sitting comfortably beside a fireplace, a steaming cup of tea in my hands, and my mother serving a plate of salted codfish, simply boiled with carrots, green beans, bread, and olive oil. Not a common dish, although popular in Oldterra, so I had grown fond of it. I would have gobbled it instantly without choking on a bone and drifted off to sleep in my soft bed.

I opened my eyes, forcing myself back to reality. I needed fire, food, and a bed before sunset. Grumbling, I stood and picked up a rusty axe that had been resting by the door. I threw it over my shoulder and headed out, drawn to the gurgling of a brook.

Its crystal-clear water cascaded over smooth rocks, and I could see small fishes swimming past. Greenish in color, they had yellow spots and a pinkish shine on their sides. If I was not mistaken, they were trout. Now, the trick was in catching them. Flapping wings made me look up. The raven was perched on a tree overlooking the brook.

"You came to watch the misery show again, huh? Or are you hoping I will catch dinner for you, too?"

The bird was silent, watching.

I sighed resignedly and kneeled on the brook's bank. The fish scattered, and I waited like a statue, eyeing them. They eventually returned, darting through the aquatic plants, out of reach of my arms. Clenching my teeth, I eventually sank my hands in as fast as I could, grabbing the fattest one by the tail. As I yanked it out of the water, it wriggled from my fingers and escaped.

I moaned in frustration, and the raven emitted a series of short caws.

"Laughing at me now, eh?" I glowered at it.

The bird was genuinely mocking me, and I could not help a smile. This was absurd.

It took me several more tries, during which the raven cawed harder each time. Finally, I clasped a smaller trout that stayed in my hands as I pulled it from the water by the tail, its mouth opening and closing in suffocating shock. I would have tossed it back in pity if it wasn't for the excruciating rumbling of my stomach.

Instead, looking away, I smashed its head with a rock, wishing it a swift death. It made me realize that I had never attended hunting trips with my father because I knew that if I had to hunt and kill my own food, I would have probably starved. *Too weak for this world,* my father had always said of me. I had considered refusing to eat animals more than once. But in Sol City, most who did not eat meat died young or became so sickly and weak they eventually returned to meat-eating—even those who had abstained for years.

"Sorry," I apologized to the fish as I covered it with leaves. "Do not even think about it …" I scolded the raven, hoping it did not fancy fish. The bird simply looked away with disdain. Then I stood and gathered a bed of bark and dry pine needles to sleep on, and enough logs and kindling to make a fire.

My arms burning in pain, I gathered up everything along with the fish and carried it into the cottage.

The sun had nearly set, leaving just a few purple rays to penetrate the dusty windows, just enough to allow me to spot the flintstone and iron fire striker on the mantel. At least I had learned how to make a fire.

The fire was easy compared to the other tasks. I skewered the fish on the iron poker and grilled it. I knew most animals had to be gutted before cooking them, and something my mother had said about the scales came to mind, but I was starving. Once it was cooked, I just peeled away the singed skin the best I could, sprinkled on some salt I found on the table, and devoured the pink flesh.

Discovering old, stale-smelling furs inside a chest, I gave them a good shake outside in the moonlight, accompanied by the sound of crickets. Finally, I shut the door, securing it with the back of a chair, tucked myself under the furs on the improvised bed of pine needles, and watched the flames dance in the hearth.

I hugged the axe close to my chest, as I had once hugged Saphyr, and fell asleep as soon as my eyes were closed.

CHAPTER 16
A GIFT FROM THE FOREST

The next morning, the raven was still there, and the morning afterward. The days trickled like the ever-flowing brook nearby. Eating and keeping myself warm were the order of the day—every day. I despised repetitive mechanical work, but this simple, natural work of existence soothed my mind. I found it did not bother me to be isolated in the woods. Occasionally, I would stare up beyond the trees, hoping to see another creature, but so far, the raven was my only company.

Sometimes, I wondered if everything else had just been an odd, distant dream. But when I thought of Galbreg, my chest constricted with the need for revenge. I could almost see Kanis rolling his eyes, telling me, "*I told you so.*" I wondered how Saphyr was faring. I missed her.

On the day of the battle, Galbreg had not followed my signal, had not sent his soldiers in. Seeing Brenen, he had stayed behind. Had he ordered the arrow that had catalyzed Brenen's attack?

I sighed. It seemed all was lost. Was Delphino alive? Had my guard perished? Was it my fault? Sometimes, I thought of my return, playing the role of the hero, saving them all. But I was no hero. I was selfish. Powerless. Lost.

As content as I was here, guilt and shame corroded my heart. I had abandoned them all—Kanis, Saphyr, my parents, Delphino, and my guard—to live as a hermit in a forest no one else would dare enter.

Several times I had tried to return to the prairie. But my feet had dragged me inside the forest until unyielding darkness forced me to return. I had left markings on the trees to trace a path home. The forest seemed to twist and turn at will, doing everything it could to prevent my escape. The markings vanished or swapped to a different tree, and fallen branches blocked the path. I resorted to stacking stones on the ground instead, but they toppled and disappeared. I had grown lean, my hair unkempt where it hung beyond my jawline, and my hope of ever returning dimmed.

I stood inside the cottage, evaluating the inches of snow that covered the ground. As the snow bed grew, food became scarcer. I had set traps for rabbits, but the few times I caught one, I had let it jump away on release. At this rate, I would starve. I sighed again as I stepped out of the cottage.

The immaculate layer of snow and ice extended to the woodland's edge. I adjusted the axe strapped to my back and crossed the clearing between my home and the forest, snow crunching underfoot. The fresh air flowing through my lungs kept my head clear and alert. The crowns of the trees glistened under a mantle of frost, a treacherous beauty. Entering the forest was a necessary evil, although my previous encounters with wild animals had taught me to always remain on guard.

A sudden caw cut the crisp morning air. Feathers, as I had baptized the raven, glided above me, spreading his magnificent dark wings. I was grateful for his company on my outings through the Dark Forest. The majestic bird would screen the land, shrieking if it spotted danger, and serving as my only friend in these isolated lands.

The labyrinth of tall pines consumed the wind and spun it into silence. Opalescent snow burdened the branches, except for a dry snag that had fallen to the ground.

As I raised the axe, Feathers cawed sonorously from the sky, bringing me to a halt. The last time he had cawed like this during one of our expeditions, I was forced to spend the night in a tree, waiting for a territorial boar to leave. I cautiously studied my surroundings but found nothing.

Feathers cawed a second time and flew further into the forest. I hoped he had chosen to go on a hunting journey, and I began chopping logs off the snag.

In minutes, Feathers returned and ascended to a higher branch. I wiped sweat off my forehead as the bird tilted its head and stared at me with astute cobalt eyes, the color such a contrast to the bird's gleaming black feathers. The imposing depth in the raven's eyes always gave me the impression it held secrets and wisdom for which many searched far but never found. Feathers opened his beak, and something fell to the ground.

Probably one of those tiny, lustrous rocks the bird often brought me as a tribute, which I treasured. My smile disappeared as I extracted a broken necklace from the snow. A painfully familiar golden tube and a miniature carved bear dangled from it, almost unchanged by time. Flashes of the Stella Islands—bright sunsets over whitewashed houses and whispered goodbyes in the salty sea air—left me breathless. My eyes widened, fixed on the necklace, and my mind froze. How had this come to be here?

Feathers spread his wings again and took flight in the same direction he had come from. I chased after him, my mind whirring, the necklace gripped tight inside my fist.

The trees blurred as I followed Feathers through the forest, jumping over small bushes and dead branches, trying not to lose sight of him until he plunged suddenly into the trees and disappeared. I came to an abrupt stop, listening over my heavy panting. Crude silence filled the woods, the only exception an almost imperceptible, sluggish breathing. My hand curled over the axe's handle as I shoved the necklace inside my pocket and prowled toward the spot the bird had vanished.

The dark tree trunks and branches parted to unveil a path of pristine silvery snow leading to a clearing. A colossal crimson tree stood in its center, one of the last to succumb to the winter slumber. Feathers was perched on top, a stark contrast to the fiery branches. I followed the raven's gaze to the ground.

My breath halted in my throat, and my heart hammered as I approached the tree. It would have been better to face a wild boar than to see the necklace's owner materialize amid the glacial forest. Adrenaline tingled through my body, and I put a hand to my throat as I saw her.

Asleep on the scarlet ground, her skin made the snow look dark in comparison. Saphyr's curls sprawled over the thick crimson bark and leaves, and her eyes were closed, her lips parted and pale. My blood froze.

Was she ...? I kneeled to touch her neck. Her pulse was incredibly slow, and her skin dreadfully cold. I went still, forgetting why I had even entered the forest. My mind leaped from disbelief to wondering how she had come to be here to swirling thoughts of what I had to do—thoughts racing so quickly that it made me nauseous. I steadied myself with a deep breath and carefully slid my arms under her body. Then, with shaking hands and my chest burning, I rushed out of the frozen woods, clutching Saphyr to my heart.

CHAPTER 17
ABLAZE

She was so still. How had she come to this Godforsaken place?

Fire crackled in the cottage's hearth, and Saphyr lay unconscious on furs next to its warmth. I crouched before her, burying my head in my hands.

I pressed the back of my hand against her temple, noticing her temperature had increased a little, but not alarmingly so. Her clothes were soaked, and I wondered how long she had lain unconscious in the snow. If she survived the cold, she would probably still get sick. It was a miracle that a dangerous beast had not discovered her before I did.

I watched her, still deliberating what to do. Her sleeves dripped water where they thawed in the heat. The layers of frosty clothes kept her shivering. Although she would hate me for what I was about to do, there seemed no better alternative to keep her alive.

"Saphyr …" I murmured, hoping she would wake. My fingers froze midair as they hovered her brown cape. I shook her shoulders kindly. "Saphyr, you must awaken."

She was still, an exquisitely sculpted statue gilded by firelight. The cloak's rough fabric dampened my hands as I unclasped the brooch.

As if feeling the draft through her open cape, Saphyr trembled violently, and my throat tightened. After all this time, I would not risk losing her again.

I held my breath as I slid her arms from the cape with utmost care. Placing my hand on her nape, I lifted her and pulled out the cape. Her shuddering worsened.

"Saphyr, please wake up!" Nothing. I pulled the lacing off the gown, which gave way to her corset, damning my trembling fingers for brushing against her skin.

A blazingly powerful slap suddenly stung my left cheek, and I drew back as a knee flew into the air where my ribs had been.

"What on—

"What on Earth do you think you're doing?" She jolted up. "Are you out of your damned—" Her mouth shut, and her eyes widened as they recognized mine. Her cheeks took on a sudden rouge as her eyes lowered to my guilty hands.

I clenched them in a fist, wishing I could disappear in a spiraling puff of smoke.

"Corvus?" Even disheveled, she was more beautiful than I remembered. I was, however, but a shadow of myself—a tired ghost next to her glowing, alabaster beauty. I feared my ganglier appearance would drive her away, but instead, she crept cold fingers up to caress my protruding cheekbones and entangle themselves in my hair, as dark and devoid of light as the new moon.

I remained motionless while Saphyr explored strands of my hair as if they were midnight silk. She observed me, absorbing the changes in my body, as if to be sure I was not an illusion.

When her fingers brushed my jaw and neck, I unwittingly winced at her chilly touch, causing her to pull back.

My stomach clenched as I grabbed her wrist, wrapping my arms around her, hoping to infuse her with warmth.

"I have finally found you," she whispered, shrinking my heart. Not a day had passed without her memory permeating my mind.

Drunk on her sweet scent, I nuzzled her hairline beneath her ear. When Saphyr froze in my arms, I pulled back softly, only to lose myself in the caramel of her eyes. My gaze dropped to the floor, ashamed. I had left her.

A gentle kiss on my cheekbone made me glance up.

"I remembered you … every day and every night. I never forgot you." Saphyr's eyes sparkled with determination, the fiery gaze igniting my heart until it hurt.

I clenched my fist, hesitant and afraid. Would she forgive me?

As if to answer my unspoken question, she embraced me. Pressing every inch of her skin against mine through the wet clothes, her nails digging into my arms. I inhaled her fragrance, relieving the excruciating pressure in my chest from all this time without her.

I had missed her laugh, her company, her lips. I wondered if they tasted the same. Noticing my gaze, she parted them invitingly, and I pressed my lips upon them, pushing down the selfish hunger that threatened to take her, until the ache in my heart was extinguished. She gasped for air, her body flushing warmer than the blood in my veins as my tongue delved deeper into her mouth.

"Saphyr." I groaned, inhaling her breath as if it were the cure for what had been poisoning me all this time. She turned, exposing her neck. Like a famished wolf, I let my tongue and teeth graze the delicate skin of her neck.

I was not myself. I was losing the little honor I had left, becoming the animal that had taken over during my endless solitary days in the woods. I pushed back out of her reach, panting.

I wondered what she saw in me, as she also panted for breath. Did she see the same Corvus who had left her crying on the steps of the pavilion? Did she see the same bastard who had loved her to the depths of his heart but had abandoned her without looking back? The selfish beast who had left her behind to fight a war that was not his?

"Forgive me, Saphyr. I died ... that day on the prairie." It had never been my intention to abandon her.

"I know. They said that God himself sent lightning to take you down. But I never believed them." Her voice trembled. "I refused to believe that you were dead. They never found your body."

"I lived." I smiled softly. "Somehow, I survived."

"Fool," she cried, returning my smile. "You fool!" She punched my chest softly with her closed fist. "Never. Leave. Us. Again!" She punctuated each word with a punch.

I chuckled, knowing I deserved each one. "I promise ..." I said.

What an idiot I had been, trusting Galbreg instead of my friends.

"I suppose I deserved it." My mouth went dry at the memory of the lightning striking through my body.

Saphyr narrowed her eyes. "Do not say that. You may be a fool, but you did not deserve to be struck by lightning."

I grinned. She was a gift sent from heaven. I cleared my throat. "Saphyr, I have many questions for you, and I am sure you have many for me. But I think you should change into dry clothes first." I gestured to her drenched gown.

She nodded, and to my surprise, began unlacing her corset. The soaked white shift clung to her breasts. I gasped at her brashness, and she halted, narrowing her eyes. "Would you mind ...?" she asked with an amused expression, her tone mocking.

"Yes, of course," I stammered, damning my idiocy as I turned away to grab some of my dry clothes from an old wooden dresser.

I stood with my back to her, staring at a spot in the wall and holding the pants, shirt, socks, and woolen cape in my hands. The small mirror on the dresser gleamed, and from the corner of my eyes, I saw her slim arm toss the sodden clothes at the foot of the hearth. I immediately closed my eyes in case the mirror decided to show me something else. After hearing her dump more wet clothes on the floor, I tossed the dry garments over, blindly aiming them nearby.

"Saphyr," I said, my back still turned. "How did you find me?"

"I—" she began, but three hard knocks on the door startled her.

I clutched up my axe and stood behind the door. Saphyr frowned as she finished tucking my loose shirt inside the pants. I put a finger to my lips, suggesting she remain quiet. I had never seen another human besides her in the Dark Forest.

Before I could move to the window to see who was outside, someone knocked again.

"Corvus, open up! It's me."

I recognized the voice instantly. My eyes widened at Saphyr, and she nodded with a smile.

"I tried to tell you before you shushed me." She smiled.

I unlocked the door and pushed it open.

Kanis's eyes were as wide as mine, but his face was weary, and icicles dangled from his short hair. I stood aside, signaling for him to enter. He did, and I shut the door.

We stared at each other for a few more seconds before Kanis flashed a smile and crushed me within his arms.

"I have missed you." I grinned, patting his back as he squeezed me in a bear hug.

"Me too," he said, punching my arm. "You have lost weight."

"A diet of trout and wood chopping will do that," I chuckled. "You are welcome to try it."

"It seems I'll have little choice." He laughed and turned around to the hearth. He froze midway, discovering Saphyr clad in my clothes. "Oh, thank God!" He engulfed her in a hug that made my hand clench with a savage need to punch him in the gut. I shuddered, harnessing the feeling. Loneliness had made a savage of me.

"How did you find me?" she asked. "I … what happened?"

"You fainted from the cold," he explained. "I went to search for wood to light a fire, and when I returned, you were gone. I followed the trail of steps in the snow to this place." He looked around the cottage.

"She could have died, Kanis," I said.

"I know." He held my stare. "She refused to give up. At the prairie, I warned her that venturing into the forest would be dangerous, but she threatened to come alone." Kanis eyed her and whispered, "You know how stubborn she is."

Saphyr glared at him.

"I knew you were alive. Only the good die young." He winked at me, and I huffed. "I am happy you survived."

"Me too," Saphyr and I said simultaneously, and we chuckled.

"You took a risk knocking on the door. What if this was the home of some foul creature? This is the Dark Forest, after all." I frowned.

Kanis cleaned his throat uncomfortably. "Since we were looking for you, I hoped Saphyr had found you. But to be sure, I listened outside the door before knocking."

My eyes moved to the dirty windows, wondering how much he had seen. I was disinclined to ask how long he had been standing there.

"Do you know the way back?" I asked Kanis.

"It took us several tries. We set up camp on the prairie for days when we first tried entering the forest."

"The impenetrable dark wall ...?" I queried.

Kanis tilted his head. "It opened up. Slowly, but it did. I left markings on the trees. But we took so many turns it may take us days to head back." He plopped down in a chair by the hearth. "Why? Do you want to head back now?"

I did not answer. Now that I had them here, everything seemed brighter.

"Care to explain how you came back from the dead?" Kanis joked.

"I don't know." I ran a hand through my hair. "One moment, the soldiers were barreling against us, and the next, lightning hit us, almost like a warning. I fell with the second strike." I swallowed.

"You were lucky. Most would've died."

"I should've died, Kanis." My throat closed. "I'm not sure what happened, but I know I should be dead."

"Don't say that." Saphyr frowned.

"It's definitely odd," Kanis agreed. "That and the fact that you're here." He motioned to the forest.

A strange notion crossed my mind. "Do you think, maybe ..." I could not find the words.

"What?"

"Remember what we talked about at midnight, back in Sirenibus? Well, I took your suggestion. Before I went onto the prairie, I prayed none of us would die."

Kanis's eyebrows arched up. "You prayed?"

I crossed my arms, looking away.

"I'm not judging, especially not something I suggested you do in the first place."

I frowned. "I wonder if it had anything to do with it."

"Well, oddly enough, none of us died—not even you, which was rather unexpected, huh?" Kanis smiled.

My chest heaved, but I held in a breath.

"Don't be mistaken, though. Prayer is not sorcery—it's not a power you can control to get what you want without fail. Sometimes, the lack of an answer is an answer in itself. Sometimes, what you want is not what you need, although you're not able to see it until much later. You must learn to accept that."

"Well, look at you," I said, sitting next to him. "Here I was thinking you cared only about fighting, women, and drinking."

"Careful there, or I'll charge you for the advice." His eyes flickered with amusement, and I chuckled.

Perhaps it was just a coincidence, but my heart felt calm to think God was looking after us like a father guiding his children back to him, like lost sheep. "Why a second chance at life, though?"

Kanis sighed. "That's for you to discover, I guess."

"Here." Saphyr plonked a flask on the table.

I raised my eyebrows, wondering where it had come from. She opened it and served a drink into three wooden cups she took from the cupboard. "Enough talking about death. Let's celebrate life and that we finally found you."

"Is that uske?"

"The finest, stolen from Brenen's personal collection and aged in the pockets of my dress."

I chuckled. "Now *that's* a story."

We all downed the fiery drink immediately. Ah, how my blood sang to it.

Saphyr sighed. "Where should I even begin to tell it?" She came and sat next to me, and a smile formed on my lips.

"Let us start at the beginning. What happened after I met with Brenen at the prairie?"

Kanis and Saphyr exchanged worried glances. I poured more uske into my cup, expecting it to be a long night.

CHAPTER 18
REGRET

Brenen had left my presumably dead body on the prairie, taken Delphino and my guard as prisoners, and ascended the mountain with a willing Galbreg and his army, they explained. Within days, Galbreg's soldiers marched on our pavilion at the Stella Islands and forced Saphyr to return to the palace. Kanis had hidden and then followed her home, after which he helped her escape and they both came to the prairie to find me.

It was late, and we were all exhausted well before we tired of the details and fell asleep.

The next morning, sunlight peeked through the windows, awakening me. The morning air chilled my bones as I crept from the cottage in silence, leaving Saphyr and Kanis sleeping by the hearth. A caw from Feathers greeted me. The sun had barely risen, sparking ripples over the snow on the ground and the trees. Waking up at sunrise had become a habit.

I approached the raven and caressed the back of his head by way of greeting. Feathers pulled his head up, pleased, and pressed his forehead against my fingers. It had taken some time for me to become used to the raven, but now, this was our morning greeting. Curiously enough, I had never fed the bird. It stayed with me of its own volition, which I appreciated.

The crunch of snow behind me heralded Kanis approaching. With a ruffle of wings, Feathers took off to a higher branch.

"You're up early," Kanis greeted me.

"So are you."

In the light of day, his face looked ashen, a glint of something akin to guilt in his eyes; he averted them before I could identify it. Perhaps he was just tired.

"I can't believe you two found me." I knew I had been the one to find Saphyr, but how had they come so close inside this wicked woodland? The serpentine forest had a mind of its own, I knew.

"After wandering in the forest for so long, we were beginning to lose all hope of finding you. We thought you were dead."

"I also thought so. When I first awoke in the middle of the forest, I wandered it like a ghost." My shoulders tightened. "And remained as one."

My previous life had been shucked, left behind as I embarked on a solo journey. How could I explain that my only concern had been to keep breathing, to keep eating, nothing more.

"Why did you not come back?"

I kept silent.

"We mourned you, Corvus! Saphyr even refused to attend your funeral. When she received the news of your death, she cried for days. She kept praying for a miracle—hoping you were still alive since we never found your body on the prairie."

"I tried to return, but this forest ..." I gestured around me. "It has a way of confusing you, of not letting you know north from the south, nor east from the west. I tried many times, but I always ran out of food or energy, or it was impossible to find my way back."

This second life, a second opportunity, what should I make of it? It was a relief to breathe again. Perhaps the emptiness of this life had given me a newfound peace, a numbness I had not imagined I would crave, but one that I could not easily let go of.

"Why are you and Saphyr here, Kanis?" The question sounded cold on my lips, so cold it surprised me.

Kanis sucked in a breath, as if my stoicism hurt him. "We came for you."

I held his gaze indifferently, masking my guilt and regret. "Saphyr disappeared one night after we set camp on the prairie," Kanis continued. "We had not found your body, and she was growing restless. I followed her footsteps into the forest. However, I didn't expect we'd come this far, nor for you to be hiding so deep within." He stopped and studied me carefully. "How did you manage to survive?"

I knew he would not give me more information until I provided some of my own. "I'm unsure. Feathers had something to do with it—with my survival."

"Feathers?"

And as if in answer, the magnificent raven cawed above us.

"You named *that* thing Feathers?"

I nodded.

"For someone so serious and calculating, you have a ridiculous way of naming pets. I don't know what's worse, you naming it Feathers or that it actually answers to it." He rolled his eyes. "Although nothing surprises me after Snowball."

I laughed. "I was a child when I named him," I said in my defense.

"Not much has changed then." He teased me.

"Thanks."

"You mean to tell me that this beast somehow saved you?"

"Look, after that lightning hit me, I died." My voice trembled at the memory. "Or at least it felt like that. I was out for some time. I can't remember exactly, but I woke up in a clearing inside this forest—completely healed but disoriented. The raven was there; one of its feathers lay on my chest. I thought it was waiting to eat my corpse—such a large raven within this eerie place—so I stood. There was no sign of life; all animals were gone. I looked at Feathers, and the entire forest came alive."

"Hold on, the forest was dead and came alive? That could not have been the bird. In the beginning, the forest looked barren to us, too, but as its twisted branches opened, we delved deeper in, and it slowly became alive."

"Well, in my case, it happened within seconds." We studied each other, confused.

I sighed and slumped against the trunk of a tree opposite to where Feathers was perched. Kanis sat next to me, gazing at the snow-covered trees.

"I think I may have gone crazy. Perhaps I was still in shock, but I think the bird had something to do with it. It guided me to the cottage. Feathers has stayed with me since."

Up in the tree, the raven preened and fluffed out its plumage proudly.

"Are you sure it doesn't talk?" Kanis asked with a bit of annoyance, glancing at the bird.

"Not a word yet." I smirked.

"As incredible as your story is, it does not explain how you went from being dead in a prairie to well-and-alive in the middle of the Dark Forest." Kanis stroked his stubbly chin.

"Who knows?" I said, remembering the earth-shaking shout right before I lost consciousness.

We kept silent for a while.

"Brenen was lucky. He did not even have to fight you."

"Galbreg betrayed us. There's no question this time," I snarled.

"Did he?" Kanis stroked his chin again. I waited for the *"I told you so"*, but it did not come. "He couldn't go after his own son after all," he concluded.

"I suppose you were right." My jaw clenched, remembering how his soldiers had not come to our aid.

"Did I mention Brenen put him in the dungeons?"

I arched my eyebrows.

"Yes, so much for *betraying* you." He scoffed. "Now Brenen has full control over the army, including his father's."

"Our families, how are they?" I rubbed my temples.

"They are … fine. Holding up."

I frowned. "What about—"

Saphyr stepped out of the cottage, interrupting us.

"Good morning," she sang, beaming. Her curls bounced off the fur she had wrapped around her like a shawl.

I returned her smile, glad she was not sick, as I had feared.

"I guess it's time for breakfast." Kanis decided.

I groaned. "Trout?"

Kanis let out a huff. "I'll start feeding you properly, boy."

We took off for a proper hunt, while Saphyr agreed to stay in the cottage. After her fainting episode yesterday, we did not want her anywhere near the snow.

I munched on the delicious crackers he and Saphyr had brought for the journey. My eyes scanned the forest while Kanis cleaned the pheasant he had caught a thousand yards away in the woods.

"I guess your father had a point about you skipping the hunting expeditions," he said.

I exhaled a contemptuous breath. "Thanks for the reminder. I never liked the idea of hunting for fun."

"I didn't hear you complain while you feasted on that hog stew last winter."

"Ha, it was that or rabbit-mince pie."

"Corvus," Kanis called in a more serious tone.

My head jerked up. This could not be good. "What?"

"I think we should head back tomorrow."

"It's too soon," I said curtly.

"You *like* being here in the unknown. I'm surprised you survived this long."

That stung. "I've managed, as you can see."

"I can see bones in your face I couldn't before," Kanis countered.

Scoundrel. "Look, it is not like I haven't thought of returning, or that I particularly enjoy living in misery. But now that you are both here …" I hesitated. A strange peace had lodged in my heart with their arrival. The two people I cared the most about were with me. Sure, we were not living in a palace, but we were together. We were alive. "We could be happy here, don't you think?"

Kanis's jaw went taut. Perhaps he was considering whether I had gone mad.

"Do you not miss your home? Your family? Your wolf?"

"All of that is gone now, is it not?" I looked down, hesitating. "I've fought the battle, Kanis, and lost. It is up to them to fend for themselves, just as we are doing." I gestured to the dead pheasant and the bow resting against the tree trunk. "They can take everything and move back to Oldterra or head north. My mother is powerful; they will know what to do."

"Do you really think they can keep everything under the current circumstances? Brenen won't even allow them to sell the estates, much less take caravans full of belongings down to the port."

"I left with *nothing!*" The roar escaped my teeth before I could stop it. "I took *nothing!* Nothing but a dagger and a satchel with food and coin for the way. We were alone when they tried to murder us at the palace and when we almost drowned and were captured by sirens. And, finally, in that prairie, I died *alone.*"

"You *left.* You left us!" My friend's eyes blazed with rage.

"To protect you! To protect my family from my failure, and to protect you and Saphyr from danger." My nostrils flared with disbelief.

"Your problem is *you* do not believe in *yourself,* nor in others. You must control *everything,* and you do not trust anybody to help you."

"Says the bastard who is accusing me of fleeing like a coward and leaving everything behind!"

"I did not say that!" He seethed.

"*You* talked me into it, Kanis." I knew it was not entirely true, but my ears pounded, and my thoughts were muddled by inexplicable rage. "Why should I have even tried to defend those who abandoned us? Those who left me to die on a battlefield for them. Where are they now, Kanis?" I shouted to the empty forest. "I don't see them here, do you?"

"Your so-called guard, the one you collected at the islands, those men are also in the dungeons! Do you even know their names? Besides, we came back for you, Corvus."

I winced at the mental image of my guards trapped behind bars. I did know their names. I had personally talked to each and learned about their families before recruiting them. Had Brenen tortured them?

"No, Kanis." I regretted the words even as they came out. "*Saphyr* came back for me. You said yourself that you ran after her into this forsaken place and put her in danger." I could tell my words sliced through him like daggers. "And now, you have the nerve to ask me to return, to fight and die for them again. When, exactly, will it be enough for you, Kanis? When I finally die and cannot miraculously survive?" I spat out the last words, standing. "No, my answer to your request is *no.* I am not going back."

I stormed back to the cottage. He could leave me again, for all I cared. A sonorous caw echoed through the trees as Feathers kept up a steady flight above me.

CHAPTER 19
BROKEN

Nothing, I had *nothing,* and yet, here I was free. Somehow, I had misplaced the true meaning of happiness. It was not in power, wealth, or notoriety. It did not live in the mountain manor or in what I had lost; it was not even in my family nor my friends, although they helped. All this time, it had been hidden right under my nose, as all good things are. My happiness lay within me. This realization gave me peace. No longer did I need to keep running, to keep jumping hurdles. No more sacrifices needed to be made in the name of things I supposedly needed to be content.

Saphyr was also happy. We had nothing, but she was shining like the sun. A basket filled with pinecones swung on her arms. The light reflected off the snow and burnished her hair and skin.

We were happy. After so much, after losing everything—including my life—we were finally happy. I would not let that end too.

We had everything we needed here in the forest. We had each other. What more could we possibly want?

Kanis was mad. The Empire was not worth it. The people were not worth it. Nothing was worth our happiness or our lives. It pained me to think of those without a roof or without food, people I knew we could help by uncovering the lies Brenen fed them, and providing them with jobs instead of promises. But it would be to save a crumbling Empire. All was lost. Brenen had already won. I had already failed.

Still, I had Saphyr. Even with so little, with this simple life, we had each other. I did not want it to end.

I smiled at her as she strolled toward me. We took a seat by the brook's edge, and I studied the forest with a frown. Kanis had not returned.

I was certain Saphyr knew something had happened, but she ignored it at first, giving me time to cool down.

"Did he ask you to go back?" She started.

"How did you know?"

She sighed. "I knew it was too soon to ask you. He means well. He just lacks … tact sometimes."

"Sometimes!" I scoffed.

"Most of the time," she agreed with a grin. Then her words took on a more serious tone. "That doesn't mean he doesn't care about you. He loves you, truly. While we searched the prairie, Kanis was preparing a rescue team to enter the woods and search for you, but I couldn't wait any longer, so I rushed in alone. I feel bad. My reckless decision put him in danger."

My stomach turned. I had wrongly accused him of only following after Saphyr.

"So … what else did he mention?" Saphyr's voice lowered to a whisper, her eyes on the moss. Two white butterflies fluttered down and danced together in small circles before us. Somehow, we always found our way back to each other.

"None of it matters." I enclosed her warm hand in mine. "What matters is that we're together." I swallowed nervously at a new thought. "I know it is not much, and that I can't offer you what I could before, but if you still wish it, my life is yours."

Saphyr's gaze remained on the moss, an air of sorrow enveloping her.

"Saphyr, I promise I'll take care of you. I'll make you happy. We could do a handfasting ceremony right here. Kanis could be our groomsman. It would be simple but all we need. You'll be mine, and I'll be yours forever—finally." I smiled at her, cupping her chin to lift her tearful eyes to mine. "Nothing and no one will separate us again."

She tugged her gaze away, clearly fighting to contain her tears. Was she overwhelmed, as afraid of losing me as I was of losing her again?

My arms enveloped her, and she rested her forehead against mine, sobbing. "What's wrong?" I murmured.

"I …" She tried, but her sobs drowned out the words. "I …"

I caressed her hair, waiting patiently. Maybe she was crying at her shattered dreams of a wedding fit for a Crown Princess, or maybe she despised this life too much.

"If this simple lifestyle doesn't please you, I'll take you wherever you want to go. We could go north to you sister, as we had initially planned, or into Oldterra. Wherever your heart desires."

It pained me to leave the peace I had found here, but I would give it up for her.

"It's not that. This place doesn't bother me. I …" Another sob broke her words. "I want *you*."

She did not care about where we lived. She wanted *me*, just as I wanted *her*. We no longer cared about nobility, about titles, or riches. We could love each other for who we were.

"I want you too," I breathed, my chest about to burst with joy.

But Saphyr just sobbed more deeply.

"What's wrong?" I searched her eyes, alarmed.

"I had to marry," she cried desperately, tears cascading down her cheeks.

My world shattered in a second, my dreams destroyed. I stared at her in shock, doubting my ears, doubting my sole existence.

"You …?" The words would not come out right. I reordered my thoughts. "You married someone else while I was gone?"

Again, her tears would not let her speak. She nodded instead.

Air stopped flowing through my lungs, and I felt a coldness fill my heart like ice. Almost automatically, I retreated, my arms falling away from her.

Had she been forced by Brenen or by her father? Had she met someone else?

"Who?" Was the only question my mouth could form.

"Me." The voice that came from above us lacked any trace of shame.

My gaze flew up to Kanis. He looked down on us, a bloodied pheasant hanging from his hand.

A glacier of ice inched over my body. I was not miserable, furious, or even stunned. I felt nothing. No thoughts crossed my mind. It was as if I were watching myself from above, my body inert before Kanis. And for the first time in my life, I raised my fist and landed it cleanly on his jawline, knocking him to the ground.

Saphyr gasped and rushed to him, checking his face. Kanis's eyes widened in disbelief and then narrowed at me, as if I had been the one to betray our friendship.

"You shouldn't have come," I whispered coldly to them both. And then I turned to leave.

"Corvus, no! Wait! You don't understand. There is something—" Saphyr rushed to me, grabbing my hand to stop me.

Feathers suddenly cawed and flapped down to us, making Saphyr lose her hold on me. I started forward again.

"If not for *us*, you must return for your mother," she pleaded, her eyes swollen with tears.

I turned, frowning. *My mother?*

"She's dying," Saphyr explained.

My mouth fell open, and I took two steps back. I could tell her eyes spoke the truth.

Despair and pain grappled with me, numbing my thoughts. I did not need to be dead; my entire world had been destroyed in seconds.

Perhaps, I was supposed to be dead, after all. Maybe I was never meant to survive the lightning that had carved through my body. It had been a gift from the heavens, to ease the pain that would later come knocking on my door. And someone had taken it. Someone had stolen that gift away.

My feet itched to run, to bear me away from life itself, to detach my body from this wretched world.

I stopped running only when my legs were ready to give out. I dropped to my knees, shutting my eyes. Sweat ran down my forehead and dripped into the snow. I wished I would freeze. I wished I would forget everything. If I could only stop loving and hurting and simply start anew.

A roar escaped my lips. I shouted until all air evaporated from my lungs. The few birds nesting in the tree crowns flapped away, alarmed.

"Why …?" I whispered, my throat feeling singed.

I frowned at the muddled gray sky, beseeching whoever was watching to end the misery of us pathetic humans on Earth.

"Why!" I shouted again, shutting my eyes.

Fire expanded from my core to the tips of my fingers, releasing a pulse of power through my body. I gasped for air, opening my eyes. If I had the power, I would have probably destroyed everything around me. I was glad I did not have it.

The distinctive figure of Feathers swooped to the ground before me, bringing some serenity to my heart. I raised my hand to pet Feather's head, as I usually did, but the raven shifted before my eyes.

Its dark feathers enlarged and morphed into a human body, transforming into skin. Its beak became a straight, pointy nose and small, full lips. Soon, the body of a woman kneeled before me. Long platinum hair fell to her hips, covering her nakedness. Morgana's icy eyes, the only characteristic remaining of Feathers, returned my wide-eyed gaze.

The frozen hand I still held up for Feathers now touched her forehead. As if I had not had enough already. It was *her*. Feathers was *her*.

"You! All this time, it has been *you*?" I growled.

Morgana bobbed her head, frowning at me. "Stop throwing a fit," she said coldly, folding her hands over her chest.

"Throwing a fit!" I repeated, astonished. "Is that all you have to say for yourself?"

She signaled to the surrounding woodland. "I'm surprised it took you this long to burst. Well, not really, after what just happened to you." She glanced about disapprovingly. "Those idiots. I thought they'd actually help."

I frowned. Had she lost her mind? "So, was it you? Why did you bring me here?" I asked, turning the blame on her. "Why didn't you leave me to die on that prairie?"

She paused, as if considering whether to give me more information. "What a waste it would've been."

"Speak," I said, and she glared at me.

"You wouldn't have survived if I hadn't dragged you into the forest. It would have been only a matter of hours before real ravens began plucking out your eyes." She snarled out every word. "After that lightning hit you, your heart stopped beating. And so, the battle ended. I went to you as soon as they took off. Brenen left you for dead." She dissected me with her stare. "But somehow"—she poked at my chest—"your heart beat again, ever so slightly. So, I dragged you inside the forest, where you'd be safe and recover. I tended to your wounds and shielded you from the cold as you slept for hours. You should be grateful you're still alive."

She had taken care of me while I came back to this world. Now it was my time to let out a mocking huff. "Grateful? For what? For my best friend marrying my betrothed? For my mother lying alone on a bed, waiting for death to take her? For the entire Empire falling into the hands of a murderer? You should have let the ravens finish me!"

At the thought of Brenen, my body felt like it was going to combust again. Oh, how I would have preferred to remain ignorant, living detached in the woods, oblivious to the life outside the forest. Perhaps, after all, I should be grateful that she had brought me here.

Her cold hand cupped my cheeks, touching a lone tear of rage that leaked from one corner of my eyes. I locked eyes with Morgana's. "I don't need your pity," I snarled, looking away.

"You are brave," she said. "You went to the prairie knowing it could mean death, and you protected your friends by leaving them behind. You left your home to protect your family. You are not a coward, nor are you to blame for anything."

I gazed back at her. She knew exactly how I felt and spoke the words that would soothe my torment.

"I feel like it wasn't enough. I made so many mistakes. I should never have abandoned my mother. She's dying alone." My voice broke, and I tried to swallow the knot in my throat.

"It is not your fault," she repeated, suddenly embracing me. As my hands rested on her chilly back, I wept like a helpless child. "You did your best," she whispered. "I'll take you to her."

I imagined myself in my mother's chamber, kneeling before her bed, taking her hand, and begging her forgiveness.

I nodded. It was time for me to go to her. "What else should I know about?"

She sighed. "It's … complicated."

"Try me," I said.

"Very well," she agreed. "But first, give me your coat. This will take a long time."

Heat rushed to my cheeks, remembering that all that separated her skin from my body and the cold was her silver hair. I had been so overtaken by grief that I had not noticed the impropriety. I immediately tore my coat off and covered her.

"What if I go back to being Feathers?"

"And then what? Are we going to the cottage?" I grimaced, not sure I was ready to go back.

She raised an eyebrow. "Do you even know your way back?"

I looked at where I had come from. I had not paid any attention to where I was running to. "Probably not." I sighed.

"It's a miracle you're alive." She shook her head, and I wondered whether she was referring to the lightning strike or to my poor survival skills—probably both.

Morgana stood, and I looked away. "Follow me," she said. "I'll guide you to a different place."

I heard wings flapping above me. Without a second thought, I sprinted after her through the Dark Forest.

CHAPTER 20

MISTWOOD

I was no longer sure of where I was. Morgana had led me deeper into the woods for hours. The trees were so twisted, so clumped together, that it was almost impossible to see her flying above me through the canopy.

My mind kept repeating my last moments with Saphyr and Kanis. Her confession, followed by her betrayal. Kanis's outraged face. The news of my mother. It all spun into an unbearably miserable gyre in my mind. None of it made sense.

Eventually, my feet stumbled to a halt, tired of walking. The cold was excruciating, and my stomach complained savagely. I had eaten nothing but the crackers this morning. My head spun, threatening to shut down my body. I steadied myself against a branch.

Morgana cawed twice. She was close, just a couple of trees away. I forced my feet to move again through a thicket, hoping we had finally arrived.

The thicket suddenly cleared, and a mysterious world opened before my eyes. The earth stopped beneath me, ending in a mossy cliff. At my feet, a single white bridge was suspended in the air. Beyond it beckoned a new forest of ancient trees of surprising height.

Their ochre crowns gleamed with pale blue light and were all devoid of snow. Elegant wooden dwellings had been built below the trees' crowns and around the thick trunks. Arches marked the walkways and landings, and oval windows glistened from the second floors. Polished stone bridges, held up by arched columns, connected the dwellings and treetops.

I had seen nothing like it.

"Beautiful, isn't it?" Morgana stood next to me, back in her human form. I immediately took my coat off and threw it over her slender figure.

Her mouth curled up smugly.

"It is," I agreed.

"Shall we?" she asked, padding gracefully over the bridge toward the biggest structure in the heart of the woodland realm.

"Where are we?" I marveled.

"Mistwood, home of the dryads," she replied. "The nymphs of the forest," Morgana explained, anticipating my question.

"Relatives of yours?"

"You could say that" She shrugged.

I frowned. Nothing would surprise me anymore. If a troll jumped out from under a bridge, or I saw a leprechaun at the end of a rainbow, I wouldn't even blink. But what intrigued me was her—Morgana. Why had she pulled me into the Dark Forest, and why had she now chosen to unveil this enchanted realm to me?

She led me into the main structure. The hall was wrapped up in beautifully carved vines that served as arches, holding up the vaulted ceiling. Inside, the air was warm, with no need for coats. It was as if winter did not exist in Mistwood.

Our steps echoed as we climbed a set of stairs to a throne set in the heart of the hall. It was carved in white wood and topped by massive elk antlers sprouting outwards. It looked harmonious, yet somehow dangerous.

A figure, submerged in partial darkness, was sprawled on the throne.

"Welcome, Corvus, son of Colthus, sole heir to the House of Alba." The shadows unveiled the man's face, and he sneered at me with an unnatural gleam in his eyes. "Morgana." He nodded to her.

He seemed young, about my age. The sides of his head were shaved, which highlighted his pointy ears. A long ponytail gathered his black hair on top of his head, and thin eyebrows framed his obsidian eyes. All his features were sharp and slightly unsettling.

"Fergus," Morgana greeted him.

They seemed familiar. To my surprise, Fergus rose and sauntered down the stairs. His stealthy movements reminded me of a cat.

He grinned at Morgana, walking around her and circling our backs as if evaluating us. Morgana did not bother to follow his movements; she simply waited for him to face us. A shiver tightened my spine as he approached and inhaled too close to my throat.

"Brought your pet?" He purred to Morgana. "Rather tart." His nostrils flared, and his lips curled as if tasting my scent.

"Finally ready to go home in a few days." Morgana studied her fingernails.

"How dull," he agreed. "Yet, an exciting addition to our circle." He grinned, eyeing me up and down. "Can't wait to see his talents bloom."

"What talents?" I asked.

"You're the future Emperor of the Sun Empire, are you not?" Fergus raised one eyebrow and pointed to Morgana with amusement. "*She* picked you."

I recalled the first conversation I'd had with Morgana in Sirenibus, and then what had happened earlier today. "Not anymore."

"The Crown Princess married his best friend in an attempt to save herself from Brenen," Morgana explained.

"Ugh!" Fergus clicked his tongue in disapproval several times. "Ungrateful wench, after everything I did to set her father on the throne."

I controlled the urge to bare my teeth at his insult. "What do you gain by playing this power game with humans?"

Fergus tilted his head, leaning in. "It's not about what we gain, but what we keep." His icy breath chilled me.

I raised my chin. "What do you want from us?"

A dangerous smile curved his lips. He caressed my cheek slowly with one finger, the long, pointy nail threatening to pierce my skin. "We want peace." He bared his teeth after the last word, his gaze fixed on my eyes. I looked straight ahead, ignoring his menacing attitude. "And the new Emperor shall keep it."

Morgana sighed and strode to a nearby table, where she took a seat and plucked a grape from a display of fruits.

"Morgana knew all about your original plan to put Galbreg on the throne. Boy are you naïve," Fergus said. "Not only did you underestimate the General's son, but you risked your life thinking his father would ever take him down. No matter how strained the family ties are, blood runs thicker than water." He whispered the last words to me, his mocking gaze still fixed on Morgana.

She simply popped the grape in her mouth and focused on the ancient trees and connecting bridges through the open arches.

Fergus approached the wooden table, grabbed a cluster of grapes, and leaned back against an arch. "If only you had taken Morgana's offer instead of running away with the help of that foolish selkie, you'd be Emperor by now." He tossed a grape in his mouth.

"Why didn't the sirens follow us then?"

"Oh yes, Morgana, why didn't they?" He winked at her.

"Because I ordered them not to." She shrugged, her expression blank as she locked her gaze on mine. "I wanted you as an ally, not an enemy, so I followed you myself."

"Then why didn't you show yourself in the islands?"

"Because I lost you there," she snarled. "When I found you, you were already on a ship headed here."

I frowned at her. "You didn't need me," I said. "You could've taken Saphyr and made her an Empress."

Morgana's blue eyes narrowed. "Perhaps I should have, given the little faith you have in yourself."

"That means she likes you," Fergus said, blinking.

"It means he is a better fit to rule the Empire than her," she corrected. "Corvus would have actually succeeded with his plan were it not for Brenen. The lousy job of your current Emperor caused this change, breaking the peaceful balance of the human realm. A new person is bound to occupy the throne of the Sun, and it should be him."

I observed Fergus. "I'm not easy to control."

"Clearly." Fergus chuckled. "But she insisted we should put someone on the throne who would do a decent job of ruling the humans." He rolled his eyes. "Morgana sometimes forgets the interests of Sirenibus come before her personal interests."

"Enough!" Morgana said, standing.

Fergus laughed and strolled back to his throne.

"Must I remind you, Fergus, that Corvus survived death and came back?"

Fergus scoffed quietly and said, almost to himself, "He won't lose anyone who belongs to Him." His words held a hint of jealousy. Who was he speaking about?

"Perhaps he's destined for the throne," Morgana added.

"We shall see." He sat gazing down at us. "You can stay for as long as you need. Are the newlyweds joining us?"

I flinched, wanting to kick him off his throne.

"Not for now," Morgana replied curtly.

"Very well, then. Go as you please." He waved his hand, bidding us adieu.

Morgana turned on her heels indifferently, and I felt Fergus's gaze on our backs as we exited the hall and moved onto the web of bridges.

Morgana clearly knew her way around as she guided me toward a treehouse nestled at the zenith. A cozy inside greeted us: walls, floor, and ceiling of cherry wood, with an arch opening to a balcony and an astounding view of the realm below.

A magnificent spread of bread, cheeses, fruits, and nuts awaited us on a table on the balcony. My stomach growled loudly, and my mouth watered. I could not remember the last time I had eaten such a meal. We sat cross-legged on the floor, and I immediately tucked in, moaning with pleasure.

Morgana handed me a cup of deep ruby wine, which I chugged down at once. She sniffed, and sipped hers more delicately.

"You try living that way for several months," I grunted. "I'll never think of trout the same again."

She chuckled in agreement.

"Is Fergus to Mistwood what you are to Sirenibus?"

Morgana nodded.

"What are his powers?"

"He keeps the Dark Forest hidden to human eyes and keeps Mistwood safe. The grim glamour of this forest and its impenetrable dark wall is all his work."

I remembered the uninviting presence of the forest, with its protruding naked branches and unsettling silence. "No wonder." I tore a piece of bread.

"He raised the glamour and opened the forest for you, and then for Kanis and Saphyr. Quite the exemption. I asked him to do so, considering the circumstances."

I munched on the bread, considering her words. They were equals, working together. "Do all dryads have powers?"

"They're a unique, peaceful kind. They can live for eternity, like sirens. But they can't shift or manipulate the elements, if that's what you're asking." She glanced at me. "My talents are my own."

"What about Fergus? How old is he?"

"Millennia older than I am."

"And how old are you?" I asked, remembering she had dodged my question back in Sirenibus.

"About your age, slightly older."

"Slightly?" I scoffed. "I thought you were at least one hundred."

"I am not ancient," Morgana drawled, annoyed, and I grinned.

Even with her glacial, ethereal beauty, she looked young. But I had assumed she was ancient. She tucked her hair behind her ears, and I noticed they were not pointy like Fergus's. "How did you get your powers?"

Morgana observed me, clearly considering her answer.

Was she going to tell me the truth?

"I was born with them. Just like you were born an heir."

"You make it sound like a curse."

"We didn't have a choice, did we?"

I guessed she had a point. If she had been born with such powers, she could choose to be lethal, or she could serve her kind and mine. Ultimately, it was her choice. I eyed her, still unsure whose side she was on. "Are we really that different?" I asked. "You and I?"

"All beings have unique gifts—different from each other. You're special in your own way. Destined to be Emperor, I believe."

"By your hand alone?"

She smirked. "Why do you think you survived that lightning?"

"Didn't you save me?"

"I didn't make your heart beat again."

I studied her under wrinkled brows.

"You died and came back. I had nothing to do with it."

Who had sent me back? And for what purpose? I could not remember anything except waking up in the forest.

"That lightning came down and stopped Brenen from killing you. The moment you fell, the battle ended. Do you really believe that was just a coincidence?"

"The weather can be unpredictable," I joked, but my smile soured. I had prayed none of us would die, and none had. Had it been God's will?

"Deep down, you know there *must* be a reason. Where did you drift to when your heart stopped beating?"

"I don't know," I answered. "After I fell, I felt a rumble on the earth. I heard a shout. Then everything went dark." I pondered, trying hard to remember. "Why would I be sent back?"

"To finish what you started."

"You sound too certain about it."

"I've seen glimpses of your life throughout the years. I've kept an eye on the palace. You're more capable than you think, and you were born in the right place. The throne of the Sun Empire is yours to take."

The last time I had been cocksure and considered the throne would be ours, all hell had broken loose. I undusted my memory of the night I had visited the Crystal Palace for Saphyr's birthday. The figure I had seen spying on the palace ... the cloak that had dropped, and the raven that had flown out. *Feathers.* Morgana! My pulse stilled. I narrowed my eyes at her. She had been there from the beginning, hidden in the shadows.

"How long have you been spying on us?"

Morgana smiled smugly. "It's my job, don't take it personally."

"And what is your job, exactly?" I growled.

"To ensure our safety."

"From what? Us? How are humans a threat to you?"

She drew back, her smile fading. "Who said you're a threat?"

"Then why spy on us? Why lurk in the shadows?"

"Why not ask Kanis and your adopted gang of scoundrels?"

I pressed my lips flat. That was different.

"It's the same. *You* spy. *We* spy. Trick of the trade." She grinned. "In any case, we're allies now, and Galbreg must die."

"Listen, Morgana. I'm done with all this," I said, pouring myself more wine. "I'm not a murderer. Dead or alive, destined or not, I'm through. Tell Fergus I appreciate his warm welcome, and I'm honored he listened to your advice to choose me to become your new puppet, but I'm not interested. You creatures can keep your secrets to yourself, and I'll keep my freedom. I promise I won't tell humans about your existence. It's not like they'll believe me anyway." I downed the wine.

"You will take the throne, and Galbreg will die," Morgana said, her jaw clenched.

I sighed. "Even if he's a lying treacherous bastard, I won't kill him."

"I will." She laughed. "I'll do it for you."

I rolled my eyes, grateful for the warmth of the wine and the feeling of it numbing my nerves. I stretched my neck on both sides, releasing the muscle tension as I poured her more wine. "Do you not have the slightest appreciation for life? Can you create it out of thin air? People always discard it, as if it's nothing but spare currency. Why do people choose the easiest route? It's not the right one."

"He doesn't deserve his life."

I cocked my head. Galbreg had once been my mentor. I had admired him for his intelligence, kindness, and determination, until his ruthlessness overshadowed his humanity. He had lied and betrayed me. But was he deserving of death? "And who are you to say?"

"It's his fault Brenen turned out like he did."

"Sure, he was a terrible father to Brenen, but he was a good one to me when mine wasn't there for me."

Morgana looked at me with a hard expression. "He's a murderer."

I pressed my lips together. That was a truth I had always found difficult to accept. "A trick of the trade for a general."

"He tried to murder an innocent child," she added.

I frowned. "That's a grave accusation."

"And killed the child's mother." Morgana's hand on the table curled into a fist. "She was his wife. Her children did not look like him, so he drove a knife into her heart and abandoned the children in floating baskets on the river."

My mouth fell open, but I shook my head. "That can't be true. Galbreg's wife died months after giving birth, from health issues."

"That's what he's had everyone believe."

My muscles tightened, and I held my breath, refusing to believe her.

"Do you think he still deserves to live?"

I hesitated. "There must be more to the story."

"You can't justify what he did," she hissed, the blue of her eyes turning to daggers.

"What does it have to do with you, in any case?"

Morgana looked away, holding her chin high. "He betrayed you. Brenen tried to kill you, and Galbreg stood there watching. I should've killed them then and there, but I had to choose between saving you and let them live. Your heart was barely beating." She eyed me, as if wondering if she had made the right decision after all. "Now that you're alive, I'll impart the justice they deserve—after I secure the throne for you."

"You're absurdly stubborn," I replied, downing the last drop of my cup.

"You will recover what has been lost and return to your normal life."

"And what's in it for you?"

"I'll gain an Empire," she sang, as if it were obvious, but a shadow in her eyes tied a knot in my belly. Fergus's words came to mind: *Morgana forgets the interests of Sirenibus come before her personal interests.*

I shook my head. *Nonsense.* They were all insane.

"Very well then, your Emperor needs to sleep now," I said mockingly. I was not interested in anything anymore. All I wanted to do was sleep for days—years.

Morgana smiled, and she stood. "I'll see you in the morning." In a flash, she morphed, and my coat fell to the ground as she flew away.

A sigh escaped my lips, and I poured myself another cup of wine, hoping to soon drift into a deep sleep. This all had to end someday.

It was afternoon again when I awakened next to the same table I had fallen asleep at. I eyed the empty jar of wine and took a chunk of bread from yesterday's supper for breakfast, if only to settle my stomach. Leaning my back against a column, I groaned. Tonight, I would ensure I slept comfortably on a bed. My days of sleeping on the floor by the fire were over.

Feathers's—or rather Morgana's—sudden caw did nothing for my headache. I glimpsed her gliding into the room through the open arch, transforming midair into her human form. I remained seated, purposefully ignoring her, my eyes on the forest below instead.

I blinked several times as I discovered Saphyr and Kanis standing on a bridge far below, watching with frowns on their faces the bird flying up into my chamber. Not that they knew these were my chambers, nor that I was even here, watching them.

Another figure on the bridge, a dryad, invited them to continue along the path, probably toward their own chambers. Saphyr seemed as astonished as I had been at seeing Mistwood for the first time. Kanis studied every route in and out of their tree dwelling.

They were here. Morgana had brought them. My head pounded.

"Did you guide them here while I slept? In your raven form?" I ground the words out, my eyes still fixated on Saphyr and Kanis.

"They don't need to know I'm the raven. I have my reasons, and I wish to keep it that way," she warned me, sitting next to me on the floor. "And you need to hear them out. I'm sure there's an explanation."

I rested my head back against the column. What did she care? Saphyr and Kanis strolled toward a dwelling opposite ours, a few floors down. Relief and pain twisted together in my chest.

"Are you sure or absolutely certain? Because I'm certain you eavesdropped on their private conversations in your raven form."

"Perhaps." She grinned. "They were relieved to see me, thinking you were near. After they realized you weren't, I signaled them to follow me, and they did so immediately. They never even stopped on their way here." Her tone turned sour, and I detected a hint of jealousy. "Such good friends."

I eyed her curiously, immediately regretting my choice of taking my eyes off the forest.

"Can you put some clothes on?" I grumbled.

She sneered, standing to grab a knitted white throw. At least her hair covered almost everything. As she returned and sat next to me, I glared at Kanis and Saphyr's chambers.

"Jealous much?"

"I could say the same to you," I scowled at her. Morgana was a loner, and I wondered if she had grown tired of it.

She held my stare with cold eyes, and then turned her stare toward the treehouse. "We're different from them," she said.

"Bitter and lonely?"

"Smart and powerful," she corrected me with a sneer, without denying my labels.

"I guess the two descriptions go hand in hand. Why did you bring me here, to Mistwood?" I asked her. "Actually, why didn't you bring me here before rather than let me starve in that cottage?"

Pity flashed briefly in her eyes. She squinted at me, clearly considering whether to tell me the truth.

"Don't answer that," I said, mortified, shutting my eyes. I did not want pity—although it surprised me she was capable of such sentiment.

"I wanted to protect you." Her eyes shone earnestly. "To keep you safe … until your friends decided to risk their lives and enter the forest, that is. Then I realized it was time to put everything back in its place."

"You can be quite contradictory, you know? First, you abduct me and drag me to your underwater palace, then you secretly nurture me back to life, after which you leave me in an abandoned magical forest to both starve and recover." I took a quick breath. "Then, you guide me to Mistwood after I punch my best friend in the face, and now you lead him here with his now-wife, who was first my betrothed. Oh, and let's not forget, you also collect selkie skins for a pastime. Just *who* are you?"

Morgana snickered. "Am I not allowed to have pets?" She puckered mockingly.

My eyebrows shot up almost to my hairline. After all I had just said, had she just called me her pet?

"Is it not a seal we're speaking of?" she clarified.

I stared at her, remembering she had not corrected Fergus when he branded me her pet, but I chose to dismiss it.

"A *talking* one," I emphasized. "You could've at least asked Ean before stealing his selkie skin. Just how many more skins are you hiding in your palace?"

"Ha!" she said dismissively. Her demeanor was that of a spoiled child—a lonely, spoiled child.

"You must free them."

"I care for them." She shrugged. "They live in a palace."

"And they must remain there only out of their own volition. You can't keep abducting people at will," I insisted. It felt like I was explaining to a child that not everything in sight was hers.

"You owe me a selkie," she replied. "A beautiful crimson one."

I howled a laugh. "Dry me dead if you want to, but I'm not returning Ean to you. He's free now, as the others should be. You can make friends, but not prisoners."

She rolled her eyes. "Well, get ready to meet your fabulous friends later tonight," she said bitterly, standing.

My head pounded again, and my stomach turned at the thought of meeting them. What explanation could they possibly have that could fix things?

Morgana let the white throw drop, and I looked away, annoyed. Did she have no decorum? Such a wild creature!

"Fergus is throwing a party tonight, and you're all invited," she announced before turning into a raven and gliding away.

Son of a ...!

CHAPTER 21

MINE

At night, Mistwood was true to its name. Thick vapors covered the ancient forest, snarling at my feet as I strode over the bridges. The mist wafted in white clumps, forcing me to halt in fear of stepping off the bridge in temporary blindness. It was difficult to breathe through such thick air, but even if the clumps stopped me in my tracks now and then, they were wickedly refreshing in the cool night air.

I knew I was close to the gathering when the soft melody of harps reached my ears. Mist rose from the forest floor to my knees, blue fireflies twinkling through it. Mistwood was an enchanting icy-blue haven of peace at night.

Opalescent light streamed through the canopy and bathed the dryads where they sat scattered beneath the trees. Tall and elegant, they had long, straight hair of tawny, copper, and ash, and looked similar to the sirens, although warmer and more welcoming.

They smiled, clearly intrigued as I passed them, and I nodded back in acknowledgment. Exquisite food filled several tables, and wine flowed from tall silver fountains.

Neither Fergus nor Morgana were in sight, but a familiar bright laughter caught my attention. *Saphyr.* She stood as elegantly as the dryads who surrounded her, all of them clearly dazzled by her confident beauty and amusing stories.

Saphyr was wrapped in emerald velvet, her skin dazzling with its usual pearly sheen. Gold thread was embroidered over the gown's bust and waist, highlighting her curls, which were kissed by the starlight. She looked every bit a true Crown Princess of the human realm.

Behind her, almost undetectable in the shadow of a tree, Kanis stood, his shoulders squared and both hands clasped behind his back. A frown creased his forehead as he observed all those around them, clearly protective of Saphyr.

I sighed bitterly and continued walking through the crowd. At the far end, a massive fire crackled near a waterfall and a river. The harps had given way to resonant drums, their thrilling beat reverberating in my chest. I leaned against a tree. A young dryad in charge of passing drinks handed me a glass and kept it filled for a while as the fire blazed and rose above the dancing crowd. Disgusted by everything, I stared at the bonfire, emptying another cup of fiery uske down my throat, no longer even feeling its burn.

"Well, you look positively miserable," Morgana hummed brightly as she nudged me with a bare shoulder. She had morphed her hair into long, raven curls, and her silky, midnight-blue dress had a plunging neckline and slits at each side of her hips. A shiny belt coiled heavy from her belly to her knees.

I scooted myself to the left so our shoulders would not touch and looked longingly at my empty cup. The dryad who had been keeping it filled approached with the jug of golden uske, but Morgana was quicker. She snatched the wooden cup from my numb fingers and sent it flying over to the bonfire with a swift move. The flames engulfed it angrily, roaring up into the night sky. The dryads dancing around the bonfire cheered and laughed.

I gave Morgana the most hateful side stare I could muster, and she smirked in return. All of this was a waste of time. I strode across the crowd, planning on getting as far away from everyone as I could, but Morgana followed. She was not one to give up.

A group of graceful dryads made way for me as I cut through them and made a sharp turn toward the river, away from the gathering, hoping Morgana could not follow.

After walking for a few minutes, I took a seat on the riverbank, exhaling a deep sigh. I lay down and stared at the stars. Had I stayed dead on the prairie, I would not have to deal with all this nonsense. It was exhausting, pointless.

Fireflies gleamed above me, providing a beautiful spectacle of lights suspended above the grass until muffled steps made me sit up. Expecting to send Morgana away, I instead found the dryad who had filled my glass before.

"Care for another drink, Milord?" She kindly extended an empty cup.

I took it suspiciously. Why had she bothered to follow me into the darkness of the river? Did she know I was human?

"Mind if I join you?"

Ginger curls swung over her full breasts as she sat next to me and fixed her brown skirt over her crossed legs. She cradled the jug with both hands in her lap. I frowned at her and let out a hopeless sigh. *There goes my peace.*

She poured me a drink and took a swig from the tip of the jug herself. "Thought we could both use a drinking companion tonight," she said.

"I suppose so." I grunted, downing half of the cup at once. If she was drinking from the same jug, it was probably not poisoned.

Dark thoughts were entangling in my head. I was sure that if I kept up her pace, I would be an unconscious drunkard by the night's end. I sneaked a look at her. Fainting alone in the woods was fine—maybe a wild beast would put me out of my misery. But losing consciousness next to a cunning magical creature? Unacceptable.

She smiled at me as if sensing my suspicion. "My lord sent me."

Fergus. I snorted. Surely it had not been Saphyr. I chuckled at the idea of her sending a pretty dryad with a jug full of uske my way. I sighed, remembering she still did not know I was here.

"I'm Ruby."

Well suited, I thought, eyeing her shining mane of red curls. A passing firefly lit her green eyes, and I drank to the appreciation of her beauty. Ruby swiftly refilled my cup and took another swig from the jug.

Ruby was trouble, and Saphyr's scornful eyes kept appearing in my mind. A nervous rasp left my throat as I prepared to rise.

Ruby put a hand to my chest, holding me down. "Where do you think you're going?"

I grabbed her wrist to push her away, but she leaned close to my ear and whispered, "He has already waged me for you." The scent of strawberries filled my nostrils.

My throat went dry as I understood what she meant. Fergus could not have possibly done this. Ruby's lips moved from my ear toward my face, but something else wrenched her away before I could.

"He is *mine*," Morgana growled, clutching the back of Ruby's dress.

Ruby stood gracefully, sneering at the siren from a few inches above her. "Very well, but I keep the pay." She took the jug and sauntered away to the bonfire, as if nothing had happened.

"Yours?" I repeated, stunned. "Since when am I *yours*?" I laughed, amused at Morgana's daring.

"My new pet?" she teased with false innocence.

I roared with laughter. Then I grinned at her dangerously. She thought she could toy with me?

I cupped her jaw, my thumb caressing her cheek. Although Morgana stood still, holding my gaze, a rush of heat warmed her skin beneath my fingers. "Since when am I your pet?" I whispered in her ear as I pressed my forehead against hers. My head was spinning with uske. Her lips parted and I was drawn by the sweet aroma of wine; Morgana had also been drinking. I dared closer, searching for the taste of uske on her lips.

But the clear image of Saphyr in my head froze my entire being. I could not do this to her, even if she was no longer mine. *Had she ever been?*

I savored the memory of our last moments together, before everything went to hell, Saphyr and I, devouring each other by moonlight on the Stella Islands. Guilt caught in my throat.

Morgana was not Saphyr. Nobody would ever be her. And I only wanted Saphyr, no one else. I could not betray her trust, even if Saphyr had betrayed mine.

I pulled myself away and turned my back on Morgana. "Why did Fergus send her?" I asked coldly over my shoulder.

"Perhaps it is just his way of helping. Or perhaps he's just trying to pry information out of you. He sure is testing you."

"Huh, how absurd. None of us can be trusted, anyway," I said indifferently.

"They're not together," Morgana said, referring to Saphyr and Kanis.

"I'll see that for myself," I snarled as I left.

The train of Saphyr's dress flowed behind her as she glided over a white bridge toward her tree dwelling. I followed her stealthily through the bouts of mist, which helped clear my head a little.

After the riverbank incident, I had gone to see Saphyr at the gathering but had stopped to observe her from afar instead. To my surprise, Kanis was gone, and she had not seemed to notice. When she finally turned and did not find him, she darted back to their chambers. She must have thought Kanis had left to return to their dwelling too, so I had followed her.

We were close now. No lights dressed the windows of their chambers. I waited on the bridge as she went through the door. Only the soft glow of the forest illuminated the surrounding tree crowns. I approached her door with curiosity. It was ajar.

I sneaked inside. It was submerged in darkness, lit only with a single candle. It took my eye a second to adjust. To my right were two doors, and to my left, a sitting room. Saphyr stood silently by the window, gazing out at the canopy sprinkled with twinkling blue lights. I positioned myself against the wall behind her. She sighed desolately. Was she disappointed at not having found Kanis here?

How close I had come to making a mistake with Morgana gripped me. I wanted only Saphyr, even if she ... Even if she was now with Kanis. A throbbing pain pulsed at the back of my head. *This was a mistake. I should leave.*

Yet my feet moved of their own volition toward Saphyr.

Like a lion sneaking toward prey, I prowled over to her. Did she care about Kanis the way she cared about me? Had she kissed him the way she had brazenly kissed me in the cottage?

I stood behind her, letting my fingertips caress the velvet over her waist, stroking her collarbone with my other hand. Would she welcome the touch, thinking I was him?

Saphyr stiffened and spun, slapping me for the second time. My cheeks burned with pain and embarrassment as I recoiled.

Sapphire light coming through the window exposed me. Saphyr's eyes widened at the sight of me. I was dressed in a black velvet tunic, my skin pale against my loose obsidian hair. I waited for Saphyr's screams, her shaming, and recriminations, but they never came.

Instead, she crushed her lips to mine. I froze, slowly understanding that she had seen me and had changed her mind so drastically. She had clearly slapped me thinking I was Kanis or a stranger. But she had kissed me on realizing it was me.

I gave in to her kiss, to her hands roaming over my hair and shoulders. A grunt escaped me as she closed the distance between us, feeling every inch of her skin aflame through her velvet dress. I burned too. My thoughts scattered. There was only her.

Unlike before, this felt infinitely right. Her lips against mine, setting me ablaze.

"You are mine," I said, as Saphyr panted for air.

"And you are mine," she replied.

I leaned to her kiss again when a shout broke the silence.

"Corvus!" Kanis's warning reverberated from the bridge.

"Bloody bastard …!" I breathed, and she smiled.

"You must let us explain," she murmured.

"Very well, then." I let space back in between us but firmly kept her hand in mine. Let Kanis explain why he had married my betrothed.

"It's simpler than you think."

"We'll see about that," I said bitterly between my teeth.

Kanis erupted through the door like a raging fire. "Get away from her," he snarled. "*You* have no right to touch her."

My blood boiled. An excruciating need to punch him again rose in me; this time, I would not stop at his face.

Saphyr clutched my arm. "Why on Earth would you say such a thing?"

"I just saw him with a dryad. He almost kissed her," Kanis said with revulsion. "I followed her, and she's now waiting in his chambers."

I felt as if a glass vase had fallen and shattered into a thousand shards.

I looked to Saphyr, pleading.

"Is it … is it true?" She gasped.

I inhaled, shutting my eyes for a second, trying to order my thoughts.

"No! He doesn't know what he saw," I said. He had not recognized that the dryad was Morgana. I groaned, annoyed that I could not even disclose it was her, recalling how she had kept me alive and guided them to me. I owed her, and I had to keep my word.

"Tell us, Corvus. What did I see?" Kanis insisted.

I faced Saphyr, who returned a worried expression. "I know it's not an excuse, but I've been drinking … far more than I should've." I sighed. "I was going to talk to you, but then I saw you together, talking to those creatures, and I thought …"

I did not know what I had thought. Irrational jealousy had driven me away. "I just left," I continued. "I kept on drinking. She came to me, and I was so upset at the thought of your having married … *him*." I spat the last word. "That I almost made the worst mistake of my life, but I didn't. I came to you, Saphyr." I clasped her hands in mine, silently begging for her understanding.

A tear trickled down her cheeks, and I caught it with a finger.

"I … I need to rest." Saphyr plucked her hands away.

"No," I begged.

But she turned and strode past Kanis, her eyes fixed on the door to her chamber. I heard a lock turn on the other side of the door.

I glared up from where our hands had been joined, to Kanis. Hell-bent on murdering him. "You!" I seethed. "Wasn't it enough to marry her?"

"If I had married her out of love and not out of duty, don't you think I'd be even more irate to find you here all over my supposed wife?" he roared back.

"That was payback, wasn't it?" I knew him well enough to see he was still mad about the fist I had thrown at him in the forest.

"You could say that," he admitted. "Not just for the punch, but for your tremendous idiocy and lack of faith in me."

I took another deep breath, shutting my eyes and forcing myself to calm down. "We need to talk. Follow me," I hissed. I left their treehouse without bothering to see whether Kanis would follow.

CHAPTER 22

HOME

I marched back to my chambers and glimpsed Morgana flying away through the arched windows as I crossed the bridge. My stomach tensed, but with Kanis on my heels, I had no time to think about that. We had to mend things. Tonight. Somehow.

A hearth fire blazed inside the dwelling. Kanis took a seat by it as I closed the door. He did not waste time pouring us two glasses of uske from the glass decanter. This night already seemed endless.

I flopped down on a winged chair next to him, and we clanked our glasses out of habit before downing them.

"You first," I said, leaning back and closing my eyes.

"I see her as a sibling. A sister. Like you're a brother to me. But you— you selfish, egotistical cad—never allowed me to explain that." Kanis closed his fists as he continued. "I merely did what you requested of me. Although I didn't agree with it, I let you go and die at the hands of Galbreg and Brenen, so I kept my promise of looking after her. It was never what I wanted; it was always what *you* wanted. I only did what you asked of me before you left the islands."

I moved uncomfortably in my seat. My friend's loyalty had always been unbreakable.

"You asked me to protect her, and that's what I did. Bloody Brenen tried to force her to marry him after he declared you dead. He confined her family members, one by one, until she agreed. I couldn't bear watching it. Saphyr was desperate. I couldn't kill the bastard myself, so I helped her escape one night, and the next day we proclaimed ourselves married. It was the only way Brenen would leave her alone. He wants to rule the Empire, Corvus. The Emperor himself is being held hostage in his own rooms as we speak, and the people don't realize. It wouldn't surprise me if the Emperor were already dead and Brenen proclaimed himself the new Emperor. The entire army is under his command since he took Galbreg's as well."

I rested my forehead in my hands. It was worse than I thought. Her father, her entire family, was being held captive. I had been such an idiot to ask Saphyr to stay in the Dark Forest with me. I had been so afraid to hear the truth that I had not allowed them to say it. Now I understood why Kanis had insisted we leave. Saphyr was so considerate she was willing to wait until I was ready to hear it.

Kanis squeezed my knee. "There is something else ... as you know, your mother is unwell. But your House could not recover its stolen wealth after your father's astronomical ransom. Your father is ... well ... he's not the same. He hasn't been there for your mother."

I remained silent, a proper imbecile indeed. Had I listened to Kanis from the beginning and not gone to that damned prairie, we would have saved all this unnecessary pain.

"I'm sorry," I uttered.

"I'm sorry too," he replied. His eyes flashed in the firelight. "We'll get through this. I have a plan. If you'll only listen this time."

"I will," I promised. I clearly had not been making good decisions by myself. I had no wish to keep fighting alone.

"I hid the satchels of siren tears we stole from Sirenibus," he explained.

I winced, looking around for a spying raven, but we were alone.

"Since they're worth a fortune, we can use them to reinstate your family's wealth and raise a proper army, as we should have done from the beginning. This time, we'll recruit soldiers in the desert and send diplomatic envoys to—

"Just a moment," I intervened. "I know I said I'd listen, and I will, but before you continue, how about we infiltrate the palace and go directly for Brenen's head this time? You must consider all the lives that will be lost in a battle of such magnitude."

"I understand, Corvus, but the man is armed to the teeth. He never spends a minute alone. He is surrounded by guards. Trust me, I considered that route when he threatened Saphyr."

"What if we plant spies? Learn his routine, his weaknesses? There must be an opening."

Kanis sighed. "Perhaps. But it'd be tremendously risky. If we fail again, I doubt we'll get a third chance." He eyed me thoughtfully. "The only reason I'd agree is because every day we spend is another day Saphyr's family remains captive. It's another day Brenen will use to tighten the leash on his soldiers. Another day closer to him snatching the Crown."

I thought of Morgana. She may have a way to help us.

"Fine. We'll leave in the morning. First, I must go home. Then, we'll figure out the rest."

Kanis nodded. "That's enough for today," he agreed with a sigh. "We should rest before the journey."

"You both must be exhausted." I eyed him, considering they had just arrived here.

"We're fine. You, however, could use some bread, and perhaps less uske. I see even more bones protruding than before."

I grumbled.

"Here," he threw me an apple he had snatched from a nearby fruit bowl.

"Thanks." I bit into its sweet flesh. "I missed you both, you know. I spent way too many days alone in that forest."

"I don't know how you managed to survive." He shook his head.

I rolled my eyes. "What if we spoke to Morgana?"

Kanis cocked his head, frowning.

"No, I have not gone mad," I drawled. "It's just an idea." I watched closely for his reaction.

Kanis clenched his jaw. "Well, she had a plan for us when she abducted us to Sirenibus." He scratched his stubble. "To make you Emperor," he recalled. "What does she want with the human realm, anyway? Do you see this place? They feel so different from the sirens. They live peacefully here, have nothing to do with us, although they were rather interested in Saphyr's stories about our world."

I recalled Fergus's wild presence. How could I describe him to Kanis without mentioning Morgana?

"Where's that raven of yours, by the way? Intelligent animal, but incredibly untimely. Had it not interrupted Saphyr in the forest, she'd have explained the truth about our marriage. That raven guided us to you. Did you send it? How did you come to this place?"

God. I ran a hand through my hair. Why had Morgana interrupted Saphyr? I guessed she felt bad about it since she had brought them here and insisted I allow them to explain. And how could I now lie to Kanis about Morgana?

"The bird guided me here," I admitted. "Then, it came back to you two." It was technically not a lie. "I was surprised to see you both here."

"Huh, how interesting. I wonder if it's magical or just unusually canny?"

"Well, you know how smart ravens can be. They can mimic human words and remember human faces. Feathers also brought me small treasures from time to time." I frowned at the thought of Morgana bringing me precious stones or small flowers whenever she wanted to cheer me up. Oh, how pitiful must I have looked to her? And I had thought I was bonding with a wild animal. "They can be cunning, though," I added. "Not to be trusted."

Kanis laughed. "Enough raven chitchat. Let's go to bed."

I stood, unsure of what to do.

"I'll sleep here," he added. "Saphyr and I have always slept in separate rooms, so you and I can share now."

"Of course," I appreciated the clarification. Then I sighed, recalling Saphyr's hurt expression when Kanis told her I had almost kissed a dryad. Thankfully, he had not realized it was Morgana. "God, she must hate me."

"I know that was unnecessary on my behalf. We should've talked first."

Kanis was a man of honor. He had protected Saphyr by telling her the truth about what he had seen just like he would have done for a sister. "I understand. It's my fault anyway."

Kanis stretched out, ready for sleep. "If it makes you feel any better, I haven't touched a single strand of hair on her head since you left."

We left Mistwood the following morning. Saphyr had opted to ignore me, and Morgana had not shown herself in her true form again. She had simply perched on a chair as a raven and eavesdropped on our breakfast conversation about returning home.

By the time Kanis and I went to find Saphyr in her chambers, a dryad had prepared three horses and satchels filled with water, cured meats, cheese, crackers, and apples for the way. I was certain Morgana had made the arrangements.

The dryad silently guided us out of Mistwood, weaving through the twisted mossy trees to the edge of the Dark Forest. After we entered the prairie, I glanced back in time to see Fergus's glamour come alive. The trees turned dry, and thorny branches tangled back into an impenetrable black wall, the taciturn dryad disappearing behind it.

I lifted my chin and tightened my hold on the reins, pushing down the gloom that threatened to overtake me. Then, eager to get out of there, I pressed my heels into my horse and sent it galloping through the prairie.

The speed cleared my mind, and a thrill shot through me whenever the horse leaped—suspended off the ground, it felt like flying. The hoofbeats of the other horses followed closely behind as we galloped up the mountain path. From time to time, I glanced up, searching for the glossy raven flying above the trees, but Morgana was nowhere to be seen.

We rested for a few hours during the day before continuing our journey. We were all so exhausted that we barely talked before we resumed our travels, finally arriving at the manor by sundown.

There were no guards or servants in sight. We dismounted and guided the horses over the bridge, water trickling below. As we tied the horses to the columns of the portico, I grew increasingly worried. The main door was ajar. I pushed it, and it creaked open. I swallowed.

Our family manor was the shadow of what it once had been. All its glamour and decadence had faded. The hall was empty, the furniture gone. White curtains flapped mournfully in the wind from the arched windows. Vines tangled their way up to the ceiling. Spiderwebs clung to the chandeliers, and a thick layer of dust on the once-polished floor drowned out our echoing steps. My chest hollowed.

Kanis and Saphyr followed me in solemn silence as I navigated the empty halls and corridors of my former home, now sacked of its life and happiness.

The door to my mother's chamber was also open. The sun's rays shone through it, and a glint of hope lit my heart. Saphyr and Kanis stayed outside to give me privacy. As I crossed the threshold, a pungent smell assaulted my nostrils. Where were her maidens? I sniffed.

My mother lay in bed, her hair loose over her pillow. She glanced through the open archways to the mountains, which were gilded in sunlight.

"Mother," I whispered, trying not to startle her.

She gaped, taking in my appearance. For a second, fear burned in her eyes as if I were a ghost. Then she beamed with joy and extended her arms toward me.

"My son!" she yelled, her voice quivering. "My son! Come here, my boy."

I fought back tears, letting her engulf me in the tightest embrace she had ever given me.

The putrid smell came from her, not the room. This realization was accompanied by fury and despair. What could I do for her? How could I help her escape the claws of death?

"I'm sorry," I said. "I should've never left."

She framed my face with her bony fingers. "You did what you needed to do, and what I asked you to." Her voice lowered, and I felt unable to breathe as she said, "I place no blame on you."

Her words undid me. I did not deserve to be happy. I did not deserve her. Even if she said otherwise, my conscience told me that if I had never left, perhaps she would not have fallen sick. If I had been taken, instead of my father, perhaps she would not be lying in this bed. Believing she had lost my father forever had taken its toll on her. I was a selfish, worthless son who had abandoned his mother.

"Let's leave. I'll take you back to Oldterra. I'll find you the best doctors. You'll recover." My throat ached.

"No. There's nothing left for me there. You have your entire future ahead of you. You're just a boy. I am old. This is my home." Her eyelids fluttered as she glanced out at the mountains, longing in her eyes. She had a love for this place that I had never fully understood. Perhaps it was the fruit of her life, building such a beautiful manor for herself and her family. Now that our House had crumbled to pieces, there was nothing left.

"Why not? We'll be at peace there."

"No. You go and have a good life. I'll stay here."

My throat closed. I had already abandoned her once. Even if I had to throw away my future and die again at the hand of Brenen, I would not leave.

"No. I'll stay here with you," I insisted.

Tears of gratitude and guilt rolled from her eyes. My mother took my hands within hers, holding them tightly. "Do not throw your future away."

"Where is he? Where's my father?

The last time she had taken sick, about five years ago, it had been after my father's dalliances with other women. My mother had found out but had somehow forgiven him. She had fought once already with this disease, which had come back to haunt her. With my father's love and mine, perhaps she stood a chance at recovery.

My mother's eyes dropped to the bed. "He is not here. I haven't seen him in a while."

My ears pounded, and my blood sent rage roiling through my body. How long had he abandoned her? "How have you been fending for yourself?"

"Thali has been here with me. She comes every afternoon. And the doctor every so often."

I thought of her maiden and felt a deep sense of gratitude.
"I'll go find Father."

Thick tears slid down her cheeks.

"What's the matter?" I asked, wiping her tears away.

"He is not here," she said. "And I prefer it that way."

My face tensed. I would drag my father here by his hair, if necessary, but my mother shook her head gently. I had to respect her wishes, so I just nodded. "You're going to be fine." I placed a kiss on her forehead and caressed her cold cheek with my fingertip.

She shut her eyes, smiling.

So, this was what was left of my home. I put a hand to my temples, trying to appease my throbbing headache.

They would pay for this—for all of it.

CHAPTER 23
A PROMISE OF FREEDOM

The hem of my ragged coat dragged over the dusty floor of the main hall. My chest felt hollow. The house felt neglected, dead. My father had abandoned my sick mother.

I stared around the empty hall, yearning for the days when it had brimmed with life. Slowly, I collapsed to the dusty floor, hugging my knees. A spider crawled away from me.

Alone. I was truly alone.

If my mother died, I would have no one to lean on except for my friends. It was terrifying to feel so forsaken in the world. Would I end up like this house? Abandoned. Empty.

The sage and crimson color of the walls was still there, hidden beneath the dust. I would cherish every moment I spent in this house: the meals shared with family, its protection, its hidden peaceful places, all would live forever in my memory. But it did not feel like home anymore. There was no happiness, no peace here. Grief and pain had stolen it. I had no home, only a seething thirst for revenge that would dry me dead if I did not quench it.

Steps heralded someone joining me in the hall. I stood, facing the arched windows that overlooked the mountains and Sol City nestled at its feet. On the horizon, the sea glimmered in the sunset.

As the steps approached, I glimpsed Saphyr.

"I'll rip him to shreds," I growled under my breath.

"He's descended into the city's fortress. He no longer dwells in the Crystal Palace."

Of course not. Brenen was not a fool. The fortress, with its limestone towers, stood tall and proud, high walls surrounding it. Penetrating it would not be easy.

"Are you all right?" Saphyr was clearly referring to my mother.

"No." Why lie?

"What about your father?"

I raged at the memory.

I had gone to find him at midnight, after seeing my mother, and had spied him at the house of his mistress. Alcohol had triumphed over the man. He wept to the dark sky, kneeling in the yard. Understanding, I left without letting him see me. All hope gone, he still remained unwilling to accept his mistakes, to fight back. Fear and grief had devoured him from the inside. His desperate screams still rang in my ears.

"He made his choice."

"Nobody knows you're alive. The people think you're dead."

"We'll use that to our advantage." I thought of the miserable condition of the manor and wondered whether the townspeople cared at all. Had they offered to help, or would they have raided it if given the chance?

"We only put ourselves in more danger by leaving. We are completely exposed and at their mercy," I said ruefully. "He's taken your family, crumbled mine, and betrayed his own father twice. We're not Brenen's only victims."

Kanis had discovered that many other Houses had suffered the same fate. The people were more oppressed than ever. "Children starve, and sickness bleeds through the streets. Any whisper of revolt is crushed without mercy. We must act soon before Brenen decides to rid himself of your father and declare himself Emperor."

"I feel we are nothing but a pair of children whom the world has abandoned to luck or forced to grow overnight to face nightmares." Saphyr rubbed her goose-fleshed arms. "There must be a purpose to all this."

"I'm sure there is. Even if we don't see it now, I'm sure we will. Everything happens for a godly reason, even this hell."

"Corvus ..." More footsteps joined us in the hall. "Everything's ready."

175

Confusion glinted in Saphyr's eyes as Kanis stopped before me. I held Saphyr's hands in mine.

"Please take care of my mother tonight," I whispered to her ear, placing a kiss on her cheek as I pushed down the pain stabbing my heart. "I have something urgent to attend."

The large studio was partially hidden by darkness. Cherry-wood panels covered the walls, and books were stacked almost to the ceiling, from which a sun of wrought gold reflected the light cast by iron candelabras. Crimson curtains covered the shut windows.

I stood in front of the fire, which crackled, illuminating the grim faces of those seated around the room.

I had traded my ragged clothes for something more suitable for the heir to the House of Alba to host a secret meeting with what remained of the Alliance. A dark overcoat embroidered in gold fell to my knees, and my shoulder-length hair was tied with an obsidian ribbon at my nape. Kanis stood tall to my right, his shoulders squared.

The lords and ladies of the Alliance stared at me, slightly unsettled, as if I were a ghost. They all had thought I was dead.

"So, it is you ... I wondered whether Colthus had called us in," said Ansel, the eldest, who was old enough to be my grandmother.

"It is I," I replied hoarsely.

"Brenen proclaimed you dead. Even your guard gave an account of your dead body after the heavens took you down with lightning," said a younger lord.

"Yet ... here I am." I twisted my lips in a dangerous smile. "I've called you tonight, ladies and gentlemen, to resume the work we had so carefully put in motion before Galbreg's son fooled us all." I studied the wary eyes throughout the studio. Not all leaders of the Houses were here. Some Houses had already fallen, like mine.

"Time is of the essence. Brenen holds the Empire hostage, but not for long. He *will* become the Emperor if we let him. If the Empire was crumbling before, Brenen has now reduced it to ashes. The people continue to starve, now more than ever. Their freedom dims like a spent candle after midnight. His soldiers patrol the streets, beating anybody out past sundown. He fears a revolt more than anything."

"What do you suggest? Your father has gone mad, your mother is ill, and you've lost your fortune. We let you oversee the initial plans of overthrowing the Empire with Galbreg's help, but his own son slipped right under your nose and took everything you had. He decimated you. What do you have to offer us, Corvus, son of Colthus? Why should we trust *you*?" Borgia, an older lord, joined in.

I recalled the same words from Galbreg. Why should anybody trust me? I did not place my trust in anyone, not even my own shadow.

Kanis took a fistful of the blue pearls from his pockets and threw them on the table opposite. They rolled to the edge, gleaming in the firelight, reflecting the widened eyes of the Alliance.

"I have not lost all my fortune, and there is still hope. I know you have secret militias spread throughout the mountains. Give them to me, and I'll recover the Empire for us."

Silence followed as they weighed up the offer. The Crown had sacked most of their chests, and the fortune they had initially paid Galbreg was lost. They needed the pearls as badly as I needed their militias.

"And who will sit as the new Emperor?" asked Ansel.

Before I could answer, an orotund voice replied, "Corvus."

I held my breath and gaped at Saphyr.

She glided in through the shadows, letting the hood of her ruby cloak fall, her face taut.

A collective gasp travelled through the room.

"If God himself had wanted to take him down, He wouldn't have failed. Instead, Corvus was resurrected. The throne must be given to the one chosen by God. And, here, we have a ghost with enough power and courage to take down the impostor and recover what's ours. The throne should be his by right. There is no one more fit to be the Emperor than Corvus."

I received her heartfelt answer with surprise. Morgana would have been proud.

"We will rule together." Saphyr intertwined her fingers with mine.

"And what about him?" Ansel stared at Kanis contemptuously.

Kanis glowered at her. "I merely saved the Crown Princess from Brenen's claws. The marriage is null. And I too believe that Corvus should be your new ruler."

"And what will you do with the current Emperor, your father?" Borgia asked Saphyr.

"Exiled, if he's still alive," I replied sternly.

Saphyr shifted next to me. She would not be happy, but better exiled than dead.

The Heads of the Alliance studied each other; some nodding, but others clearly hesitant.

"Let me seal this matter for those of you who are still unsure," I said firmly. "As your new Emperor, not only will I return everyone's lands and coin to their respective chests, but I will also allow you to have private armies. No longer will the Emperor hold sway over the Empire with a single army. I will stand for no more rogue generals, moronic emperors, or bastards like Brenen threatening the wellbeing of the people with the Empire's army."

Gasps left the Heads' mouths, and their eyes shone ravenously. It was a promise of freedom.

"Very well, then." Ansel stood gracefully, followed by the son of the House of Vilmir.

"All those in favor say aye," he shouted.

The chairs and sofas creaked against the floor as the Heads of the Alliance stood together.

"Aye," they replied gravely in unison.

"All those opposed say no."

A solemn silence followed.

"The ayes have it. The militias are yours," Ansel concluded.

Saphyr glared at me. I bit my lips, holding back a smile. When we were children, I used to make fun of her angry face. There was something about the way she puckered her lips and frowned in anger that I found adorable.

Noticing my distracted gaze, she poked my knee. "You lied to me."

I swallowed. "You knew about the Alliance?"

"You created it to get Galbreg under your control. I gathered as much. But, to exile my father *if* he is still alive by then?"

I rubbed the back of my neck, looking around the rose bushes of the garden. Sighing, I moved on the bench to face her and enclosed her hands in mine. It was time to tell her the truth. "After the Emperor took you away from me, I worked with Galbreg and funded the Alliance with the purpose of getting you back. The night of your birthday, I met with Galbreg to set a date to dethrone your father before everything went down the drain."

Saphyr gasped.

"Your father created enemies, turning a blind eye to things he shouldn't have. He spent the Empire's coffers and the people's taxes on lavish parties and excess, ignoring his citizens' needs. The Sun Empire was crumbling, Saphyr. It still is."

Saphyr gritted her teeth. I could tell she knew this was all true. She had despised her father for his greed, but her love for her family, her desire to hold it together was stronger.

"So," I continued, swallowing the knot in my throat, "we planned to have your father exiled and put Galbreg on the throne."

Saphyr's eyes widened, and she pulled back.

"Of course, I regret it now," I added promptly. "I didn't know Galbreg's true intentions, nor those of his son. Our plan fell through because of everything that happened."

"You're an idiot!" she snapped. "Putting Galbreg on the throne! What was supposed to happen to my family?"

"I was going to marry you! The night of your birthday, I had hoped you'd agree to marry me; that way, I could keep you and the rest of your family safe."

"So, you planned to marry me to keep me and my family safe while you overthrew the Royal Family and exiled my father?"

I winced. "After you married me, our Houses would be joined. With the work of the Alliance and Galbreg, I had hoped to grow stronger than my father, so you and your family could enjoy the same lifestyle."

Saphyr's face hardened. "You know I never cared for such things. What truly hurts is that you planned to exile my father without even telling me."

I had been scared. If I asked her and she refused, what could I have done to help her?

"I couldn't bear seeing you forced into an arranged marriage, nor could I bear to let the Empire crumble under your father's hand."

Saphyr fumed. "My father may be a useless Emperor, but he is not an unfaithful drunkard like your father!"

This time, I pulled back. I gaped at her in disbelief. Her vile words had stabbed me right in the heart. My worthless father *had* abandoned my ailing mother, and I *had* let the fear of losing Saphyr get in the way of telling her the truth. Her words were true, all true. Yet, they only made me feel empty, as if everything had been in vain.

"So, you'd rather keep your father on the throne even if your people starve? Even if you're forced to sacrifice your freedom and be sold into a loveless marriage? Is that what you want?" *Not me?* I thought, holding my breath.

Saphyr clenched her hands into fists. "I know what I don't want, and that's a liar!"

My ears pounded, and something inside me shattered.

She looked at me with a pained expression, one pale hand against her breastbone.

I stared at her, my shoulders held back. "I will dethrone the Emperor and have him exiled. Brenen and Galbreg will pay for their crimes with life sentences, and I shall be the Emperor," I told her coldly. "You may still be my reigning Empress, if you so desire."

Saphyr winced, giving me a long, sad look before leaving.

Standing, I marched back to the manor, repressing my need to beg for her forgiveness.

Fragrant jasmine vines on a balcony outside the studio eased my anxiety. I rested my back against the cold marble column, watching Sol City bathed by moonlight, trying to forget Saphyr's words. The Alliance had already left the manor.

The militias were mine. On our way out of Mistwood, Kanis mentioned that the Houses had been gathering secret militias after the raid on the Crystal Palace. I knew that an offer of private armies would seal the deal for the Alliance.

I studied the mountain range surrounding the valley. No random fires illuminated the forest; only the other manors produced any light. Commanding all the different militias in secret and under a single House, my own, would be a logistical nightmare. I would have to get Delphino out of the dungeons sooner than I thought. With him and Kanis together, we had a better shot at organizing the militias.

A caw cut through the crisp night air, and Morgana materialized in the balcony.

"Missed me?"

"For goodness' sake, someone could be watching. Put some clothes on," I snarled, taking off my overcoat and placing it over her naked shoulders.

"Nobody is," she said in a silvery voice. "I already checked from up there." She pointed to the sky.

I studied her warily. Our last encounter had not been pleasant, yet she acted as if nothing had happened.

"I'm glad you've sorted things out with your friends." She said the last word mockingly.

"Thank you. I know you asked the dryads to help us leave Mistwood."

She shrugged. "I told you I'd bring you to see your mother. I'm sorry," she said, eyeing me.

"It's not your fault I left her." I frowned, shaking away the miserable thoughts that crawled on me. "What about you? Is your mother in Sirenibus?"

She shook her head rigidly. "She is dead. Murdered shortly after giving birth to me."

I did not know where to look or what to say. I regretted asking the question. "My apologies."

"I'll soon kill the bastard myself."

A heaviness lodged in my chest for her.

"I have a present for you," she said brightly, abruptly switching the subject and piquing my interest. "You'll find him inside. You can thank me later." With that, she shifted back into a raven and flew away into the night.

I snorted and headed back into the studio. It was a surprise indeed to find Delphino standing before the fire, just where I had stood moments ago. His back was stiff as he ran a hand through his long dark curls, resting the other on his hip. He turned at the sound of my thudding steps, and his eyes gleamed with joy.

"So, the rumors are true." He gasped. "But how? You died after that lightning hit you! You couldn't have possibly survived."

We hugged and patted each other, content to discover we both lived.

"I see I'm not the only one who's lost weight," I said, eyeing his previously glowing skin, now almost as ashen as mine.

"You look like a skeleton." He smiled.

"I could say the same about you."

He ran a hand through his hair again, his smile tarnished with unease.

"How did you get here?" I asked.

"Well, a bird helped me escape. A raven. It dropped the keys to my cell just as the guards had their shift change. I still can't believe it myself."

"Huh, clever bird," I said distractedly, noting I would have to thank Morgana later.

Delphino studied me. "I can't believe you're alive." He rubbed his hands over his face. "I followed the rumors here. There are whispers of you among the people. They even reached the guards in the dungeons. The people call you the *death conqueror*. I had to see if it was true, to see for myself that you were alive."

"Well, I am. And you've come to the right place." I placed a hand on his arm. "There's much to catch up on. I need your help."

His eyes widened even more. "Anything," he said, nodding solemnly. "Anything to kill the bastard. Saphyr's family …"

"Captured. I know." I completed his thought. "Everything will be fine. Things will go back to how they used to be. We'll get the rest of our guard back from the dungeons. But for now, take a moment to rest and recover. You may stay here with us from now on. Kanis will show you to your room."

Kanis emerged from the shadows behind us and guided the overwhelmed Delphino to his room. After a bath and a good night's sleep, he would be himself again. Sure, his bitter memories of the fight and the dungeons would never fade, but at least he would feel safer here.

I sighed and took a seat by the fire, a glass of uske in my hand more from habit than the desire to drink it. After seeing what alcohol turned my father into, I was not sure I wanted to drink ever again. I shut my eyes and tried to empty my mind for several minutes.

"He'll be fine," Kanis grumbled, walking back into the studio and taking a chair next to me.

"I hope so. We need him," I said, my eyes still shut.

"If the rumor already got out to the dungeons that you're alive, it'll be just days before Brenen or his minions show up."

"I know." I let out a heavy sigh. "But now we have the militias. Let Brenen march his entire army if he wishes."

"Wouldn't it be easier to leave the manor and hide somewhere in the city? We don't want Brenen to know you're alive and vulnerable."

"I won't run away again," I said. "Should Brenen show his face around here, I'll kill him myself."

Kanis watched me from the corner of his eye as he swirled a glass of brandy. We remained in silence for a moment.

"About Saphyr, I mean, what did you expect, seriously?"

I scowled at him.

"You did plan on exiling her father behind her back." He pointed at me before taking a sip.

I turned to him. "What would you have done? Do you see a different way, even now?"

The corner of his mouth twisted down in a grimace. "No, not really."

"Then *shut it*."

I could not believe Saphyr had called my father an unfaithful drunkard to my face. She knew more than anyone how much damage my father had wreaked upon me. Perhaps I had deserved it for implying her father was a failed Emperor, but what good did it do to wound us both with the truth?

"She won't marry me now, that's for sure." I let myself drop on a chair next to Kanis and buried my face in my hands.

"I'd say at least you don't need her in order to become the Emperor now, but that would be unfair." Kanis sighed. "Perhaps she'll come to terms with it and accept it is the best solution."

A dreadful possibility crossed my mind.

"What if she can't forgive me? What if she wishes to keep her father on the throne and—"

"Stop the nonsense. She has no way of doing that, even if she wanted to. And I believe she won't. She loves you, even if you've been fighting with her like a complete moron."

"Over the destiny of her father," I said between gritted teeth.

"Who tried to sell her off to the highest bidder! And trust me, she's well aware of that. More than out of love for her father, she's acting out of fear. Saphyr values her family more than anything, so we must guarantee her they'll remain together. You must also consult with her from now on. You can't keep leaving her on the sideline."

"I've been trying to protect her! I've asked her to marry me more than once! You must understand how hard everything has been for us. The world has forced us to come together and realize our feelings for each other overnight and during great chaos. Normal couples would have months, if not years, of courtship before marrying!"

"You've known her half of your life, even if it took you so long to realize your feelings for her. Are you now having second thoughts?" Kanis raised his eyebrow.

"Of course not," I replied bitterly. "I'm just saying—"

"And you're not just any couple," Kanis reminded me. "We're talking about the one and only heir to the House of Alba and the Crown Princess to the Sun Empire."

I frowned, staring at the fire.

"Look, before you became attracted to her, you must remember that you always enjoyed her company first. She was there for you during the good and bad times. You used to follow her around and listen to her counsel. But now you've kept her aside. You did the same to me back at the Stella Islands, remember?" Firelight flickered in his stern eyes. He was right. "As your closest friends, we don't like being ignored."

I opened my mouth to defend myself.

"No matter how badly you want to protect us," he added, rolling his eyes.

"Well, I hope you're right. I hope she'll forgive me and stand with us. Do you think she wants me still?"

Kanis raised his eyebrows. "I think you should ask her, not me."

I shuffled incessantly on the large bed. The air inside the chamber was hot and heavy. I kicked the sheets off the bed and sat up, hand over my heart, trying to ease the pain. It felt as if someone was crushing my heart in their hand. I tried to breathe, but the air barely filled my lungs. It was obvious that lying in bed trying to achieve peace was pointless.

I stood and walked out to the terrace. The mountains were silent in the frosty night air. I let it singe the skin of my bare chest and inhaled deeply. Neither the valley city below nor the sea beyond was visible from this side of the terrace. Instead, the endless mountains glimmered, their snow-covered peaks pale under the moonlight. Far below, the Dark Forest waved its naked mist-covered branches to the moon. I wondered whether Fergus had to attend to it constantly to keep up the grim glamour.

I had to mend things with Saphyr, so I set my bare feet into motion down the cold stairs before giving it a second thought.

I knocked on Saphyr's door once … twice. Nothing. I exhaled in disappointment. She was probably asleep. I left the house and walked to the bridge. The guards on it nodded as I passed them. I rested my elbows atop the rail, recalling our earlier disagreement.

What was I going to do about Saphyr and her father? I sighed. She had a right to be upset. Even if her father was a despicable man who would force her into an arranged marriage, she still loved him for what he was: her father.

Had I done irreparable damage? Would she forgive me for casting her aside, making such an important decision regarding her family without her input? Hard as it was for me to lose control over the matter, I had to let it be her decision or God's will. I would put it in her hands and accept the outcome.

Having made my decision, I ascended the stairs to my domed chamber. To my surprise, a cloaked figure waited before the tall doors.

I approached carefully as a delicate hand appeared and pulled back the cloak's hood, uncovering blonde curls. A shy smile adorned her face.

"Saphyr. I went to see you, but I thought you were asleep."

"I wasn't."

"Here." I opened the door and let her in.

"I couldn't sleep." She shook off her cloak, leaving it on the chaise.

"Neither could I," I said, dropping my chin.

She approached me, her hands interlaced on her chest. "What are we going to do?" Her smile turned bitter.

I went to her and took her joined hands in mine.

"I'll respect your wishes. It's your father, your family—it should be your decision, no matter how that changes tomorrow's plan."

"Thank you." She stared down at her hands. "I wish it was easier."

"Nothing ever is."

She rested her cheek against my chest, bare where my cloak had opened, and I enclosed her within my arms. She was delightfully warm.

She grinned up at me, the melted honey of her eyes inviting me in. Saphyr bit my bottom lip, making me gasp. Then she pulled away, and I caressed the tip of her nose with mine.

"I'm sorry ... what I said about your father," she said. "I didn't have the right."

"I'm sorry too. We know each other so well; we know which words will cause the most damage."

She nodded, and I nestled my chin on her head, closing my eyes and inhaling. Her scent of nectarines felt like home. Saphyr always felt like home, regardless of where we were.

CHAPTER 24
RAVEN WINGS

I had forgotten who I was, had been too deep in slumber. But not anymore. Fear and uncertainty no longer held me back. I no longer feared death. I had succumbed to it once and lived to tell the tale. No man would ever step on me again. I was going to take back what was mine, and no one would stand in my way. I had nothing to lose. It was death or victory.

The passages of the dungeons were empty. Morgana had timed the shift changes to the second. She flew high above as Saphyr guided us through the entrails of the fortress.

The fortress, impenetrable as it looked from atop the mountains, was not unsurmountable now. We navigated the hallways, stopping at each corner. Morgana would clear our way into each new passage by clicking her beak once, twice for danger, and then Saphyr and I would emerge from the shadows. We reached the top in minutes, spiraling up the stairs used by the servants.

Brenen was supposedly in a meeting in the throne room. He had been acting as the General, sending out diktats in the name of the Emperor, whom he kept sedated in his chambers.

In the short time after leaving Mistwood, Morgana had amassed information from inside the fortress. We brought Saphyr since she knew the passages and could help us secretly navigate the fortress. Kanis and Delphino had stayed behind to meet with the secret militias. All the pieces were falling into place. And I was now on my way, a crucial part of the puzzle.

Brenen had taken a chamber on the highest tower of the city's fortress. The round room was as piercingly cold as its owner. Its stone walls were naked, and he had furnished the room with nothing but a four-poster bed, a chaise lounge, and a desk, which would make my task easier. I approached the desk, and Morgana perched herself on the lancet window behind it, the wind ruffling her feathers.

Saphyr followed me closely.

I opened the drawer beneath Brenen's desk, and there it was: the Imperial Seal glinting in the sunlight. Saphyr gasped, recognizing it. My fingers traced the gold engraving of the sun on the seal with reverence. I could conquer any land with this. It was the key to any door in the Empire. And now, to our freedom. I slipped it inside my pocket.

Morgana cawed, clacking her beak twice to alert us. We were not supposed to linger, but a unique item on the desk caught my attention. A parchment with elegant handwriting, signed at the bottom with Brenen's name and seal.

It was a list of names, lands, and their worth. Lands that had belonged to my family, and names I recognized from the Houses of the Alliance. Unfamiliar names were next to them—those who would receive such lands. My blood boiled. I crumpled the parchment paper and slid it into my pocket.

Steps clanked against the stone outside the room, and I took a step back, protectively placing Saphyr behind me. The servant's hidden door was out of our reach. It was too late.

By the time the main door clicked open, we were against the tower window. The wind rushing in whirled our dark cloaks as Brenen strolled inside.

His eyes widened with rage as he started toward me, my identity hidden beneath the black hood. His silver hair swirled back with the gusts. I stepped back until I felt the windowsill against my calves.

"It's you," Brenen said smoothly, only a few steps away. He grinned. "You must have the nine lives of a cat." His gaze drifted to Saphyr. "Oh, darling. You should have stayed with me instead of running away with that stray dog. You would have been mine by now, my Empress Consort."

"I'll be a reigning Empress, Brenen, never a consort. You can't steal what's mine by birthright." Saphyr's hand slid beneath her cloak, reaching for her thigh. "The throne belongs to us."

"You're wrong. When your father dies, it'll be mine."

I tried to grab Saphyr's wrist, but she moved faster. Her mother's ruby dagger slashed through the air with the precision of an arrow aimed for Brenen's head.

Brenen twisted his torso to the side at the last second, and the dagger plunged into the door, a full strand of his hair dangling from it. Brenen snarled back at us, his teeth bared, as I drew my own dagger.

Lunging, Brenen unsheathed his sword, ready to strike. I raised my dagger above my head, stopping his thrust. Then I ducked, punching his stomach with my other hand. My opponent's eyes bulged at the unexpected hit, and Brenen folded over, clutching his stomach. Saphyr took advantage of the moment, thrusting a knee into his groin.

Brenen grunted, his sword clanking to the floor. Saphyr spat at him, but he straightened, his face wild with anger. I stretched an arm over Saphyr's chest to move her away and aimed my dagger at his throat, but I was too late. Brenen stretched his bony fingers toward Saphyr, who tensed behind my arm and let out a gasp. I turned, and my breath froze in my throat.

"Let's see if you can land on your feet," Brenen hissed.

Saphyr fixed her wide eyes on mine, reaching a hand toward my raised arm as she fell backward through the window. I quickly extended my arms to catch her, crying out as her silken hair slipped through my fingers. Saphyr screamed. Fury and pain gripped me at the realization I had not been able to catch her. I did not care whether I survived, but I refused to let her die.

I jumped, plunging through the air after her, the folds of my cloak engulfing me in darkness. I twisted just at the right moment to catch her, her arms pressing tight around my back, her hair whirling uncontrollably in the wind. I spun and placed her atop me, sheltering her from the full impact of the drop.

Looking up, I glimpsed Brenen smiling with satisfaction as we plummeted toward the ground. Saphyr's eyes gleamed, her tears drying on her face in the wind. With one hand, I unclasped my cloak, letting it fly away, releasing us from its darkness.

The fall felt endless. Morgana hovered around us, circling and cawing frantically. I desperately wished for a way to save us both. I had not survived death and recovered Saphyr, only to lose everything again at the hand of none other than Brenen.

Rage and despair filled my every pore and exploded in a roar that shook the air. Then, something materialized from my back, dark feathers ruffling in the wind. Immediately understanding, I growled, forcing my muscles to own this strange new feeling, to spread my wings and halt the fall.

Saphyr's weight relaxed into my arms as we felt the sudden pull of flight. She slithered from my grip, but I caught her forearms and forced my entire body to push those great wings down and back up, heaving us away from the ground.

I struggled to keep us both alight, barely able to control these strange new extremities.

Saphyr looked up, confused. She took in the sight of the black wings, and her jaw dropped. Then, understanding my struggle, she placed her feet atop a terrace, her hands still gripping my forearms.

Once her weight released, I understood my own weight and knew how much effort my muscles required to beat the wings and keep myself in flight. With the strain, I shut my eyes tight in concentration and flapped the wings downwards, gathering enough momentum to pull us both up.

Saphyr squealed and then laughed in amazement as her feet left the terrace. I smiled in relief and carried us both off as far as I could from the fortress. Experiencing nothing but air around us felt magnificent; I imagined that flying alone would be truly liberating. I soared up, searching for a place to land.

"There!" Saphyr shouted.

Morgana had spread her wings wide below us, and we followed her, gliding through the sky. Saphyr's cloak swirled behind us. From high above, Sol City lived up to its name. The sun reflected itself in thousands of twinkling lights over the rooftops and the sprawling Tagus River.

I extended my wings, feeling them cut through the air. I had never felt so alive—so free. A shout of victory escaped my lips as Morgana and I gained momentum. She shut her wings, spiraling down through the air, weightless.

A couple of yards above the river, she unfurled her wings again, and we glided over the water. Her claws cut through our reflection, sending a refreshing spray toward our faces.

I laughed. When had I last felt so lighthearted? Not in ages. Flying was even better than I had imagined. Morgana was blessed to be able to shift into a bird at will.

She guided us toward the empty riverbank, where she fluttered to a stop. I turned into it, trying to land us on the grass by the shore, but it was not as easy as I thought. A cramp suddenly seized my back, paralyzing the tip of my right wing.

As we neared the ground face-first, I twisted us so we could both land on my back. My fingers grasped the grass, trying to slow us down, and my wings sent spiraling jabs of pain down my core as the power of my failed landing dragged us through the undergrowth.

When we came to a stop, Saphyr grumbled and rolled off my chest. A gulp of cool air filled my lungs, and my entire body felt heavy. I was exhausted.

"Are you all right?" Saphyr asked.

The air rasped in and out of my mouth, but I did not have the strength to talk.

She observed me from above, each hand next to my head. She frowned, her lips parted. Her eyes evaluated me with concern, but her hair tumbled around my face, cutting off my airflow. I gasped, turning my face away.

"Oh, I'm sorry!" Saphyr flicked her hair to the side, chuckling.

I laughed with her.

"Can you move?"

I tried to move my elbows backward to raise myself, but my wings twitched instead. Saphyr crouched and pulled me up by the arms. Finally learning the difference between my arms and the wings, I sat and stretched my wings out, easing the cramps.

"They're beautiful." Saphyr gasped, tracing a finger across my wingspan.

"Ah." I smiled as the wing flinched. "It tickles."

"Where did they come from?"

I shook my head, as lost as her. I thought of the lightning on the prairie and wondered whether this was a divine gift.

Saphyr shifted her attention to my face, her fingers alleviating the tension focused between my eyebrows. Warm rays caressed Saphyr's golden hair and sent sparkles into the calm river behind her. She cupped my cheeks and closed in the distance between us, her cheeks flushed.

"Thank you," she said, "for saving us." Joy sparkled in her amber eyes.

I twined my fingers through her hair, inviting her in. Her lips hovered above mine, brushing them, and I delved into their sweetness, drawn like a bee to honey.

A dark raven cawed, circling above us against the bright sky. It was time to act. Now that Brenen had seen me, the hourglass had been turned. We needed to act fast, before time ran out.

It took a few tries before I could take flight with Saphyr in my arms. Morgana had still not revealed herself to Saphyr and remained in her raven form. I followed Morgana to the edge of the city and then up the mountains to the manor.

I had stopped and rested several times on our way up, but we had still traveled twice as fast as we could on horseback. From the air, the manor still looked like a striking palace of stone arches and domed ceilings nestled atop the mountain. We soared past flowing cascades, the cold water spraying our bodies.

Sweat ran down my forehead, and my shoulders burned with exhaustion by the time I landed on the balcony of my domed chamber.

"Thank you," Saphyr breathed, leaning against the stone rail. "I'm sorry you had to carry me this far."

I shook my head. "It would have been nearly impossible for me to ride a horse back up the mountains with these things." I flapped the wings, their draft sending Saphyr's tousled hair backward.

She tilted her head. "There must be a way for you to make them disappear."

I pressed my lips into a fine line. "I've tried. It looks like I'll be stuck with them."

Saphyr sighed. "I'll go find Kanis. Maybe he'll come up with something."

My hand went to her wrist. "I need to rest. I'll meet you both in the dining hall in an hour or two. And take Snowball with you. I don't want him to see my wings yet."

She nodded. "I'll tell Kanis what happened."

"Thank you," I said, watching her enter my chamber through the balcony's glass doors and sink her fingers into my pet's fluffy hair. The white wolf's tail wagged as he spun around with happiness. I grinned; he had been ten times more excited when he first saw me after I returned home.

The wolf looked up, startled by my wings through the glass panels, and barked. I sighed. I would try to approach him later. Saphyr led Snowball out through the wooden doors and headed down to the main building.

Turning to the mountains, I stood on the terrace rail, knowing exactly what my body needed. The raven was gone. I shut my eyes and let myself drop.

Excitement coursed through my body, and I laughed at the insistent pull of the wind as I extended my wings to stop the fall and glided through the air, my teeth chattering in the wind.

I scanned the mountainside and immediately found the place I was looking for. Tall, ruinous stone arches towering above the trees pinpointed the location. I descended and landed right in the clearing. The arches, although once belonging to a temple, now surrounded a pool of steaming hot springs.

From time to time, I had come here since it was a short walk from my chambers. Few knew about it, so it was always empty. The forest encased the clearing, providing some protection from the icy breeze. I set my clothes atop a boulder, ensuring the Imperial Seal and parchment remained protected inside, and then slowly lowered myself into the scorching waters.

Once the water reached my neck, I sighed with relief. The pain eased from my muscles and cumbersome wings. I spread them and let the water take care of their weight. A moan escaped my lips, and I arched my back as it finally released its tension.

A few hours of light remained before sunset. I rested my gaze on the gray sky as I floated, grateful we were alive. Kanis would never let me hear the end of it. He had warned me not to sneak into the fortress—much less with Saphyr—but the Imperial Seal had been key to my plan of calling a siege. I had meant to send a royal command to the troops stationed throughout the Empire, commanding them to assist the militias in forcing Brenen out of the fortress. By now, he would have discovered that the Imperial Seal was missing and put two and two together. I needed a new strategy.

We had even less time to act now that Brenen had seen Saphyr and me, not only alive but also fighting back. I suspected he would gather his soldiers tonight and march them up the mountains tomorrow. I would not put it past him to burn me at the stake just to guarantee I died this time.

I let out a heavy sigh.

"You're supposed to be relaxing," a silvery voice raised itself above the murmur of the water.

My feet planted themselves on the bottom as my wings shot up, dripping water and sending a wave splashing against the edge of the pool.

Saphyr smiled as she walked under a stone arch, wearing nothing but my cloak. I frowned at her feline grace and felt a sense of déjà vu.

"We've already talked about this, Morgana," I said.

"I'm keeping my hands to myself." She raised her hands and shifted back into herself.

I grunted and turned my back on her, resting my arms on the rocks.

The siren came and sat in front of me. I rested my chin on my forearms, looking up at her. "Have you considered shifting clothed?"

Morgana snickered. "I can manipulate liquids such as blood and water, not create things out of thin air."

Goosebumps grew on my arms. *So that's what allows her to shift into a raven or another person.* I shut my eyes, my thoughts muddled.

"How do you feel?" she asked.

"Exhausted. What happened to me?"

"I grew wings out of your back."

I cocked my head, trying to understand.

"Your flesh is mostly water."

My head pounded. So it *had* been her. "Why did you give me wings?"

"Did you want to die along with Saphyr?"

"Can you make them go away? As incredible as they are, I don't think I want them permanently."

195

"They'll vanish with the next crescent moon."

"Thank you," I said. I let my wings sink back into the hot water.

"It's a pity." She grinned. "They suit you."

I rolled my eyes.

"You're insane, jumping after her like that," she said, a sullen look taking over her features. "You would have most certainly died this time, squashed against the ground."

"Lovely image." I cleared my throat. "I've been meaning to thank you for bringing Delphino back to me. So, again, thank you."

Her mouth curled up.

"How did you know I needed him?"

"I saw him fighting by your side the day you died. He is the captain of your guard, so I figured you'd need him." She shrugged.

"How did you find me the day I died on the prairie?"

"After you escaped Sirenibus, I followed you." She glanced at the forest. "I lost you after you spent the first night in a rundown inn, but I was sure you'd return home eventually, so I guarded the port. Finally, I saw you sneaking out with him and your guard. I followed you again until it was the right moment to show myself, but then you went to war. What an idiot. Maybe I should've just taken you by force."

"Well, I'm sorry for the trouble, miss," I said sarcastically. "You should consider talking to people instead of abducting them."

"Would you have come willingly if I asked you to?" She looked at me, arching one eyebrow.

"Probably not, but that doesn't make it right."

She pursed her lips.

"Why do you shift into a raven? Why not … let's say, an eagle? Or a bear?"

"My name has its roots in the words 'greatness' and 'terror.' You should know."

"Enlighten me," I said, getting comfortable and letting the hot water work its way down my body.

She sighed. "Ravens are cunning, despicable creatures, but they symbolize provision. Contrary to common belief, they can be good. They've helped uncover murderers and save innocents from poisoned foods. I guess … they can be noble or unvirtuous, like anyone else. It bothers me they're considered the bad guys. They're rarely given a chance to prove themselves."

"It's like you see yourself in them."

"The sirens found me as a baby," she said, surprising me. "They took me in and raised me as one of their own. As I grew older, I showcased uncommon gifts, unique even. In admiration and greed for the protection my powers could grant them, they made me their queen."

I frowned. "They saw you only as a weapon?"

"Nobody has ever trusted my good side. I wasn't born royal or to a loving family. I grew up alone. I fought to develop myself to my fullest potential. When given the opportunity, I took it. I have ruled the seas ever since. All my life, I've known only how to fight, tooth and claw, for survival. That doesn't make me inherently bad, you know?"

I nodded. "I believe in you, Morgana—if it makes a difference. You're not *that* bad, and I owe you in more ways than I feel comfortable with."

She chuckled.

"So, are you even a siren? What are you?" I asked.

"A human, of sorts. Just not your average kind."

"Well, that's for sure," I said, eyeing her round ears.

Silence followed, and her eyes locked with mine. Morgana had opened up to me more than usual. I wondered whether it was because she had saved my life earlier.

"What do you know of your origin? I've never heard of a human with the power to shift or manipulate water."

"I have a rough idea. My mother was a siren, and my father was human. I'm a half-breed. A moonchild."

"A moonchild?"

"From what I gathered, my mother made a bargain with the moon to conceive me, but the moon told my mother her firstborn human child would belong to the moon in return. My shifting ability is amplified by the moon, so my powers are greater than normal sirens."

The moon? Morgana was a moonchild. A child of the dark. My jaw clenched. Anybody who tried to strike supernatural bargains always ended up in a pit of darkness. I eyed her, worried. Was she doomed? No, she could still choose. Her mother's mistake should not be hers to inherit.

"Is your father alive?"

Her jaw hardened, and she nodded.

"And why do you collect selkie skins?"

"I needed to find out more about my parents. The selkies travel the oceans at a greater speed than sirens; hence they can gather information faster. That's how I learned of my mother's story. I stopped looking for her after learning of her death. I began looking for my father instead."

"I hope you find him soon."

She flashed her teeth in a dangerous grin. "I will. But there is something else I need to take care of first." Morgana's gaze trailed my wings.

"Don't consider yourself evil," I said, thinking of my own experiences. "Like a raven, you can choose to be good, even if others perceive you as bad. People are afraid of the unknown, of what they haven't seen before, what they can't control. They may see us ravens and fear us."

"Perhaps they should." Morgana's eyes glinted, the glacial waters of her eyes swirling in a storm.

I straightened, raising my wings slightly.

Morgana remained silent. "Would you like to know what I spied at the town's market earlier?" she asked.

I nodded.

"An old man poured every single coin out of his pocket, but all he could buy was a single potato. One potato. When the stall owner asked him if that was all, he shrugged and said it was all his pension allowed him to buy for the week. How can an old man survive an entire week on a single potato?"

"Brenen promised the people our lands and our riches, so why are they now starving?" I hissed.

"I think you already know the answer …"

Of course, neither Galbreg nor Brenen would have kept their promises. I remembered the list of names, families who would receive our lands, Brenen's new Court. My fists shut tight until my knuckles turned white.

"It'll soon be over," she reminded me. "We're closer than ever to returning to normal." Morgana placed a hand on my shoulder.

She was right. I sighed deeply. Soon, his time would come.

CHAPTER 25
BROKEN PROMISE

I awoke to the fragrant scent of jasmine and frowned, disoriented. It was already dark. The clock told me I had slept for almost two hours. Cursing under my breath, I wobbled to my feet, supporting my weight on the bedhead. My wings spread wide and knocked over a small table, scattering its books on the floor. I cursed again, trying to get myself together, knowing Kanis and Saphyr would be waiting for me down at the hall.

The persistent sweet scent confused me even more. Servants had not replenished the vases of fresh flowers in weeks. Soft, rhythmic breathing suggested I was not alone. Glancing around, I found Morgana asleep on the chaise, tucked under dark furs that contrasted with her silver hair. A vine had crawled through the window and wrapped itself around her sleeping form, sprouting snowy flowers.

I adjusted my black robe over my chest, and I went to her. Her pink lips were parted, but a frown creased her forehead.

"Wake up." I poked her shoulder twice.

Her eyes slowly opened, her eyelashes fluttering sleep away.

"Oh …" Morgana clutched the furs against her chest.

"Is that normal?" I pointed to the magical vine.

"It happens sometimes." She sighed, pulling the vine off, its jasmine petals falling off to the floor. "The water in plants overreacts sometimes when I sleep. I guess I was cold."

She sat up, and her long hair fell over her naked back.

I cleared my throat. "What are you doing here?" The last thing I wanted was Saphyr to find Morgana naked in my chambers. "Must I remind you of the impropriety of your nakedness, especially *here*?"

"Oh, do shut up." She groaned and ran a hand through her hair. "You fell asleep first. What was I supposed to do? Sleep in a tree?"

That did not sound like such a bad idea. I tried to recall what had happened. My memory of dressing and flying from the hot springs back to my chambers was hazy. I remembered entering my chambers and deciding to nap before heading down to the manor. Morgana had agreed, but I thought she had left before I collapsed on my bed.

"Is there any tea? Black as midnight and bitter as your tongue?"

I scowled at her. "No, Milady. Unfortunately, my servants are on permanent leave." I moved to a pitcher of water and served her a glass.

"Your future Empress is running away," she rasped.

The water overflowed the glass. I put the jug down and glared at her. "What?"

She jutted her chin toward the door. "She opened the door, saw us, and turned away. I suggest you run after her." Morgana yawned.

It felt as if someone had pulled the rug from under my feet. "That's precisely why I said you were not welcome in my chambers!"

Her eyebrows drew together. "It's *your* fault. You forgot to lock the door."

Locked or not, she was still not welcome inside, but I did not have time to argue with Morgana. I ran after Saphyr, my wings slapping the walls, doors, and furnishing. I cursed again, feeling the cold stone of the bridge against my bare feet.

"Saphyr, wait!"

She continued running down the stairs.

"Wait!" I fumbled my way down, my wingtips bouncing with each step, pain stabbing my shoulder blades. This would not do. I growled as I sent my wings down, soaring up. My back throbbed excruciatingly, but I ignored it and flapped down to her.

Saphyr gasped as I landed next to her on the grass, dropping to my knees with the impact of my landing.

"Please," I begged her, extending my hand.

Tears glittered in her eyes as she took a step toward me and then stopped, hesitating. I clutched her hand before she changed her mind and I pulled her to me.

"I'd never do that to you," I muttered against her hair. "I didn't even know Morgana was there until I woke up."

"Is that true?"

"Yes." I stared into her eyes. "I thought she was gone before I fell asleep."

Saphyr tilted her head. "She was there before you fell asleep?"

Shoot. I looked around desperately. How could I explain it to her without digging myself into a deeper hole?

"Why was she half-naked, Corvus?" Saphyr's voice turned steely.

"She is Feathers. She can't shift back with her clothes on. Believe me, I've asked."

Saphyr made to leave.

"No, wait!" I pleaded, holding her by the arms.

"You mean to tell me," she said, her tone scarily calm, "that Morgana has been with you all this time, and you never told me?"

A cold shiver prickled my neck.

"And that most of that time she was *naked*?"

That was it. She was going to leave me. There was no way to explain any of it logically. "I didn't know she was Feathers at first!"

Saphyr raised an eyebrow. "She tricked you?"

"I found out after you told me you had married Kanis."

She flinched.

Good! I desperately needed her to hear me. "I was devastated. You had married my best friend; I was losing my mind."

Saphyr looked at the ground.

"That's when Morgana showed herself to me. She even guided you two to Mistwood, against my wishes, and insisted I listened to you. She was the one who dragged my body into the forest and helped me recover. And today, she saved us, Saphyr. These wings"—I spread them wide, and she tipped her neck back, observing them with awe—"are gifts from her. We wouldn't be alive today if it wasn't for Morgana."

Saphyr pressed her lips tightly together.

"Please, give her a chance. She wants to help us regain the throne and defeat Brenen."

Saphyr raised her chin. "Kanis is looking for you—that's what I came to tell you." She turned, jaw clenched, and marched down the stairs.

I sighed, knowing better than to follow her. I would let her cool down before I sought her out again.

I paced the study like a caged beast, my drooping wings brushing the maroon carpets and the polished hardwood floor.

"What have you been up to?" Kanis studied me, standing by the window.

I sat on a chair by the hearth.

"There are rumors of you flying over the Tagus."

My eyebrows shot up. How were rumors traveling so fast across the city? The riverbanks had been empty. "Who?"

"Some farmer who used to work for your family recognized you." Kanis opened and closed his mouth, staring disconcertedly at the wings I was unsuccessfully trying to press against the chair. "What are we going to do about those?"

"They'll vanish with the next crescent moon."

"How do you know that?" Kanis narrowed his eyes at me.

I sighed and stood, gesturing to the chair. "You may want to sit. I can't with these darned things anyway."

Kanis continued staring at me as he lowered himself into my chair. I could tell he smelled trouble.

I angled my body away from him, knocking a vase onto the carpet as I did so. Clenching my teeth, I crouched to pick it up and almost poked a wingtip into the fire.

"Can you just stop? Stay still."

I glowered at Kanis and perched on a wooden stool, crossing my arms to tuck the wings in tightly.

"The people think you're some sort of fallen angel."

"That's absurd." I swallowed, terrified at the thought of being cursed by God. What sort of evil act would get a divine being cast out of heaven?

"Well, they romanticize it."

"Being evil? How moronic."

"They whisper your name with reverence. They call you *death conqueror.*" Kanis made a flourish in the air.

"No!" I glared at him.

"It's great publicity." He grinned. "They won't doubt that God has sent you to take the throne."

"I suggest you stop making assumptions."

"You came back from the dead parading yourself around with a pet raven on your shoulders."

I held in a chuckle. Morgana had taken a liking to perching atop my shoulder, as if I were some kind of pirate. I found it ludicrously funny. *A pet raven—if he only knew.* "I didn't *parade* myself around."

"And now they see you flying over the Tagus on enormous black wings. People are noticing, Corvus. They're nervous, but they believe you've returned to stop their misery."

I stared blankly at the fire, ignoring him.

"I say we play along. Use it to your advantage."

"You should sell goods at the market rather than advise me on my public image."

"It's all the same." His smile twisted.

I rolled my eyes, although he was probably right. Reputation was nothing more than smoke and mirrors—all a matter of perception.

"Here." I slipped the Imperial Seal from my pocket and extended it to him.

Kanis grabbed it and examined it in the firelight, gasping. "You got it!"

"Not only that, take a look at this." I passed him the rolled parchment.

Kanis opened it and went completely still.

"Yes, a detailed list of our assets, your family's included. And the names of those supposed to receive them."

Kanis looked at me, astonished, holding an item in each hand. He lifted the parchment. "This will open our way to other Houses, not just those of the Alliance. And this ..." He held up the Imperial Seal. "Heck, this will open any door, really."

"But Brenen saw us. He threw Saphyr out of a window. Hence, these." I pointed to my wings, my face taut.

Kanis furrowed his eyebrows, understanding what it meant that Brenen had tried to kill Saphyr for the second time. "He knows you're alive."

"How long before he arrives here?"

"With the battalions he'll bring." Kanis caressed his chin, "He should arrive tomorrow afternoon. We're lucky he can't move the troops up the mountain by night."

"So, what now?"

Kanis sat quietly, shaking his head. "How do you know those things will disappear with the next crescent moon?"

"Morgana," I said.

My friend's eyebrows shot up. "You've seen her?"

"It turns out it was Morgana who moved my body from the prairie into the forest and took care of me until I woke up."

"When did you find out?"

"She's Feathers."

Kanis gaped. "Morgana, the Nightmare Queen of the Seas? *That's* your raven pet?"

"I found out after Saphyr told me she had married you."

He crossed his arms, clearly upset. "You didn't think to tell me this until now?"

I sighed. "Saphyr said the same. But I promised Morgana I would keep her secret. I owe her."

"Saphyr knows?" Kanis's pitch increased in disbelief.

"She, um, saw her in my chambers moments ago."

Kanis arched an eyebrow.

"The main issue is that … well … Morgana was sort of naked."

He brought a palm to his face. "I'd smack you myself, but I'm sure Saphyr already has."

I shook my head. "She took it rather calmly."

Kanis sank back into the chair, letting out a deep breath. "I need a moment." He sat with his elbows on his knees, burying his head in his hands.

My foot tapped incessantly on the stool, and my gaze flew around the room, up to the bookshelves, around the windows, and over the velvet chairs in the wood-paneled studio. Then I stared into the fire. We had retrieved the seal, but now Brenen was coming here. He was gathering all his soldiers to march on us. Keeping Morgana's stupid secret was going to cost me. And now I had wings. *Wings!*

As if in answer, my wings spread, knocking something else to the floor. Then it hit me.

"That's it!" I snapped my fingers.

Kanis looked up.

"He's coming to us, and we know when. We don't need a siege anymore."

It took Kanis a moment to fall in with my line of thought. "Most of our militias are already stationed around the city," I reminded him.

"Are you suggesting we take the fortress tomorrow?"

"He leaves the fortress; we attack it. Brenen remains unaware of the militias."

"And what are you planning to do with him?"

I pointed at the seal. "We can hunt him down after we secure the fortress. His soldiers are not loyal. They will obey whoever sits on the throne of the Sun."

Kanis breathed, leaning back. "It'll have to do. We don't have the time to come up with a better plan."

My lips curved into a smile. At least we had a new strategy.

"I'll head down tonight to prepare. Delphino and I will send the word out."

"Thank you, but please stay for dinner before you leave."

Kanis nodded. "You still have a tremendous issue at hand."

"Saphyr."

"Yes. The people won't stand with us unless she's there."

I massaged the bridge of my nose. "She's furious. I think I'd have preferred a slap than her calmly walking away like that."

"Crawl. Beg. Do what you must."

"I told Morgana back in Sirenibus to stay away from my chambers," I said, shaking my head. "Why does she keep doing whatever she pleases?"

"Maybe it was on purpose. I wouldn't put it past her, especially after she tried to pry information out of you while disguised as Saphyr in Sirenibus."

I put my hands on my hips, looking away. "But why would she do that? She saved me back in the forest, and today as well. She's made it her mission to set me on the throne, no matter how many times I've refused."

"I'd say she's into you."

I let out a huff. "You're joking, right? I'm nothing but a tool to her— a tool to achieve peace and restore the balance of the human realm or whatever ridiculous excuse she keeps using."

"Send her packing. Make Saphyr happy."

I roared with laughter. "Send the Ruler of the Seas, Queen of the Sirens, packing?" I emphasized the impossibility of the last word with a flourish of my hand. "Did you forget about her powers?" I pointed to my wings. "We're stuck with her."

Kanis eyed me suspiciously. "You like her."

"Don't be stupid."

"Then stop justifying her."

"I'm not. I'm simply stating the facts." I sighed. "I need to talk to Saphyr."

A soft knock on the door silenced us. Kanis went to it, opening it only slightly, so my wings remained out of sight.

"Dinner is ready, Milord," Thali said. "I've already taken Milady's dinner upstairs." My chest expanded with a warm feeling. I was grateful to her for continuing to care for my mother and Snowball.

"Just in time." Kanis smiled.

"Yes," she said. "The ladies are waiting."

Kanis's smile disappeared just as quickly, and he glanced in my direction.

My mouth hung open. Uh-oh.

"Thank you, Thali."

"I'll go back upstairs to Milady."

We waited until Thali disappeared to rush out of the study to the dining hall, ignoring the flying books, vases, and the trail of broken things my clumsy wings left behind. Morgana and Saphyr alone in the same room meant only one thing: trouble.

CHAPTER 26
SIREN TEARS

Saphyr sat at one end of the long table and Morgana at the other, their eyes shooting daggers at each other. Across from me, Kanis stared austerely at Morgana as I awkwardly observed the tension between us.

"It all makes sense now," Kanis said bitterly, shoving a hunk of meat in his mouth.

I sighed, stretching an arm toward my glass of scarlet wine, and then hesitating. My head, although better, was still pounding. I took a sip of water instead.

"So, it was you who kept him alive in the forest."

"You're welcome." Morgana snickered.

"Morgana, the Nightmare Queen of the Seas," Kanis mused. "And raven pet."

"Watch it," Morgana growled, showing her teeth.

I scowled at Kanis, knowing he was trying to get on her nerves. Morgana seemed more than eager to remind him why we had nicknamed her the Nightmare Queen in the first place.

"Morgana not only kept me alive back in the Dark Forest, but she also had the Dryad King open the forest to you so you could find me. She also had them guide us back home. Let's please remember that Saphyr and I would be dead if it wasn't for her help today."

Saphyr watched the firelight reflect in the glossy black feathers of my wings, her face taut.

Kanis clenched his jaw and sipped his wine in silence.

"Although," I added, "I would like to know what you were thinking, Saphyr?"

She raised an eyebrow.

"As admirable as it was, throwing your mother's dagger at Brenen's head and failing was an extremely risky move."

"*I* answer to no one. I am your Crown Princess and future Empress, and *you* should not forget that," she said stoically.

It felt like a slap to the face. My fingers stretched for the wine before I could stop them. Morgana glared at her calculatingly. And Kanis straightened in his chair.

"You could've killed him, but you gave him warning instead. You failed on purpose. Why?" Morgana pressed.

"I'm not a murderer. I simply wanted to give him fair warning. I spared his life so he would step down on his own."

Kanis choked, coughing and hitting his chest. His disdainful laughter had lodged the meat in his throat.

Saphyr glared at him as Kanis downed his wine, finally breathing again.

"He is not a man of honor," I tried to explain to Saphyr. "He already tried to murder you once, on your birthday, nonetheless."

Morgana shuffled uncomfortably in her chair.

"God did not choose him to occupy the throne," Saphyr said. "I grasped his life within my fingers, and I showed him the mercy of a true and just ruler."

I studied Saphyr from across the table with a frown. Yes, she spoke like a true Empress, but Brenen did not play by the rules. Saphyr had been born into royalty, but her fate was on the line. I glanced at Morgana and wondered: *Was I struck by lightning to avoid death at the hands of Brenen? Had Morgana appeared in our lives to protect the Sun Empire and establish a new just rule?*

I rubbed my chin, deep in thought. I had tried to depose Saphyr's incompetent father by working with Galbreg and the Alliance. Perhaps, I would have eventually vanquished both Galbreg and the Emperor anyway, and Saphyr would have become Empress. Maybe fate had put me in her path after all, and she in mine, in order to protect her and the Empire.

"Corvus?" Kanis pulled me out of my thoughts.

"Brenen probably doesn't even believe in God, Saphyr," I said. "He doesn't believe you're a ruler chosen by God. He thinks everything is there for his taking. He doesn't believe in justice nor goodness. He made false promises to the people to gain their support and tossed them aside. He spread his lies to everyone through the post offices, official dispatches, and letters."

"But soon, everything will change," Kanis said.

I nodded. Tomorrow, the throne would be ours.

"Brenen is so close to the throne that he's desperate to grasp it before it slips through his fingers. Saphyr, he knows you could've killed him. Do you think a man of honor would've pushed you from that tower to your death? He could've called for help and sent us into the dungeons instead of trying to kill you so miserably for the second time." I clenched my teeth.

Saphyr dropped her chin to the chest.

"It was not a waste, however. You were brave and smart. You acted like a true Empress." I tried to grin at her, but she frowned and looked away. "I'm surprised you knew of secret passages that even Morgana couldn't discover," I added, trying to coax a smile out of her, but I perceived Morgana's scorching eyes upon my face instead.

"The same passages I've used all my life." Saphyr shrugged. "My father and I traveled through them instead of the public hallways. Secret passages exist in both the palace and the fortress."

I remembered the passages I used to travel through the Crystal Palace and nodded.

"Tomorrow, we'll strike. As Brenen heads up the mountains, we'll charge the fortress," Kanis explained to Morgana and Saphyr. "I'll travel ahead tonight to get things in order, and you three can fly down tomorrow morning."

A wooden chair screeched against the floor as Morgana stood. "Marvelous," she drawled. "Now, if you'll excuse me, I'm off for an eternal slumber in one of the *empty* rooms," she emphasized, looking at me disdainfully from the corner of her eyes. "Please stay alive while I'm gone, will you?" She grinned.

I returned the sour smile, noticing the deep purple shadows under her eyes, but Kanis and Saphyr said nothing.

"Oh." Morgana stopped by Saphyr. Her gaze fixed on her hand. She raised Saphyr's hand, examining the pearl ring I had given to her. "That looks awfully familiar."

"Are you going to cry we give it back?" Saphyr's lip curled up in a cruel smile.

Morgana studied her coolly. The air in the room turned dry. "It means nothing to me." She laced her words with disdain as she sauntered from the dining hall.

"Saphyr, may I speak with you in private?" I asked.

She nodded and stood, frowning.

Kanis leaned back on his chair, pouring himself another glass of wine. "I'll instruct Thali to take your mother and Snowball in the carriage to my mother's, and I'll head to the city."

"Thank you," I said.

"Goodnight."

I accompanied Saphyr out of the dining hall.

We walked the hallways in cold silence. I guided her out of the manor and stopped at the highest point of the arched bridge, the water rushing calmly beneath us. Guards from the militia were stationed on both ends of the bridge, and they gawked at my wings. I gave them a warning look, and they turned away to give us privacy.

Inhaling the fresh air, I placed my elbows atop the railing. Saphyr did the same, both of us appreciating the sparkling light and flowing water.

"I apologize if I made you feel inferior or incapable during dinner," I began.

She shook her head. "I'm sorry I put you in danger today. And thank you for saving my life."

I smiled. I wanted only to protect her, to make her happy, even if I failed at communicating it correctly.

"How's Mother?"

"She's doing better," Saphyr replied softly. "She enjoys the company, although I can tell she misses your father …"

I chewed the inside of my cheek. I wished he would come to his senses and be there for her.

"You could visit more often too, you know."

She was right. I had thought of going back myself, but it was hard for me to push back the tears when I saw her bedridden, and that putrid smell was a constant reminder of the death that was coming for her. I forced myself to act jolly, like all was well, because I did not want to cause her pain or worry. Every time I left my mother's chambers, I hid in a corner to wipe away silent tears. If I could just make her sickness go away, but ... I was useless. I hated seeing her draw closer to death every day and being unable to fight it off.

"I'll try," I said hoarsely, pushing the bitter memories down my throat.

We let the rushing water fill the silence for another moment.

I thought of Morgana, sleeping somewhere off in the manor. My debt to her grew larger by the day. She had manipulated the blood and flesh of my body to grow my wings, just like she did with hers. I wondered about the limits of her power.

Saphyr followed my gaze toward the guest rooms. "I guess your opinion about her has changed," Saphyr said.

"Are you upset about the ring?"

She studied the blue pearl twinkling under the starlight. "It's made of her siren tears, isn't it?"

I flinched. She knew.

"I know you and Kanis took them. And this kind of gem is not that common."

"I'm sorry."

She shrugged. "It reminded me that you have always done everything you could to keep us together, even at your lowest. But now that I've seen her in your chamber, I—"

"It surprised me as much as it surprised you to see her there. I did not invite her to stay."

"It was you who told me in Sirenibus not to trust Morgana."

"You were right. But there is a good side to her, even if the bad overshadows it." I told Saphyr about Morgana's mother, and how the siren had been collecting selkie skins to dig out information about her.

"How horrible it must've been for her to grow up lonely with unique magical gifts such as hers. I can only imagine." Saphyr took pity on her.

"She feels like the sirens only used her for her powers," I added. "But she still didn't hesitate to take the throne. Power in exchange for offering them protection."

"What a pitiful life." Saphyr watched water flow down the stream. "Perhaps that's why she has taken such a liking to you, and you to her. You both led lonely childhoods."

I clenched my jaw. Saphyr was right. Morgana and I understood each other on a deep level. We had both experienced the loneliness that comes with power.

"But she is nothing like you." I turned to Saphyr, tracing her cheekbone with the back of one finger. "Such a brave, beautiful, and intelligent future Empress."

Saphyr smiled softly.

"And such an important part of my life. You've been there for me since we were children. You and Kanis are my only family besides Mother. Thank you for always being there for me. You've cheered me up when I needed it the most and never allowed me to fall. It remains a mystery why you'd be with someone like me. And I'm sorry, Saphyr. I'm so sorry I didn't tell you about Morgana earlier."

I recalled how wretched I was back at Mistwood and the terrible mistake I had almost made. "I'd never forgive myself if I lost you. I'm truly sorry."

"Have you kissed her?" Saphyr frowned at me.

"Never," I replied solemnly.

She tensed, looking away.

I pulled my fingers away from her face and turned back to lean on the rail. My chest caved in, my wings cocooning me in darkness.

Had I lost it all? I had fought and died. I had returned to an abandoned home housing my dying mother, and now, the very person I had done it all for perhaps did not want me anymore. I wondered if I could keep going.

Even sleep evaded me. Only exhaustion finally drove me to sleep every night, and then only a little before the cold sweats and dreadful nightmares woke me before sunrise. The lack of sleep was driving me mad. I dreamed of Saphyr dying, of my mother dying, of soldiers cutting my throat with their knives. Would I ever go back to normalcy, to feeling safe, content, to being able to sleep at night?

"How could you ever love me when I'm utterly broken?" I murmured.

"I'll always be here for you," Saphyr said softly, placing her hand over mine on the rail.

I glanced up at her, my wings opening to encase her within. Suddenly, I felt like a child again. She had said the same thing whenever I had stormed from the manor after a fight with my father.

"Thank you." I gently touched my forehead to hers.

CHAPTER 27

FREEDOM

Saphyr gasped for air as I pulled back from her lips. She rested her head on the wall as I held her by the waist. I did not care about the ring or what we would have to face tomorrow, I only cared about her.

"Can I stay?" She looked around my chamber.

"Of course."

"I'll keep you company until you fall asleep."

"You can stay for as long as you wish."

She went to my bed and sat over the covers. "It is absurdly hot," she said.

I chuckled.

"Should we leave the door to the terrace open?"

"That's probably best."

I walked to the veranda and left the door ajar, a cool current making its way into the room.

Saphyr lay down on the bed, her curls spreading loose over it in all their splendor. Her beauty spirited my breath away. I glanced at the chaise. Perhaps it was best I slept there.

"Don't be silly. We've shared a bed before. We can do it again. Come." She tapped the open space next to her.

I sighed and obeyed, wondering how it was so easy for her to lie near me. I felt like my desire would consume me at any moment. The last time, I was drunk with exhaustion. Tonight, I felt as wide-awake as an owl.

I sat upright, resting my back against the tufted bedhead. Saphyr moved closer, nuzzling her head onto my chest. A sudden memory of us napping together when we were young brought a smile to my face. Everything was so much easier back then.

I stroked her soft curls, letting my gaze move up to the sparkling stars visible through the arched terrace.

"Thank you for being here," I whispered.

As she laced her fingers into mine, I felt like everything was right once again in the world. Swiftly, we let go of our worries and fell into a deep sleep.

A sudden gasp and a brush of skin pulled me from my slumber. Saphyr's fingers dug into my skin, alarmed.

I jolted to discover Morgana standing over me. She gazed down at us, her face hard. For a second, I feared for Saphyr. My head pounded, still half asleep.

Morgana stood still, unbothered, the silky strands of her on platinum hair covering her nudity. I studied the door I had left ajar. She must have entered in her raven form and then shifted back once inside.

"What is it?" I snarled.

"It's time," she said curtly. "Brenen's soldiers are moving up through the mountains. They'll be here in a few hours."

I sighed in resignation, running a hand through my hair. *Not a moment of peace.* "I guess it took him long enough." I straightened.

Morgana studied Saphyr coldly, and Saphyr frowned back at her.

"You could've at least knocked," Saphyr said sharply, standing. She took her discarded cloak from the chaise and handed it to Morgana.

"Oh, I'm sorry for keeping you all alive while you slept so soundly," Morgana retorted, throwing the cloak over her shoulders.

"How long do we have?" I asked.

"They should arrive before sunrise."

"Is everything in place?"

Morgana nodded. "Everything is as we planned. We'll fly to the city before they get here."

"Kanis?"

"He sent me here. The scouts hidden in the mountain sounded the alarm. Kanis and Delphino have mobilized the rest of the militia down the mountain through an alternate path. They're outside the city, waiting for you."

"Very well, then. Saphyr?"

She nodded. "I'm ready."

"Is the manor empty?"

Morgana nodded. "Everyone has already left. Your mother and Fulffbolt are with Kanis's mother."

"Thank you," I said, standing and throwing my robe on the bed. I looked to Saphyr. "Would you like to change and pack a set of clothes for Morgana?"

"I won't need them." Morgana shook her head.

"At least a cloak."

She crossed her arms, looking away.

"Fine, I'll be quick." Saphyr set out through the doors.

I glowered at Morgana, who sat by the cold fire, ignoring me. I changed into a fresh attire behind a screen, and then taking my dagger I sliced through my cloak twice, one slit for each wing.

"About the ring—"

"Keep the pearls. I was going to give them to you anyway."

"I'm sorry."

She fell silent.

I felt there was more, but it was best if I left it at that.

"Gliding down is easier than flying up, even with the extra weight," she said, changing the subject.

"Good to know."

"Do you have the seal?"

"Yes," I tapped my pocket, feeling the seal against the parchment. I approached Morgana, her pale hair reflecting the starlight, as if shining in place of the absent moon.

"I'm glad to see your Empress is back."

"Happy to put her back on her throne."

"It's yours too." Morgana narrowed her eyes at me. "Everything I've done is to put *you* on the throne, including saving her life."

My jaw tightened.

"Just remember that." Morgana stood, facing me. "She is not fit to rule; you are."

"I suggest we focus on staying alive. Brenen is marching with all his force, but there are some soldiers left at the fortress."

Morgana cackled with laughter. "And you're worried about them?"

I frowned. "Are you not?"

"I'm never afraid."

"Not even of death?"

"No such thing exists to us." She grinned wickedly, placing her hand on my shoulder. "You'd do well to remember that."

Steps approached from outside, and I took two steps back.

"Let's go," I said, stepping onto the terrace.

Morgana followed me, still smiling.

Saphyr entered the chamber and met us on the terrace.

"Are you ready?" I smiled, extending my arms to her. She nodded, throwing her arms around my neck and placing a soft kiss on my cheek.

A flash of light was followed by flapping wings as Morgana rose above us.

I lifted Saphyr and put a foot upon the stone rail. "Close your eyes and hold on tight," I whispered. She nodded as I let us fall through the mountain air.

When we arrived at Sol City, the sun glowed ruby and amber, setting the cloudless sky ablaze.

Morgana led us to the riverbank on the city side, where Kanis and Delphino waited under the shade of a tree. Somber expressions clouded their faces hidden beneath the hoods of their chestnut and moss-colored cloaks.

I landed smoothly, still cradling Saphyr. I filled my lungs with her scent as I set her on the ground. Then, I strode to Kanis and patted his arm. "Thank you," I said.

His eyes glistened with pride. "They're ready." Kanis jerked his head to the fortress that towered over the city's houses. "The brats carried the word through the night."

I thought of the gang of little spies with gratitude. I would thank them properly later.

"The people are gathered at the iron gates of the fortress. Mostly young men and women. No children."

"Good. Go! I'll meet you there."

Kanis eyed my wings and nodded, his face taut.

Saphyr glanced back at me as she walked with Kanis and Delphino through the trees lining the riverbank, headed for the fortress. I soared up, following them from above.

The crowd was thousands strong. They pointed to me with awe, gaping and shouting. I circled the city as Saphyr, Kanis, and Delphino shoved through the tight crowd to its core, where an obelisk crowned by a wrought gold sun rose up. Then, I descended, landing softly on the rim of the fountain that surrounded the obelisk. I straightened, spreading my wings. The crowd's gasps faded to utter silence. I glanced over them to the iron gates of the fortress.

"People of the Sun!" I shouted.

They stared at my cloaked figure with apprehension. "Today, your Crown Princess stands with you!"

Saphyr stepped forward from the shadow of the obelisk and into the light, letting her emerald hood fall. Her hair gleamed bright in the sunlight.

An audible gasp flew through the crowd.

"Yes, she lives," I said. "And so do I." I flicked back the hood of my obsidian cloak, revealing my face. My hair, in contrast to Saphyr's, consumed the sunlight instead of reflecting it.

"It's him—the dead heir to the House of Alba," a young man shouted.

"The *death conqueror*," another added.

I glanced at them sternly, a storm raging in my mind until the loud caw of a raven cut the air. Morgana swooped down from the fortress, her wings sweeping over the crowd, her talons almost scratching their heads. She perched herself atop my shoulder, and the crowd went silent again, mute with fear.

"They have betrayed you," I continued, without needing to shout anymore. "They have lied to you! They have manipulated you!"

The citizens frowned and squinted at each other.

"The traitor does not sit among you. He sits up there!" I pointed to the tallest tower of the fortress. "The son of Galbreg will stop at nothing until every one of you kneels before him and the bread of your children is upon *his* table!"

I took a step down to pace in front of the crowd, my wings tucked in, my eyes briefly locking with the gaze of each person, regardless of age and gender.

"Where are the riches he promised you?" I asked softly.

The multitude stood silent.

"Where are the riches he took from our families to give to yours?"

Nobody answered.

"They are in his coffers!"

Cloaked men stealthily infiltrated the crowd while everyone's attention was on me, their clenched jaws barely visible under the hoods. Their discreet brooches marked the Houses they belonged to. The sons and daughters of the Alliance slowly seeded the militia through the people. Everything was going according to plan.

"Where are the lands, the crates of food, the free remedies he promised you? Why do you not dwell in manor houses atop the mountains?" I pointed toward the imposing houses that overlooked the valley, the homes of the Alliance.

"Why," I asked, looking at a bony old man, "are you hungry?"

His sunken eyes flickered with sorrow, and mine with pain.

Turning, I then climbed the rim of the fountain again. "This is why!" I unfolded the parchment, showing the list of Court members who were to swindle what was ours. "This is the list of exclusive individuals who will receive what Brenen promised you, all handpicked by Brenen himself."

Rage simmered through the crowd. I threw the parchment to a man, who caught it and was immediately surrounded by others wanting to examine it. They passed it around, shaking their heads at the list of names next to Brenen's signature.

"I see Marcus—the chancellor of the city!"

"I see Ruben—chief of the Royal Guard!"

"And I see Theobald—the chamberlain!"

"I don't see any of your names on that list," I shouted. "The poor grow poorer, and the rich grow richer! Their soldiers patrol the city and monitor your every move. Where has your freedom gone? As if that wasn't enough, he keeps the levies you pay, those borne from the sweat of your labors. And what do you get in return? Nothing! One measly potato for a week's worth. They don't care if you starve. They've already gobbled up your freedom."

Angry stares, teary eyes, and grave faces within the crowd caught my eye.

"So, what do you say, sons and daughters of the Sun? Will you be children of light and stand with us, or will you collapse in the dark?"

Murmurs of revolt rippled among the people.

"By decree of the Emperor," Kanis shouted to my right. "Brenen, son of Galbreg, will be brought to justice. He stands accused of treason, of murder, and of theft. All his former decrees will be lifted immediately, including, but not limited to, the nightly and daily curfews, the levies added to trade, and the prohibition of travel outside the city. We will bring all those who collaborated with him to justice. This decree shall be effective immediately!" Kanis turned and extended the decree toward the people, who fixed their stares on the gleaming sun stamped in blood-red ink—the Imperial Seal of validation.

"The rumors are true!" Saphyr raised her voice. "My father and the Royal Family are held hostage in the fortress at this very moment. I beg of you, people of the Sun, today you must fight for your Empire and for your sons and daughters in the name of freedom!"

At her last word, the cloaked men threw off their hoods and roared to the sky, swords clanking from their scabbards and blazing in the sunlight.

The people joined, all turning to the fortress gate, where the soldiers waited with pale, alarmed faces.

Within seconds, the clash of weapons and the furious cries of battle erupted.

Kanis, Saphyr, and I nodded to each other, our faces solemn.

It had begun.

CHAPTER 28

MOONCHILD

"Stay out of my way today," Morgana snarled at me.

Her plum cloak clashed against mine as we dashed through the tight corridor, delving deep underground. She had transformed into her human form right after we had entered the hidden passageway through the outside wall, well away from the iron gates where the soldiers clashed with the militia and the people.

Saphyr and Kanis marched in front of us, a torch in hand. The stomping of the troop of militia behind us echoed off the stone walls. A pair had stayed behind, guarding the entrance to the passage.

"We're close to the dungeons now," Saphyr said, her emerald cloak swishing over the stone floor.

"Why must I stay out of your way?" I glanced at Morgana. The plan was to stop at the dungeons, where we would divide. Kanis and Saphyr, with half the men, would go in search of the Emperor in his chambers. Morgana and I would take the rest and go to find Galbreg.

Morgana's mouth was set in a hard line.

"We're here." Saphyr stopped, and we all drew to a halt.

A door gave way to another flight of stairs leading down.

"Corvus," Saphyr whirled around to clasp my hand.

"What is it?" I whispered as she led me away from the others. I shot a glance at Morgana's impassive face, hidden beneath the shadows of her hood.

Everyone else remained silent, waiting for us.

"I've decided," she said.

I furrowed my eyebrows, confused.

"I will speak to my father, and I will ask him to abdicate."

My back straightened. *Abdication, not exile?* "What if he doesn't agree?" I asked carefully.

"Then we will do as you say." She looked away, sadness clouding her beauty.

I placed a knuckle under her chin and drew it up. "Look at me," I said. "Everything will be fine. I won't do anything you don't agree with."

She brightened. "I'll do my best to convince him. I am the next in line to the throne, after all. As his eldest, they have trained me to rule the Empire, and he is of old age. Perhaps he'll find early retirement appealing."

From the corner of my eye, I saw Morgana shuffle her feet.

"Very well. But," I said gravely, "if he agrees, he must understand that he will lose all power. His Court, allies, and everything he's established will no longer be his to control. I will put a new rule in order. Our rule," I emphasized, squeezing her hands within mine.

She nodded with solemn determination. "Our rule," she repeated.

"It's time, lovebirds," Morgana dragged the words out, rolling her eyes. "We have an Empire to take, if you don't mind."

I squared my shoulders and let go of Saphyr's hands.

"Let's go." Kanis approached us, patting Saphyr's shoulder to guide her forward.

I held her gaze until she turned and set off, with half of the troop marching behind them. My wings shook, and I shoved down the powerful pull that made me want to follow her.

"I hope Delphino breaks through the gate soon enough," I grumbled, mortified.

"It'll be over soon, pet." Morgana tugged the creaking iron door open, and I let out a disdainful huff.

We marched down the short flight of stairs to the dungeons.

Our militia quickly knocked out the few guards who had stayed behind to protect the dungeons. After snatching the keys off the unconscious bodies, they immediately freed Saphyr's family members one by one.

Morgana and I strode past the cells to the end of the hallway. The stench was awful. I could only imagine the horror of spending so many days and chilly nights in this miserable, fetid darkness.

"Milord!"

The largest cell, behind a thick iron grille, contained a group of men. They sat on a thick layer of straw, gaping at us from bony faces, only hope burning in their eyes.

My guard!

I smiled as I inserted the key and unlocked the door. "You're free to go."

They looked heavenward, thankful their prayers had been answered, and then jumped to their feet and rushed through the door. The men gathered outside, inspecting me with amazement.

"You're alive," one said in a gruff voice.

"I'm sorry it took me so long."

The men from the Stella Islands observed me and my wings with awe.

"It all ends today," I promised. "The reason you're here." I pointed at the hated dungeons. "It all ends today. Thank you for fighting alongside me."

"Thank you for coming back for us," the baker's son replied.

I swallowed the knot in my throat and nodded.

Then, the militia men signaled my guard to follow them into the secret passages and out of the fortress.

Morgana and I crept along to the very last cell, where Galbreg waited.

His white hair, usually smoothed neatly at his nape, fluttered loose and disheveled around his face. My once-mentor sat on his knees, looking miserable. I remembered why he was here: betrayed by his own son.

"Was it worth it?" I asked.

He said nothing, observing my wings, unperturbed.

"Betraying me, only to be betrayed by your own blood?"

He stared at me coldly from behind the iron lattice. I held his stare, awaiting his response.

"It wasn't me," he growled hoarsely.

"Then who?"

"A spy. Brenen put him within my men. He shot the first arrow from the forest and gave Brenen the excuse to attack."

"Why didn't you come to our aid?" I snarled. "You had plenty of time."

For the first time since I had known him, Galbreg looked sorrowful. "He is my son." His voice reverberated, as cold as the cell's stone walls. "My only son."

Morgana's cloak swished against my feet. Fergus's words echoed in my head. *"Blood runs thicker than water."*

"I became your son when you cast away your own. I was going to make you Emperor. But you went around my back, making empty promises to the people and planning to murder Saphyr despite giving me your word you would not. Brenen only carried on with your plans after getting rid of you. And still, you lacked the courage to take him down? You would let him kill me instead."

My hand twitched, and I moved it closer to my dagger.

"I couldn't kill him. He's my son."

I stared around his cell. Brenen had not killed him either. I supposed Fergus was right.

"You didn't need to kill him." I pointed out. "Apprehending him would've been enough. Then this would've all ended. Why put us all through hell?"

Galbreg glanced up. "That would've been pointless," he warned. "He wants complete control to fill the void I've left in him. Brenen will not stop until he feels he has surpassed me. I've been a terrible father to him. You should know."

I winced. I had never expected Galbreg to recognize he had failed Brenen. He had cast him aside, just as my father had done to me. I had never truly questioned why. Brenen had disguised himself as a hedonistic courtier, always visiting brothels. No one ever thought of him as more than the aimless son of the General. In my own quest for power, I had not spared him a glance. I had happily occupied his place as Galbreg's apprentice rather than remain in the shadow of my drunkard father, who despised my weakness. How foolish of me to have underestimated Brenen.

"So, you left me to die?" My tone was numbed by indifference.

A glimmer of regret laced with fear sparkled in Galbreg's eyes. "You were the son I wished I had. But I had no choice."

Within the blink of an eye, Morgana was inside the cell, her hands choking his throat as his feet dangled midair. Galbreg wheezed for breath.

I froze. "Stop!" I commanded her, stepping inside after her.

"You had another child," she hissed low to Galbreg. "But you let that child drown and kept the other instead."

What was she talking about? Suddenly, I recalled what she had told me about Galbreg back at Sirenibus. He had killed his wife and abandoned his two children in floating baskets on the river because he thought they were not his.

Morgana's face twisted with rage. She lifted one hand, pointing her sharp mauve claws at Galbreg. Then she pulled them back, beckoning something.

I watched with horror as multiple droplets of blood seeped from Galbreg's ashen skin.

"Morgana, *no!*"

She did not listen. She fixed her blazing eyes on Galbreg, ready to drain him to his very last drop, to kill him.

"Morgana, stop!"

I shook her shoulder, and she gnashed her teeth and put out a hand to stop me while Galbreg continued to dangle, his face turning purple.

Morgana's eyes glinted like blue fire, her pupils dilating as new droplets of crimson blood floated into the air—my blood. She was warning me.

I dropped my hand from her shoulder.

Her eyes flashed back to Galbreg.

"You're not a murderer," I pleaded. "Don't do this."

"He is a murderer! He killed my mother, and now I'll kill him."

Then it hit me: Morgana had been found by the sirens as an infant. She had been one of the babies in the floating basket. Her mother could not conceive, and once she did, she was killed. Galbreg had dispatched his wife shortly after she gave birth because the children did not look like him. Morgana was Galbreg's firstborn—a moonchild.

Pity and sadness washed over me. Morgana fought back tears, her nostrils flaring. This poor child. She deserved so much better. I put my hand to her shoulder, pressing kindly. "Morgana, you're better than him," I said, my hope set on her good nature, however buried. She had saved me more than once. Morgana was not a murderer. "I believe in you."

My words seemed to strike her. She turned her stare to my raven wings and let Galbreg drop to the floor, where he clutched his throat, still gasping for air.

We choose to be children of light, despite our origins. She did not want to be like him. Morgana despised Galbreg to her core.

"No," Galbreg wheezed. "Let her do it. I deserve it."

I tilted my head, confused.

He stepped toward her, still panting, and raised his hand to her.

"Your mother was not the problem; I was. I was told I couldn't have children, but I never told her for fear she'd leave me. When she came to me, pregnant, I knew the children could not be mine. I drove her away." Galbreg choked. "She was torn apart by sorrow. She tried to gut me in a fit of rage, and I fought back." Tears fell from his eyes. "I regret it every day. I rushed to the river after realizing my mistake, but you were already gone. I could only retrieve one."

Morgana took two steps backs, her face twisted with horror.

"You have your mother's lips and the shape of her eyes, no matter if your skin and hair are as bright as the full moon when mine was pitch black. I see some of myself in you. How stupid I was." He buried his face in his hands. "I've thought of you every day. It is why I couldn't be near your brother. He always reminded me of you, and of your mother. And oh, how I've missed her. My heart is burdened with guilt." He looked up, pleading. "But you're alive, our beautiful daughter."

I grimaced at the sight of the once all-powerful General reduced to a miserable old man.

Morgana raised her chin and recoiled, turning her body away in disgust.

I extended my hand to her, wondering if she could ever forgive him, but her gaze was cold.

"Brenen is mine," she snarled, flashing her teeth at me.

Then, in a burst of light, she morphed into a raven, and her plum cloak fell to the floor.

Stay out of my way today, my brain repeated as she flapped out the dungeons. She had been planning her revenge. I had stopped her from killing Galbreg. Was she now going for Brenen?

I ordered the men to keep Galbreg in his cell as I barreled up the stairs after her, spreading my wings to take flight. She was out of control. I had to stop her before she tried to kill Brenen as well.

A thousand curses beat like wings in my head.

I propelled myself at full speed through the sky, but Morgana was nowhere in sight. Gritting my teeth, I soared over the mountains, leaving the fortress behind. The wind froze my hands and numbed my face. My dark cloak fluttered uncontrollably behind me. At least I knew where she was headed.

The minutes passed quickly, my stomach churning with anticipation. As my house became visible through the trees at the mountaintop, I held my breath. Soldiers swarmed around it like ants. Carefully, I glided out of sight, and then flew up to my chamber. There, on my balcony, Brenen stood overlooking the Dark Forest. Two soldiers were posted at the external doors, but inside the chamber, he was alone.

I landed stealthily behind him, at the opposite end of the terrace, and unsheathed my dagger.

Brenen stared down the mountain, clearly enraged to find my home empty. His platinum hair moved in the wind. I prowled to him, relieved that Morgana was absent.

Finally, it would be over. Brenen would rot in the dungeons with the father he had betrayed. I raised my dagger, but then, for a fraction of a second, I hesitated, my hand frozen in the air. Was this truly Morgana's brother? If she knew all along, why had she waited until today to act?

Sensing my presence, Brenen spun, plunging his sword down in a ferocious strike. I twisted my dagger with both hands to block it, but he shoved my dagger aside and sent a left hook smashing against my jaw. My feet left the ground, and I gasped for air as my body slammed to the floor.

"How does it feel?" He twisted his lips up in a sneer.

I raised myself on one elbow, trying to stand, but he smashed his foot against my wrist, sending my dagger clanking to the floor.

"You were a fool to return by yourself."

"Why?" I breathed hard. "All the misery you've caused."

Brenen grinned cruelly. "Because I can." He raised the point of his sword, aiming for my chest.

The caw of a raven made him look up, and I used his distraction to roll out from under his blade. Brenen growled, once more aiming his sword at me. But, in a flash of light, Morgana materialized behind him, my dagger gleaming in her hand.

She snickered as she swiftly held it against the skin of his neck. "Hello, sweet little brother," she hissed in his ear, holding my incredulous stare.

Brenen gaped with horror.

"Drop it!" She pressed the dagger to his skin until a thin scarlet line of blood leaked from it.

His sword *clunked* to the ground.

"Morgana, don't do it," I implored.

"He tried to kill you yet again, and still you wish to let him live?"

"He is your brother."

Grief glinted in her eyes, and I saw Brenen's eyebrows shoot up.

"Perhaps you can fill the void Galbreg left in him. Think about why you shift into a raven. He may also choose to redeem himself."

Morgana tilted her head.

I trust you, my eyes begged her.

Her eyebrows knit together in thought. "Or maybe I can just get rid of him," she ground out between clenched teeth.

"Are you really her? The child he left to drown?" Brenen asked, his face taut.

Morgana and I stared at each other.

"You knew?" She pulled the dagger ever so slightly away.

"I've always hated him for it," Brenen said. "I thought both you and Mother were dead."

"I survived," Morgana grunted, tears of sorrow glinting in her eyes.

Brenen stared at me, my dark wings spread on the ground.

"Saphyr has taken the fortress with the help of the Alliance, Brenen. She has the Imperial Seal. It's done," I said.

"You're lying!"

"He's not." Morgana pressed the dagger again. "The people you starved have knocked down the iron gates. The revolt you desperately tried to avoid has happened. You have nothing."

I stood and took his sword. Brenen clenched his fists, but he turned to face Morgana. "Let me see you."

"Let him," I instructed her, letting the sword tip pierce the back of his coat in warning.

Brenen inhaled sharply, and his mouth fell open at her nakedness. Then his shoulders slumped. "Your hair, it's exactly like mine. And your ... face." He dropped his gaze to the ground.

Morgana frowned, studying his features. "Should you come with me, then?"

Brenen raised his chin. "Yes. There's nothing left here for me."

Morgana narrowed her eyes at him. "Try anything funny, and I'll dry you dead in an instant."

He stiffened.

"You may regret this later," Morgana said, taking a step back. Then, two magnificent white wings spread from her back, opening wide around her.

I gasped, fixing my gaze on the iridescent, pearly feathers, which rivaled her shimmering hair for beauty. Her feet lifted slightly off the ground, and she stared down at Brenen with menacing blue eyes, glacial as a winter morning. Galbreg's eyes.

"I'll take him to Sirenibus. Come." She shoved a stunned Brenen toward the rail.

"I'll help you," I said, stepping and removing my cloak.

She took it, donning it while inspecting Brenen's lean frame. "No. I can take him."

I frowned at Brenen, his hands clutching the rail with apprehension. "Fine, but let me at least return his kindness," I said, giving Morgana a twisted smile.

Morgana grinned, immediately understanding. Her wings flapped powerfully as she soared upward.

"The new Empress sends her regards," I told Brenen.

He froze as I raised a leg and kicked him off the rail. His scream echoed satisfyingly through the mountains as he plunged down the cliff.

Chapter 29

Immortal Souls

Saphyr grinned from her throne. Behind her head, gleaming dangerous spikes sprang up, as brilliant and golden as the rays of the sun.

The Empress of the Sun Empire finally sat at her rightful place. I returned her smile and raised my glass to her.

"What a day," I muttered, chugging another pint of beer. At least something good had come from it. We had won. The fortress and the throne were ours.

Our coronation day arrangements were already beginning. Next to her, her father sat on a wooden throne, looking ghastly and pale in a red tunic. Saphyr had convinced him to abdicate. Two guards, positioned behind him, watched his every step—under my command.

"It could've been worse." Kanis eased himself onto the long bench next to me and slid another pint of beer my way, clinking it against the empty one.

The hall roared with music and laughter. The moment the people had seen Brenen dangling from Morgana's claws as she flew toward the sea like some sort of implacable angel, their cheering had convinced the soldiers to drop their weapons and raise their hands in surrender. The heads of the Houses and the militia quickly separated the loyalists from those who were willing to accept Saphyr as their Empress. Not that there were many men loyal to Brenen.

I knew that, with time, we would also weed out any of Galbreg's traitors. We would tolerate no insurgency.

Exhausted, I rolled my shoulders, and Kanis studied me.

"What troubles you?" he asked, his face close to mine.

"It's over," I confessed, "yet I feel as if it has just begun. Are we really free of trouble now?"

Kanis motioned toward the cheerful people around us; the daughters and sons of the Alliance loudly celebrating their victory with the militia inside the hall. There was no sight of the traitorous courtiers who had made up Brenen's list.

"We'll get to the disloyal soon enough," Kanis promised, guessing the question from my concern as I watched the crowd.

"And Galbreg?"

"We'll reform the army, monitor his loyalists. Imprison as many as we can."

I sighed with weariness. "But we keep the good men. Identify those with both talent and character."

Kanis nodded. "We'll keep anyone who doesn't pose a threat."

My jaw was hurting. I had kept it clenched for so long. I drained half of the new pint and shook my head.

"What else is on your mind?" Kanis insisted.

"Morgana," I growled. "She left with Brenen after I convinced her not to kill him, but I can't shake the feeling that she toyed with me. She knew Brenen was her brother and Galbreg her father. She knew it all along. But she waited until today to act."

I had filled Kanis in on Morgana's secret family history, sparing the details since time was scarce.

"She almost throttled Galbreg in the dungeons," I muttered. "Drained the life out of him and even gave *me* a warning. This time, she didn't dry me out but actually sucked blood droplets from my skin."

Kanis gasped.

"Exactly! It's like there's no end to her power. Did you see her wings?"

"There's an end to everything."

"I'm not so sure ... She's a moonchild, unlike the sirens, far more powerful. A shapeshifter, a halfling, a queen. Galbreg's firstborn." I sighed. "I fear her and pity her at the same time."

Kanis frowned.

"She could have had her revenge from the start. Why wait until we seized the throne?"

He shook his head.

"And why put her kind's secrecy on the line with these?" My wings stirred slightly. "And by revealing her wings to the people of the sun as well?"

Kanis shrugged. "Your wings and hers hardly scream *sirens*—quite the opposite. She's crafty. She knows what she's doing."

Beneath her obstinate, crude nature was a certain goodness buried deep within her. She was constantly fighting against her darkness.

I sighed and looked up at Saphyr. "I do think Morgana acted out of what she thought best for the Empire."

Kanis tapped his fingers on the table. "What does she care about the Sun Empire? The vast oceans are hers to rule. The sirens don't need more space. They choose to remain hidden." He looked around. "Morgana is not afraid of us. For whatever reason, she made sure you sat on the throne before taking care of Brenen and Galbreg. It wouldn't hurt us to know why."

I thought of her conversation with Fergus, back at Mistwood. "Fergus, the Dryad King, said she'd picked me against his advice. He mentioned something about her personal interests getting mixed up with her royal duties to Sirenibus."

"Perhaps we should find out more about the interest these creatures have regarding the human realm, now that the Sun Empire is ours."

I nodded, my head pounding. My fond memories of conversations and moments spent with Morgana, both in her human and raven form, were muddled with distrust and betrayal.

"Do you think she'll kill Brenen?"

"I don't think so. She and Brenen seemed to bond over their shared hatred for their father. Perhaps she'll try to get to know him, her long-lost brother."

Now it was Kanis who chugged his beer. "Brenen getting along with Morgana. I fear what may come from it."

"Perhaps she'll try to make up for the family Galbreg stole from her."

"Or perhaps she'll stay impulsive, moody, vengeful ... Perhaps she'll just get rid of Brenen, and we'll never hear from either of them again."

I chuckled. "That's also a possibility." I remembered the blood magically emerging from Galbreg's ashen face. "Double down the security on Galbreg, in case she changes her mind about him."

"Of course."

"I must speak with Fergus," I said, standing. "Before Morgana returns."

Kanis studied me with concern. "Are you sure, after such a day?"

"I'll be fine. I could use the fresh air."

The din and the aromas of food in the hall were suffocating me. It also pained me that Morgana had not told me the truth. *Had she planned everything meticulously from the start? Had I been the idiot who had missed the subtle details that would have unveiled her plan?*

"You should take guards with you."

"It'll be faster to go alone."

He frowned.

"Fine," I growled. Kanis was always an overprotective idiot. I turned and marched from the hall, a pair of guards already on my trail.

The officers guarding the main doors swung them open, eyeing my wings with fear.

Stepping outside the iron gates, I took a deep breath of cold air and pushed my wings down to the ground, soaring up.

My guard chased me on foot until I glided up and away, out of Sol City, toward the Dark Forest.

I hovered above the trees, still and silent in the starlight, the moon as absent as Morgana. Had she already arrived at Sirenibus with Brenen, or had she grown tired of him during the journey and fed him to the sharks? Mist blotted the forest beyond, and I momentarily feared Fergus would not lift the glamour to let me in.

As I flew over the prairie, I shivered to return to the place where the lightning had struck me, and nausea rose in my guts. I had lain there— dead—before Morgana carried me into the forest. Had God struck me down to protect me? Or was my return merely an unfortunate incident? I exhaled, sending the thoughts away. It was pointless to wonder why; I was grateful to be breathing.

No one traveled to the Dark Forest. The people avoided it with good reason. Fortunately, I knew what its grim aspect hid. Mistwood. I drifted in until I reached the twisted trees of its impenetrable black wall. To my relief, the wall untangled, allowing me passage into the forest's heart.

The air slowly warmed, and the eerie silence was replaced with the hum of cicadas. I could sense Mistwood was near. When the dry grass became a lush, verdant carpet adorned with small flowers, I knew I had reached my destination.

I landed on the central white bridge, suspended high above the ground. My steps echoed against the floor, my dark wings trailing the snowy surface. Mistwood was as beautiful as before, its ancient trees crowned with twinkling lights, untouched by time, ever unchanging.

He knew I was here, of course. I passed beneath the spiraling high arches on my way to the throne room, and there he was. Far from the warmth and light streaming from the candelabras, Fergus sprawled apathetically on his throne in the darkness, resting his chin on one hand.

"Fergus," I greeted him, and he flashed me a dangerous leer.

"Have you come to pay me a visit? Or is this our first diplomatic encounter?" he drawled.

I frowned.

"Congratulations on your victory. Morgana must be very pleased."

"It is Saphyr who sits on the throne, not me."

Fergus leaned in. "Yet ..." He bared his teeth in a smile. "When is the wedding, or will she make your *friend* her Emperor instead?"

I winced. "What if Saphyr reigns by herself?"

"I don't care, as long as the peace is kept. But Morgana would be upset."

"Why? Why did Morgana wait all this time to carry out her plan? Why not just kill Galbreg and Brenen on Saphyr's birthday? Morgana was there; I saw her there. I saw her shift into a raven."

"She didn't intent to kill them then. She decided to do so after she saw you dead on the prairie." He mocked me. "Ask me something more interesting. I'm bored, you see." He rested his chin on his other hand. "Forever bored." He sighed.

"I'm sure there's more to it. Enlighten me."

"The reason is simple." He chuckled, flicking his loose hair over one shoulder. "Morgana spied you working alongside her father. She took a liking to you. She saw what you were doing for the Crown Princess, and jealousy clouded her heart. She wanted you for herself."

A rush of blood warmed my cheeks.

"Had you not been so set on your princess, you could've gained an empire more powerful than you'd ever dreamed of. The seas and the Sun Empire could have been yours."

An empty feeling lodged itself in the pit of my stomach. "Why then did she help me gain the throne?"

"Morgana believes you're destined to lead the human realm, but I rather think she's blinded by unrequited love." Fergus's top lip twisted up again. "In any case, you broke her heart when you left her by the river that night. Ruby told me all about it."

I clenched my fists. I had always thought Morgana was simply toying with me, like a cat with a mouse. My lack of trust in her, and in myself, had never allowed me to see her heart—not that it would have made a difference.

"Now, now, don't blame yourself." He flicked his hand. "Morgana's pride always comes first. I even offered for her to stay here with me." He clicked his tongue. "But she prefers to keep her precious talents to herself. Such a selfish woman."

Morgana was anything but selfish. She had respected my wish to stay loyal to Saphyr, and I admired her for that. "What will she do now?"

Fergus shrugged. "Return to her royal duties, I suppose." He smiled. "Why? Do you miss her already? I think it's too late to make her your Empress now."

"I'm no longer in need of power." My gaze took in the mystic forest visible through the arches. A soft breeze entered, and I inhaled it deeply. Memories of my life in the cottage came to me—of the raven perched atop a tree, watching me catch a trout; of winter days filled with solitude and peace.

"Ironic, isn't it? I started all this with a thirst for control and power, and now, I don't want it. All I want is peace ... very much like you." I raised an eyebrow at him.

Fergus huffed impatiently. "Let me tell you, it gets boring after a while, especially in solitude." He looked longingly to the sky.

"Why keep yourselves hidden?" I followed his gaze up to the glittering stars.

"We once shared the land with humans. We arrived here first in dark clouds, fallen from the sky." His fingers twirled fleetingly in the air. "Not good enough for heaven, nor bad enough for hell, we call ourselves the Fallen, although you may not call us that. Throughout the years, humans referred to us as the hidden people, the good folk, the fairies, or, in your case, your neighbors." Fergus stood and sauntered down the steps of his throne. "But humans invaded our lands. We fought and we lost, so we made a bargain. We'd go into hiding in exchange for peace." His eyes narrowed. "You keep your end of the bargain; we'll keep ours."

I held his gaze. *The Fallen.* These ancient mythical creatures were not of this world but had been cast down from the divine realm.

"Very well. Peace." I swallowed, finally accepting the truth. If an ancient peace treaty kept them here, I was more than happy to uphold it. "May I ask how our realms intersect?"

"As you multiply and seek to conquer the land, we fade into the fabric of the forest and the depths of the sea. We typically avoid humans, save for a few exceptions, such as yourself—which you may thank Morgana for."

"Will she live as long as you?"

His expression turned somber. "Another reason to not keep the company of humans. We get to know you, to love you, and then you die. You move on and leave us here, mourning our loneliness, foolishly missing you ..." Fergus sighed, the blue lights of Mistwood illuminating his pain.

"Immortality?"

"*Immortal*," he whispered, "to not die." Holding my gaze, he crept closer and closer until his nose almost touched mine.

I suppressed a wince. He smelled of pine, although I had expected his scent to be rotten. His obsidian eyes searched mine. "Tell me, Corvus, do you fear death?"

I thought of the prayer I had sent out before entering the prairie. The lightning and its excruciating pain. The thunderous roar of the earth before death consumed me. I had been terrified, wondering if I had ceased to exist, but my essence had remained. God, for some reason, had forced my return to this world.

"No," I answered honestly.

"Good. The gift and joy of eternal life is in death itself for you. Humans die and transcend because you've been blessed with *immortal souls*."

A flicker of hope ignited my heart. Humanity had been granted true immortality through what we feared the most: death. After facing our deepest fear, we had the chance to live forever.

"All humans?" I asked.

Fergus grinned mischievously. "Yes, but only those who are truly worthy will conquer death." He turned and moved up the stairs back to his throne.

"Does Morgana know?"

"Human blood runs in her veins. As long as she behaves, she, too, will conquer death."

I swallowed, imagining what it would have meant if, blinded by vengeance, she had killed her father and her brother. Vengeance in exchange of her immortality. She did not fear dying, since she thought herself immortal, but her soul had to conquer her darkness to live on past death. I walked to one of the arches and leaned against it, watching the mist travel through the gnarled trees. Tears welled in my eyes. Immortality, it could be ours.

I left Mistwood and Fergus before he changed his mind about the peace treaty and decided it was more fun to keep me locked inside the forest.

The first rays of sun cleansed the city of all darkness and warmed the air as I soared up the mountains toward my home. It was a new start, one filled with hope and light.

By the time I descended onto the terrace of my chamber, I was stiff with exhaustion. I leaned on the rail, absorbing the warmth of sunrise.

Everything was in order. We had recovered our homes, and our families were safe. With the throne, I could care for the people, although the responsibility tightened my chest. What if Galbreg's scattered loyalists caused an uprising? What if we faced new foreign enemies? What if Fergus, out of boredom, decided the Dark Forest was not enough territory for the dryads?

Sitting on the throne meant facing hard choices—choices that would not only affect people's lives but also possibly end them. I had never wanted to be Emperor. I had only wanted to find one good enough for the Empire. I did not crave the glory and all the enemies that came with it. I was already wealthy, and I was content. All I wanted was to live a long, peaceful life with Saphyr, Kanis, and my mother.

The words on the crest I had seen hanging back in Sirenibus came to mind: *Si Vis Pacem, Para Bellum.* If you want peace, prepare for war.

Morgana always seemed a step ahead. If we wanted peace, if we wanted justice in the Empire, it would come by our hands and no one else's. Even if that meant sacrificing a peaceful life.

We would not entrust others to do our job. We had tried that and failed. This time, I would keep a tight watch over the new Court, the Alliance, and any foreign threats. I would prepare for war, so we could live in peace.

My shoulders tightened at the task, and I felt older than my years. I would have a century of life at most, not millennia like Fergus. I hoped it would be enough.

I left the terrace and slipped into the warmth of my bed, abandoning myself to the oblivion of the realm of dreams.

The vast Dark Forest extended before me, devoid of life and opalescent with snow.

A cloaked figure hurried through the forest clearing, pushing through the blackened branches of frozen trees.

Suddenly, the figure dropped her hood, and Morgana's icy eyes stared at me.

I frowned. "Why?" I whispered.

She padded to me and replied, "I'm sorry, pet."

Her black cloak swished back as ivory wings sprouted from her back. She soared magnificently into the air, and then plunged toward me, her talons clawing for my throat.

I woke up gasping for air, my hands raised, protecting me from the ghostly image of her claws stretching inches before my eyes.

Everything was still in my chamber and dark. I had slept all day. The glass terrace door swiveled to the darkness, letting a draft of frozen air nip my bones. I stood, thinking to close it, but something else caught my attention.

A white envelope gleamed on my empty desk. I took it up and turned it between my fingers, discovering my name written on it. The black ink bled freshly over the parchment. I broke open the silvery wax seal shaped like of crescent moon, and my stomach flipped in anticipation.

A pearly feather fluttered from the envelope. I caught it and opened the letter.

My darling pet, it started. A smile escaped my lips as I instantly recognized the elegant cursive.

I'm sorry to have kept you in the dark. Thank you for trusting me and showing me the meaning of mercy. In many ways, it saved me. My heart swelled. *Congratulations on taking back the throne of the Sun Empire. I know you'll make for a magnificent Emperor. Don't visit Fergus again. I know you miss me.*

I huffed, rolling my eyes at her presumption. *But he is jealous and can't be trusted. My sweet little brother will be safe with me, as long as he behaves. Monitor your new Court, and I'll monitor the underwater realm and my kind. I'm happy to have a friend wearing the crown of the Sun. It was, after all, my main purpose.*

I felt a pinch of sadness at the word *friend*. Friends did not abandon each other. Another sentence was scrawled below, almost like an afterthought.

If you ever wonder about me, look at the moon. When I'm happy, it is full. The nights when I'm sad, the moon wanes as if to make a cradle for a lost babe.

I gazed at the night sky, darkened by an absent moon, and hoped Morgana would no longer feel lonely.

I will not return to the Sun Empire for now, but I know you'll be in excellent hands. Kanis will always be by your side, and Saphyr will make a beautiful bride. Be happy, my pet.'

The letter ended with no signature, but it did not need one.

I sat, brought down by sadness. It was strange. I had not realized how attached I had become to her.

I savored our memories together: her company as Feathers, her comfort in Mistwood after learning Kanis and Saphyr had married and that my mother was sick, the moment we had glided above the Tagus River, and our conversation afterward. She had saved my life countless times, and Saphyr's as well.

Morgana had been key to our victory, and I was deeply grateful. She was no longer the menacing Nightmare Queen of the Seas but a dear friend whom I would always welcome.

I banged a fist against the desk and pulled myself together. This was for the best. I would never choose her over Saphyr. But keeping her as a friend would only hurt her more.

I carefully slid the creamy feather inside the pocket of my robe and walked to the dying embers of the fire. Tossing the letter in, I watched the flames slowly lick it into ash.

CHAPTER 30
HOPE

The crystal balcony glittered in the sunlight. Below, Saphyr ran across the gardens toward a cliff. She playfully caught her youngest sister and swung her in the air, laughing at the child's giggling. Beyond the cliff, the sea shimmered. A relaxed smile slid across my face.

Kanis stood next to me in silence, also watching.

We had been working nonstop to organize our new rule. I had exiled Galbreg to a secluded house, guarded day and night. The Emperor had moved out of the Crystal Palace to his retirement house by the coast. Saphyr's mother and her sister had stayed in the palace, and our coronation drew near. Only one thing remained pending.

"Have you set a date?" Kanis asked.

"Not yet." My smile widened. "She wants a large wedding; I just want her."

"Well, you two better figure it out soon. There isn't much time left before coronation day."

"Yes," I agreed.

We kept quiet for a few more minutes. Saphyr strode to the cliff and sat on the grass by her sister. Soon, the moon would take over the sky and bathe the sea with cold silver light.

"It's unsettling to think it's our turn," I said. "Our fathers no longer control this world. We do. But we're too young, too weak for the unknown and for what lurks in the shadows."

"Where's your faith?" Kanis asked.

I slid my hands in my pockets, finding it hard to breathe.

"God has sent you friends like us to help you get where you are now. Look at everything that happened. You even survived being struck by lightning. How many people can say that? *This* is your purpose. He's created you, and He knows your strengths and weaknesses. You can handle it, Corvus. I personally think there's no better person for the task, and not just because I'm your friend. You're intelligent, loyal, and caring. We stand with you. You're not alone."

I pressed my lips together. There were so many unseen threats, so many decisions that would break me. I had died once. Would I live now but sacrifice my soul?

"There'll be sacrifices, but nothing that won't strengthen you, nothing you won't be able to handle," Kanis reassured me.

"I hope you're right." I sighed.

"Stop being afraid. Take this opportunity and enjoy it. Marry her, and be happy."

A flicker of hope ignited a warm feeling within me. "Thank you."

Honeysuckle vines draped the hedges, their sweet scent drifting through the labyrinth. A crescent moon lit up the sky.

I listened for the giggles that disappeared between the dense hedges, turning another corner to chase the joyous voice. A glimpse of a flowing white train, swishing around a second corner, intensified the anticipation building in my stomach.

I stretched my fingers out and turned, catching Saphyr by her shoulders. "I got you!" I panted as she turned in my arms, her hands pressing against her belly. She let out a burst of laughter and snorted, making me laugh along with her.

"Oh, I could do this all night. It's so much fun," she said, puffing.

"I'm not sure I'll be able to keep up." I struggled to catch up my breath, resting the weight of my wings on the ground.

"Let's take a break." Saphyr took my hand and led me through the labyrinth, which she knew intimately.

We had played here often when we were young until her father had set us apart. Now, things had changed. After so much, we were finally able to enjoy the lightheartedness of our youth. I squeezed her hand and entwined my fingers with hers. She beamed.

The arched exit of the labyrinth gave way to a secret garden. Bushes of gardenias surrounded a pond full of colorful fishes. We entered a long pergola and strolled through it, admiring the shimmering sea at the very far end of the Crystal Palace.

"Let's fix a date," Saphyr said.

"A thousand attendees sound like a bit too much," I tried to negotiate.

"Corvus, I need you." She puckered. "It's not proper we share a room in the palace before we're married, and I don't know if I want to wait until then."

I raised an eyebrow, a sense of calm and ease breezing through me. My hand went to her waist, and I pulled her in. "Do you really?" I gave her a wicked smile. "Need me? A hundred attendees."

Saphyr raised her chin and looked to the sea. "Perhaps I should arrange a marriage with an heir of Oldterra."

I narrowed my eyes at her. "You wouldn't dare."

"You know I wouldn't." She sighed. "Why do you have to be like this? You are as stubborn as a mule. This is the wedding of the century, people from all over the world will be coming over to the Sun Empire."

I smiled, and tucked her hand under my forearm, continuing our midnight stroll.

"Are you taking revenge on me with this because I had to marry Kanis? That marriage was annulled, and you know it."

I pressed my lips together. Yes, that was one of the very first things Kanis had taken care of when we recovered the throne. Since it was never consummated, the marriage had been easy to annul. However, few believed it. I heard the whispers and rumors about Saphyr and Kanis's marriage. If I did not trust them both with my life, I may have struggled to accept the truth.

"You know, I could always warn any potential suitor from Oldterra about your previous marriage. Although it was a farce, they might not believe you like I do."

"Fool." She scoffed. "With my beauty and wits, I'm sure they wouldn't mind." Saphyr whipped her hair backward and added, "Besides, if you dare, I can always send you to the dungeons."

I laughed at her childish behavior.

A gust of wind swept through, and the fragrance of nectarines suddenly set me ablaze. My hands clutched her waist, and I pulled her against a wide marble column covered in jasmine flowers.

She returned my fiery gaze with wide eyes and parted lips.

"No other heir nor princeling shall have you," I whispered against them. "Even in the dungeons, I'd make you mine."

Saphyr shivered and grasped my arms as my tongue explored the depths of her mouth.

"800 hundred," she said, gasping for air.

"500 hundred," I growled, taking her lips again.

"Tonight." She gasped again. "Otherwise, you won't have me."

I studied her, my eyebrows raised. "You want to blackmail me?" I traced her neck with my lips, and her back arched.

"You could have me tonight."

I sighed, placing my forehead atop hers. "Tempting."

"We just need to go down to the temple. Besides, I'm already dressed for the occasion."

Her white dress was disheveled beneath my hands, and I chuckled.

I imagined her at the altar, exchanging eternal vows with me, and then back at the palace, beckoning me into her bed, and my heart ached. I forced myself to breathe, and the pain eased.

"It'll be our secret," she offered. "Just you, the priest, and me. We can take Kanis as our witness."

"What about your parents and mine?"

"We'll give them a grand wedding celebration later with 800 hundred attendees, no more and no less." She studied me under furrowed brows.

"Hmm," I growled. Just a ceremony with her, not hundreds of people to deal with, no public appearances yet—just Saphyr and the presence of God. "Very tempting," I admitted. She knew exactly how to entice me.

"Say it," she whispered with a twisted smile.

I chuckled. "Saphyr."

"Mmhm?"

"Will you marry me tonight?"

"Yes!" She squealed, placing her arms around my neck and planting an excited kiss on my cheeks.

Kanis stood next to me, his eyes open like an owl's and his hair still wild from bed. Moonbeams flowing through the stained windows barely illuminated the pews in the temple, and the solemn silence of dawn reigned.

The priest, clad in a dark robe, stood next to both of us before the altar, equally stunned from being awakened in the wee hours to perform the secret royal wedding of the century.

I had not been able to stop smiling since Saphyr and I left the gardens.

My foot tapped incessantly, and I was not sure I was breathing at all.

The immense temple doors groaned open, and Saphyr stepped inside with a grin. She wore the same white gown of tulle and lace, but she had taken off the robe, her bare shoulders gleaming. Shimmering curls fell around her chest and framed her delicate face. She clutched a bouquet of jasmine and gardenia from the garden. And, on her head, a crown of golden spikes beamed like the sun.

I had been so enthralled with Saphyr that I had ignored the little girl walking in front of her, Saphyr's sister, who carried a cushion with another crown of sun rays.

When they neared the altar, the priest took the cushion and set it aside.

Saphyr gave her bouquet to her sister and faced me.

Unable to contain my excitement, my wings spread wide, slapping Kanis fully awake. He groaned, and Saphyr chuckled as I took her warm hands in my cold fingers and fixed my eyes on hers.

I could see the universe glittering in her amber eyes—a world of possibilities, a lifetime of adventures awaiting us. I had spent a lifetime enjoying her company as my best friend, now I was ready to make her my wife. I felt certain I wanted to spend not only a lifetime but also an eternity. So, when the priest asked me to say the vows, I changed the last words.

"I, Corvus Elliot Di Alba, take you, Seraphine Catherina Stella, to be my wife. I promise to be true to you in good times and in bad, in sickness, and in health. I will love you and honor you for all eternity."

Saphyr smiled, tears welling in her eyes, and said her vows in the same way.

"Saphyr, receive this ring as a sign of my love and fidelity," I said. "In the name of God and the holy triad." I slid the pearl ring over her finger. I had added more sapphire gems to it and engraved our names inside it with the date of the year in which we had first met.

Saphyr repeated the words and placed my gold ring on my left hand.

Then the priest took the crown from the cushion and raised it overhead.

"Do you, Corvus, promise to serve the Sun Empire wholeheartedly and with a lifetime of commitment to its laws and welfare after I have formally crowned you the Emperor on your coronation day?"

Saphyr squeezed my hands warmly and gave me a reassuring smile.

I lifted my chin, breathing easily. "I do," I said, my eyes glinting at the vision of returning the Empire to its former glory.

The priest placed the crown of the Sun atop my head, and I felt the burden of the entire Empire resting on me.

"By the holy power invested in me, I now declare you joined in sacred marriage. You may now kiss your Empress."

Through the stained windows, I glimpsed the sun rising over the Empire, joining the waning moon in the sky. Together, they illuminated the temple in a kaleidoscope of colors. Saphyr glowed, and I smiled, feeling the weight of my wings dissipate into thin air as the crescent moon vanished.

Now, there was nothing but her. I pressed my lips against hers and held her tight as we let our foreheads join.

"I love you," she whispered.

"I love you, too."

EPILOGUE

The Stella Islands sprawled at our feet under the sun. Saphyr and I had returned to the pavilion to celebrate our secret honeymoon. Kanis remained at the palace to monitor things. I smiled, recalling our conversation when we bid him goodbye.

We had met at my old studio, where we decided all important matters. Kanis wore a serious face after I had asked him to resume our duties while we escaped to the islands.

"Only for a week or so," I insisted. "If anybody asks, tell them we're sick."

"Their Emperor and Empress sick for several days? They'll see it as ominous. Some will see it as an opportunity to pester."

I rolled my eyes. "Nothing will happen. I have instructed our maids to say we're in fake meetings and what-not. By the time you mention we're sick, we'll be back."

"Well … in that case. I'll gladly cover for you. Simply let me know when the honeymoon is over, and you may take your rightful place." He crossed his arms, studying the stack of rolled parchments on the desk. "I'm sure you'll have tons of fun making babies while I rot here under piles of mandates."

I tried to stop the gamut of emotions, from surprise and embarrassment to outrage and finally resignation, from showing on my face.

"She's not … we're not …" I sighed. There was no point in correcting his lack of tact. Saphyr and I had not even talked about when we would have them.

Mortified, I turned for the door.

"I'll write when we're ready to return," Saphyr said in a singsong voice to Kanis, immediately catching up to me.

"Hope you name the child after me!" Kanis shouted as the immense doors shut after us. "I deserve it, after all this bull—"

The door muffled his expletive, and I chuckled.

The scent of rosemary and the breeze on my skin interrupted the memory.

Light footsteps approached me, and I shivered at the touch of Saphyr's hands on my chest.

"Is it time?" she asked, resting her cheek on my back.

I pressed her hands with mine. "Yes."

We left the pavilion and headed to the beach we had arrived on after escaping Sirenibus.

The sand was soft under our feet, but the water iced our skin as we waded into the waves. A crimson sun lay flat on the horizon, ready to set.

Saphyr hugged my body searching for warmth. I ran my fingers through her hair, embracing her until our bodies acclimated to the cold.

"Is this really necessary?" she asked through chattering teeth.

"Better to be cautious."

"Very well." She pulled away, and I held her by the elbows. "Tell me what it is I have to do, again?"

"Shed seven tears and call his name."

"Right." She took a deep breath and shut her eyes, concentrating.

I furrowed my eyebrows, studying her face as she tried to cry. After a while, she opened her eyes, returning my gaze dry-eyed.

"I can't," she said, stepping back and pouting with disappointment.

I contained a laugh. "Just think of something sad."

"I'm not an actress. I can't cry on demand."

I pondered what to do. "Well, he never specified they had to be tears of sadness," I considered, suddenly lunging at her and splashing freezing water across her torso.

Saphyr squealed, attempting to run, and I sucked in air as I chased her. I caught her, lifted her above the surface, and ignored her eyes daring me on as I dropped her into the water, drowning her curse as she submerged.

She emerged with a crooked smile, seeking vengeance. She thrust me several times into the water until I finally caught her and held her firmly, tickling her feet until she twisted in incontrollable laughter.

Tears of joy trickled from her eyes, although I struggled to count them.

"Now! Before you shed any other," I said at the seventh tear.

"E ... E ... Ean!" she breathed, gasping for air and wiping the tears of joy away.

I looked around expectantly, but the sea was empty.

She clutched my arm. "What now?" she whispered.

"I guess we wait."

We remained silent, hearing only the crash of waves and the distant squaw of seagulls. Just when I believed nothing would happen, a splash of water behind alerted us.

We turned to face a boy emerging from the sea.

"You called me, Sire?" Ean's crimson curls stuck to his skin, which dripped with water.

"Ean!" I engulfed him in a hug.

He chuckled as I backed up to study him, my hands still on his shoulders.

"Milady." Ean nodded, and Saphyr smiled.

He looked exactly the same, as if time had done nothing to him. A human child would have grown an inch or more by now.

"How's your freedom?" I asked.

"Great." He grinned. "I've been traveling the oceans."

"Has your queen been pestering you again?"

He shook his head. "She's been busy with her newfound brother at the palace."

I sniggered, certain Brenen was giving her trouble. "Could you please send her a message?" I recalled Kanis's words. "Humans have gone missing near the Dark Forest. Tell her we tried to contact Fergus, but the forest remains impenetrable."

Ean frowned. "I'll inform her immediately, Sire."

"Thank you."

"It's a good thing we selkies are fast." He winked.

I nodded, smiling. "Although it seems hard to believe, I've asked Morgana to not bother you again. And I believe she gave me her word, so you shouldn't fear her anymore."

Ean beamed at me. "Thank you."

"But be careful. She can be unpredictable."

"Yes." The corners of his eyes crinkled with amusement.

I took the boy by the shoulders and hugged him again. "I'm so happy to see you. Come by Sol City, and I'll give word to the keepers of the port to bring you straight to me when they see you."

"Absolutely, Sire. I'd be happy to visit your palace."

I raised my eyebrows.

"I caught word of a new Empress of the Sun. I trust your other friend is well?"

"Kanis is fine." I chuckled, remembering his words of goodbye. "Taking care of business while we're here with you."

"Please send him my regards."

"I will."

"I'll return to you on your coronation day with whatever message the queen sends me back."

"Perfect. Thank you, Ean."

Ean bowed slightly to us as goodbye and turned to leave. Then, he looked back. "And congratulations on your marriage!"

Saphyr and I gaped at each other. How did he know? Sunlight glinting on the rings we wore gave me the answer. Before we could say anything, Ean had disappeared.

"The boy is clever," Saphyr mused.

"I'm going to miss him."

"Me too," she replied.

We kept silent, perhaps waiting for Ean to reappear. My body no longer felt cold.

"Well, enough business." Saphyr took my hand and pulled me toward her. "I've pleased you, and now it's time you please me. Let's enjoy our time together." Saphyr placed her hand on my cheek, and my stomach fluttered.

The waves washed away my tension, and I finally relaxed. She looked stunning in the sunset, wet curls framing her eyes as she smiled invitingly.

I took her invitation. Sliding my hands under her thighs, I carried her out of the water and back off the beach.

Saphyr would forever be the Reigning Empress of my heart.

THE END

PHOENIX VIEIRA

has spent the past fourteen years reading and writing fantasy and romance, traveling, and drawing inspiration from worldwide mythologies to build a rich fantasy world for her debut novel. When not writing, Phoenix can be found wandering the woods near her backyard, forever guarded by a legendary fluffy white beast.

Find Phoenix on Facebook and Instagram
@PhoenixVieiraOfficial

THE IMMORTAL SOULS SERIES

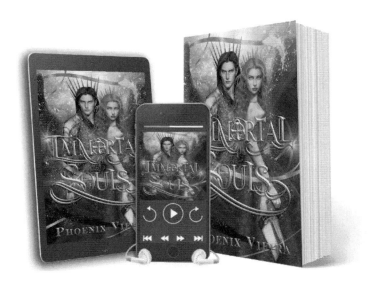

Thank you for buying this book.

If you liked this book, thank the author by leaving a review on the Amazon and GoodReads page of Immortal Souls. To learn more about the Immortal Souls series, make sure to sign up now to Phoenix Vieira's Newsletter at www.PhoenixVieira.com and stay up to date with special offers, bonus content, and info on new releases!

Printed in Great Britain
by Amazon